MW01246000

A NOVEL DEATH

A NOVEL DEATH

•

Judi Culbertson

AVALON BOOKS
NEW YORK

Published by Avalon Books,
an imprint of Thomas Bouregy & Co., Inc.
160 Madison Avenue, New York, NY 10016

Library of Congress Cataloging-in-Publication Data

Culbertson, Judi.
    A novel death / Judi Culbertson.
        p. cm.
    ISBN 978-0-8034-7663-9 (acid-free paper)
    I. Title.
    PS3553.U2849N68 2011
    813'.54—dc22

                                        2010046195

PRINTED IN THE UNITED STATES OF AMERICA
ON ACID-FREE PAPER
BY RR DONNELLEY, BLOOMSBURG, PENNSYLVANIA

To everyone who has ever been enthralled by the mystery of an old book and where it has been

Acknowledgments

Without writing a second book, I'd like to thank my tireless agent, Agnes Birmbaum, of Bleeker Street Associates, and my wonderful editor at Avalon Books, Lia Brown. Both of you had faith in this book from the beginning.

Thanks also to my New York City writers group who held my feet to the fire: Jean Ayer, Myriam Chapman, Teresa Giordano, Tom House, Eleanor Hyde, Elisabeth Jakab, Carol Pepper, Maureen Sladen, and Marcia Slatkin. But most of all to Adele Glimm, who went above and beyond with encouragement, multiple readings, and a place to spend the night.

As always to my family, whose love inspires me every day: Tom, Andy, Robin, Emily, and Andrew, as well as to the other Chaffees and Randalls. You know who you are.

Chapter One

The day my life began to unravel—like the sweaters my mother tried to knit for us to save money—started much too early. By the time the first call came, shortly before seven A.M., I was on my third cup of espresso. I was sitting in the kitchen of the Victorian farmhouse owned by the university, a hodgepodge of wide-planked floorboards, the original scarred-oak table, and Harvest Gold appliances. These were accented by an avocado-toned dishwasher that was dead when we first moved in.

I answered the call quickly. Book buyers from Australia and Japan didn't always get the time difference right. "Secondhand Prose."

"Secondhand, huh? I thought this was a bookstore!"

What do you think prose is, buddy? "This is a bookstore," I reassured him. A virtual bookshop, true, but the books were real boards and paper.

"Yeah, well . . . I've got stuff to sell."

"Great. What kind of stuff?"

"What kind? They aren't a kind. They're books! Old. Ver-ry old." He stretched out the last two words seductively. "One of them has this date in the front, 16-something?"

Be still, my heart. My breath caught, even as I reminded myself that books that old would be copyrighted in Roman numerals. "Where did you get it?"

"What—you think I stole it from some library? Nobody else asked me that!"

So he had been shopping his *stuff* around.

"They're from this old house I'm cleaning out. The guy doesn't care what I do with the stuff; he just wants everything *out.*"

1

Sadly, that sounded true. People threw incredible things into dumpsters. Of course, these books were probably mildewed, their covers hanging by threads. Even a week stored in kitty litter wouldn't kill *their* smell. But I didn't hang up. Because any book in any abandoned cellar has the potential to be the find of a lifetime. *Tamerlane,* Poe's forty-page booklet of youthful poems, which recently sold at auction for $250,000, had been tossed in a bookshop sale bin because Poe had modestly designated himself only as "A Bostonian."

"When can I see the books?"

"I'll let ya know. I'm just checking who's interested. Then I'll take bids." And he hung up.

He hung up! He didn't even give me his name! I punched in *69 to see if I could retrieve his information, but a scratchy recording let me know that "the number of your last incoming call is private."

Damn! I pressed the receiver to my chest, disbelieving. What did I say wrong? Should I have offered him money right away?

And then the phone rang again. "Yes, hello!"

He had realized his mistake. But there was only breathing.

"This is Secondhand Prose," I encouraged. *Don't be shy.*

"Delhi, it's Margaret. Something terrible happened." Her voice had the taut sound of someone using words that would not make her fall apart. "Lily passed away."

"What?" I understood "passed away," but the "Lily" upended its meaning. Forty-five-year-old women, women my age, didn't "pass away," like a calendar page being turned. An aneurysm? It had to be an aneurysm. A car accident. "What *happened?*"

"They aren't sure."

"The doctors?"

"The *police.*" Her voice veered dangerously.

I needed more coffee, fast.

"Can you come by the shop?"

"Of course!" But why would she even open her bookstore today? "Do you need someone to—"

But Margaret had already hung up, before I had a chance to even tell her how sorry I was about her sister.

Clicking the handset off, I picked up the small china cup and took an automatic sip before I remembered that it had gotten cold. *Yuck.* I clinked it back down quickly. Why would the police be involved? Did they investigate all sudden deaths?

Maybe it would be on the local cable station. I switched the TV to Channel 12 and waited. At first there was a special about celebrating the Fourth of July on Sunday. Clips of last year's fireworks at Jones Beach were shown, as well as several local parades with fire engines, Hibernian bands, and historical societies dressed up like Long Islanders of two hundred years ago. I even recognized the tall ships that had visited Port Lewis, my home village, on their way to Huntington Harbor.

Come on, I willed the station, *it's time for the news.* And then, at eight A.M., the news began.

Lily Carlyle was actually the lead story, alternating feeds between a weary-looking news anchor and shots of the railroad tracks outside the Port Lewis Station. A photograph of Lily, perhaps supplied by the Metropolitan Museum of Art, where she worked, kept flashing on. In it, Lily was wearing a leaf-green caftan that made her eyes dark as jade, a hammered-gold pendant, and an enigmatic smile. Her dark hair crinkled in charming curls around her face.

According to the tired blond reporter, Lily had lain down on the LIRR tracks in the wooded area one hundred yards west of the station and been decapitated by an engine whose engineer could not see her in time in the ten P.M. darkness.

I sat with my hand over my mouth. *Why?* Why would she do such a thing? The clichés kept coming. Lily had a wonderful life, everything to live for! I tried to blot out the image of her beautiful severed head rolling down from the track. That was even the train she sometimes came home from the city on!

I found I was clutching my upper arms and rocking slightly back and forth.

I'll say it now. Lily and I never liked each other. I rarely saw her except at the annual Christmas extravaganzas the sisters gave. Last December she accepted my box of Godiva chocolates at the door as if they were something I had picked up at 7-Eleven. It made me want to tell her how much they actually cost. But Lily took pride in never eating anything sweet; she was a tireless gym-goer who re-warded herself with exotic massages and Armani scarves. She would die before she ate a cheeseburger or a hot fudge sundae.

Bad choice of words. I made myself click off the TV, which had gone back to corn roasts and Fourth of July celebrations, and went upstairs to finish dressing. In deference to Margaret, I pulled off my coral T-shirt with a starfish that said LIFE IS GOOD! and replaced it with a black top that said nothing at all. As I pulled back my long hair and anchored it with a clip, I couldn't stop replaying Lily's last moments. What kind of despair allowed you to remain on the tracks with a train screeching down on you and not jerk yourself away at the last moment? Margaret had never hinted that her sister suffered from depression.

Was it possible she hadn't been conscious? What if she had climbed down from an earlier train and stumbled into the woods to be sick? Tried to get to her car and collapsed on the tracks instead, unable to move. What if she had had a stroke and couldn't move? I understood now why the police would be involved.

But nothing, no explanation of circumstances, would make it any less horrible for Margaret. I knew the horror of someone being alive and with you—and suddenly *not.*

To keep from revisiting my own past on this sunny summer day, I tried to think about what book from the 1600s my early-morning caller could even have. The Gutenberg Bible wasn't even printed until 1455, and even though atlases, histories, religious tomes, and natural history guides were in circulation two hundred years later, none were being printed in the wilderness that was still America. And yet it was the quest for the impossible books that kept me climbing shaky stairs into mold-choked attics and descending into basements that should have been condemned. I loved *all* books, rare or not. After a day of hunting, I would lug the boxes out to the barn behind the house and pore over their details. One of the best things about being an Internet bookseller was reuniting people all over the world with treasures they'd never hoped to find. It was what made me stand in line for hours at estate and garage sales just to get in.

In fact, I should be tracking down today's sales right now. But Margaret's shop opened at ten and I wanted to be there.

Against my better judgment, I decided to give my own village another chance. Port Lewis, like the local waters, is fished out. Because the ferry from Connecticut crosses Long Island Sound and docks here, bringing swarms of day-trippers needing entertainment, Port Lewis residents have responded by erecting permanent YARD SALE signs. If they have lobster traps or a chipped chamber pot, they'll add ANTIQUES! Any real treasures have long disappeared across the Sound.

For an hour I made my way up and down the steeply winding streets, visiting historic white Victorians with wide porches, and saltboxes whose wooden plaques gave the names and dates of the sea captains who built them. I pored through cartons of tattered suspense novels, cookbooks with translucent thumbprints, books that would be better off incinerated. I knew I was wasting my time, but I didn't stop. Part of me, the part I was not proud of, dreaded seeing Margaret. Would she weep hysterically when I hugged her and be inconsolable? Would I be able to say anything at all to her that would soothe her, that wouldn't be an empty cliché? I had never known sisters who did so many things together.

Margaret and I certainly weren't that close. We talked about what good friends we were, but she was ten years older than me. She was my mentor in bookselling: she instructed and I listened, anxious for her favorable opinion. It made me more deferential with Margaret than with my other friends. There was also something unknowable about her; we laughed at things together, but I could not tease her. Now that it was up to me to offer comfort, I was afraid I wouldn't know how.

When I could not stall any longer, I parked my van on High Street near The Old Frigate Bookshop and moved slowly past the stale-beer smell of The Whaler's Arms, the floral sweetness of Love in Blooms, and the Port Lewis Gallery, which had bad paintings but no odor at all. Then I pressed down on the bookstore latch.

At the sound of the bell, Margaret lifted her head from behind the oak counter; I was relieved to see her talking calmly on the phone. What had I expected? Moving closer, I heard her say, "I'm afraid that's all I know right now. But thanks so much for calling!"

Then I was around the counter and hugging her, though Margaret
was hard to hug; her hands always grasped my upper arms as if to
keep me from crushing her in my enthusiasm. So close to her face, I
saw that her hazel eyes had bloodshot map lines and underlying
bruising. Still, her cheeks and lips were pink and her thick chestnut
hair was held back from her pretty face in a tortoiseshell barrette.
Even on such a terrible day, she was dressed in her usual lady-
bookseller uniform, a white silk blouse and long black skirt. An old-
fashioned pendant showing a woman's face under glass hung around
her neck on a velvet ribbon.

"Margaret, I'm so, so sorry!" I burst out.

"I know. I *know*." It was as if she were consoling me. Then, re-
leasing my shoulders, she whispered, "Let's go next door. I can't answer one more phone call."

She looked around the room until she found her graduate student
assistant, shelving books in the nautical section. "Amil? Can you
handle things if we go next door? Don't bother with the phone."

Every village needs a rare book shop like The Old Frigate. Its
name was a nod to both the joys of reading and Port Lewis' whaling
past. The Emily Dickinson quote—"There is no frigate like a book
to take us lands away"—was painted in gold script across the windows. Emily herself was hanging in a small old-fashioned frame just
inside the door.

Yet the store was more like a British library than a New England
homestead, all brown leather couches and brass lamps. There was a
marble fireplace with carved figures at the far end, and lots of corners
to curl up in. You could almost smell the mingled odors of tobacco and
leather polish, and I imagined the Inklings—J. R. R. Tolkien, C. S.
Lewis, and the others—sucking on their pipes around the fire and
making ecclesiastical jokes.

I couldn't imagine my life without The Old Frigate.

Amil looked up and smiled. Wearing a peach-toned knit shirt
and khakis, he might have been an exotic model, an Indian playboy
who toned his body playing polo and sailing yachts. I admired his
breathtaking white smile and artistic features, though once in a
while I noticed that his full lips took on a spoiled—or perhaps it was
discontented—pout when he was lost in thought. Of course he wasn't

a wealthy playboy, just a young man studying British poets at the university and working in a bookshop.

When we were almost out the door, he called, "Bring me a triple latte?"

And Margaret answered. "No, Amil. Double or nothing!"

It had the sound of a private joke—but wasn't today an odd time for it?

"Whatever." His voice mocked the word's use.

Margaret and I stepped into the July morning, into the scent of caramelized nuts from the red cart on the corner and the general sweetness of summer on Long Island. Later on, when it was August and nothing moved in the heat except the sweat on people's foreheads, the smells would seem stale, even rancid. But that was not yet.

"Have a lot of people been calling?"

"Delhi, you have no *idea.* A few people really do care, but so many just want the gory details! People I haven't heard from since last Christmas." Her refined lips quivered as if she might either laugh or cry. In the end, she just gave her head a shake, dismissing them all.

Then she opened the door of The Whaler's Arms, and we moved into a cloud of fried clams and spilled beer. It wasn't my favorite place—it seemed dreary in broad daylight—but we always came here instead of one of the new outdoor cafés along the harbor. Margaret and the owner, Derek, did many favors for each other and he never let us pay for our coffee. Margaret didn't even bother to bring her purse with her.

Ignoring the red vinyl booths with their nautical paper place mats already set out for lunch, we perched on stools at one of the tiny bar tables. Derek began fussing behind the counter, and after a minute brought us identical cappuccinos. He chatted with Margaret about a proposal to require shop owners to pay for flower planters along the curb. Evidently he was one of the few people in Port Lewis who had not yet heard about Lily.

When he was gone, I expected Margaret to finally break down. She lifted the cup to her lips, and then changed her mind and set it down. "Find any books this morning?"

I blinked, and then remembered all the wakes I'd been to where the bereaved had talked and even laughed, seeming to ignore the body that lay just a few feet away. I had assumed that a kind of shock coated and denied the horror of their grief. Perhaps this was happening here.

"A total waste of time," I sighed. "But I did get an interesting phone call."

I described my conversation with the mysterious seller. Then something occurred to me. "Did he ever call you?"

"Actually, if it's the same one, he stopped by. He wanted an assessment of what he had found."

I came alive. "Did you *buy* anything?"

"No Hemingway firsts."

"But *what?*" As Colin reminded me before he moved out, I had no pride. "Did he give you a phone number?"

"He might have. I'll have to look." Then, seeing that her evasiveness was annoying me, she tossed back her hair. "You know, Delhi, these so-called 'finds' are just a bookselling myth."

"But they do happen." She made me feel like a child hoping a visitor would bring me a wonderful toy. "Look at all the things found at garage sales! Great paintings hidden under other ones because some yokel thought he was *better* than Rembrandt."

"But who knows at the time who's going to be remembered? I knew a lot of good artists when I painted."

"You painted?"

She tried to brush it off. "Delhi, at my age I've done everything! Lily always says that if . . ." But that stopped her, would not let her pretend any more that this was an ordinary Friday. Putting her hands over her face, elbows on the table, she gave deep gasping sobs. "How could she do something like that?" she moaned.

I reached over and stroked her sleeve over and over, the way I did when my children had been upset. "People—life is *hard,*" I whispered, excusing Lily for not standing up to it.

I was afraid Derek would see us and come over.

Margaret lifted her head and wiped at her eyes. "I'm sorry."

"Don't."

"If only the shop hadn't been open late last night! We would have had dinner together and everything would have been fine."

"But if she was depressed . . ." I prayed that I did not sound like the people on the phone.

Margaret traced the compass in the center of our table. "You have to understand that Lily was never completely happy. Even on the wonderful vacations we took, places that people only dream about, there was always something—the hotel, the bad weather, a museum that was closed—that ruined her day. We still had fun, of course, but . . . Being a perfectionist was great for her work, but people aren't statues."

Which people? At their last Christmas party, Lily had seemed more edgy than usual, her green eyes constantly darting to the doorway, as if she were expecting somebody who never came. By the end of the party she had even been short-tempered with Margaret.

"But why *now?*"

Wrong question. Margaret's face completely shut down.

"Why don't you just go home?" I pleaded. "I can keep the shop open."

"And do what? The police won't let me *do* anything. They wouldn't even show me the note in her purse."

"But you're her sister!"

"Tell them that."

"But who *would* they show it to? Her husband? Ex-husband, I mean."

Margaret's hand suddenly knocked against her cup, her rings clattering sharply. She was the only person I knew who could wear several rings and look as refined as Princess Grace. "What are you talking about?"

"But I thought—Lily had a different last name. I thought she must have been married, since you hadn't."

Margaret sighed. "No, we were *both* young and foolish once. But I took my own name back, and she kept his. He was an actor, if you can imagine that. But I have no idea where he is. And I wouldn't tell him anyway."

I didn't say anything. I was too surprised that Margaret had never told me she had been married. She was my mentor, true. But we did talk about other things besides books. The vagaries of my life with Colin, my shock when he moved out. Wouldn't it have been natural to share her own unhappy experiences? "How long ago was it?"

"Years. I can't even remember." She sounded sorry she had mentioned it. "And I have to get back to the shop." Her feet hit the linoleum.

I slid down from my stool too. I still didn't know when Lily had been found or what the police had told Margaret, but I knew I couldn't ask. Instead I said, "Do you need me to fill in this afternoon? If you have things you have to do, I'll be glad to help out."

"Well, you can check with Amil. See if he needs any help. And—damn! I forgot his latte." She stepped back from the door with its small porthole opening and into the restaurant again, leaving me to go next door by myself.

Chapter Two

When I opened the door of The Old Frigate, I was surprised to find the shop empty. No customers, but no Amil either. I called his name, but there was no answer.

Why would he leave the shop unattended? If there had been an emergency, he knew Margaret was right next door. He shouldn't have been in the back room, out of earshot of customers anyway.

And then there was the click of a knob and Amil stepped out of the small side office. His cheeks were an odd sunburned red and his dark eyes hard as glass. "Where is she?" he hissed.

"Margaret? Getting your latte. Why?"

He muttered something I could not understand, and then said more clearly, "You want to know something about your friend?"

"What?"

"You know what she—" But then he stopped, and I saw that he was looking past me out the window. With my back to the door, I could not tell whom he was seeing.

"Let me write down the name of that book for you." His voice was deliberately loud, meant to be heard. He patted the countertop for scrap paper, found only Margaret's neat lists of new arrivals, and then reached into his back pocket and pulled out a square leather wallet. It was so choked with bills that it could barely close. Had I interrupted him cleaning out the safe? Had he been going to tell me that Margaret owed him money? But he worked out a dog-eared white card and scribbled on the back with Margaret's pricing pencil.

Then the bell over the front door chimed and I dropped the card into my woven bag.

But it was only Margaret, holding a paper cup aloft Miss-Liberty style. "Better lat-te than never, boy-o!" Her voice was hollow, a brave attempt to mask her terrible sadness. When she saw me her smile faded completely. "What are you two plotting?"

Did we look guilty? *Amil was just about to tell me something terrible about you.* "We were talking about Colin. Amil likes his poetry."

Though I use my own last name, Laine, I hoped that Amil as a graduate student had at least heard of Colin Fitzhugh.

Margaret's expression cleared as I knew it would, and the corners of her mouth turned up. *"Voices We Don't Want to Hear?"* She quoted the title of Colin's prize-winning book mockingly. "What's the new one? *Earthworks?*"

"Earthworks," I confirmed. Colin actually taught archaeology at the university, and many of his poems referenced that.

Without saying anything, Amil moved deftly around me and approached Margaret. I saw her hold out the cup to him. But instead of taking it, he shoved it back into her chest. His force popped the white lid off and sent hot coffee spewing across her face and onto her white blouse.

Margaret gasped as the coffee reached her eyes and dropped the cup. It hit the oak floor noiselessly, sending tan streams everywhere.

Amil jerked the door open. "You've ruined my life!"

Then he was gone.

"Margaret, are you *okay?*"

"Paper towels. In the bathroom."

I doused several in cold water, and handed the wad to her. Instead of pressing it to her face as I expected, she sank to her knees, frantically mopping up the spill. "Get more and help me," she cried. "This floor will warp!"

What about your face? I decided she was in shock and ran for another wet towel. Then I knelt down on the floor and twisted her face toward me. Her left cheek and the side of her chin glowed with the cherry-red shape of a continent. "How are your *eyes?*"

"Delhi, I'm okay!"

But I pressed the towel against the burn gently.

"I'm really okay. It wasn't as hot as you think."

"But he assaulted you! We've got to call the police."

"No police! Delhi, he was upset; he bumped my arm. That's all. It was my fault as much as his."

This was too much. "But why was he so upset? He wasn't before."

She didn't look at me. "I told him I might have to let him go. For personal reasons."

And then the bell over the door dinged and we both froze. My mind raced with images of angry employees and guns. I would die too, just for being in the wrong place.

It was a smiling young couple looking for travel books about Australia.

"Domestic accident," Margaret said, pointing to her face and blouse with a rueful laugh. The tan streaks were beginning to dry, but the silk still clung to her breasts.

"You go change," I said, "I'll stay here."

"You don't have to. I'm closing up anyway. I've had it!" Plucking her blouse away from her body, she added, "Maybe I'll see you at the sale tomorrow."

"You're going to Oyster Bay?" I was surprised. Margaret didn't often make the rounds with the rest of us. When you had a brick-and-mortar shop, people usually brought books to you. You didn't have to line up hours early at estate sales and fight with other dealers. Still, the Oyster Bay sale, located on Long Island's Gold Coast, was supposed to be exceptional. The furniture from the estate had been sold separately last weekend, clearing the way for books and collectibles.

"I'll get a number for you," I promised. I was one of the ones who arrived hours before the sales began so I could be in the first group of people to go inside.

"Leave your phone on. I'll call if I'm not coming."

We said good-bye again, once more with delicate hugs, and I hoped she'd be all right.

Chapter Three

When I first started buying books, I was a crazy woman. I would pore over *Newsday* on Thursday nights, cut out the classified ads for tag and estate sales, and then lay them across the scarred wooden table like miniature Tarot cards. I studied them as if they held my future. Should I start on the North Shore—or in the Hamptons? Massapequa or Manhasset? Where could I go that would have wonderful books and no other dealers buying them? When I finally had a workable pattern, I would tape each advertisement onto a pink index card and number it. Then I would consult my street atlas, and write out detailed directions to each house on the back.

It took several years to calm down, to be able to wake up naturally just before five o'clock on a weekend morning instead of at three or four. But that Friday night, I kept jerking awake, haunted not by missed opportunities, but by Lily Carlyle. Her narrow face and tangled black curls floated over me with a tense smile. *You don't know the half of it,* she seemed to be taunting. *You'll be so surprised.* But when I woke just before daylight, it was because her expression had changed from a kind of gloating to frightened anguish.

I knew I couldn't sleep after that. Pushing up from the bed, I told myself I was mixing her up with Amil, that he had been trying to tell me something. When I got back to the house yesterday and remembered the business card he had given me, I pulled it out of my purse. It was a card for an automobile repair shop in East Setauket, Stan's Body Shop with a small red-embossed image of a tow truck. On the back, Amil had scrawled in pencil *Call me tomorrow* and a number. Because of all that had happened, I had been tempted to try him right away. But I decided he had specified Saturday for a reason.

14

Lily's ghost watched me while I dressed in black shorts, sandals, and a black T-shirt that said in yellow letters, "I am a professional. Do not try this at home!" *You killed yourself,* I told her reproachfully. *Why are you haunting* me? *Newsday* would probably have more details today, so I would not have to bother Margaret. Ghoulish. But I had always been ghoulish. I could hear my mother's gentle reproof from years ago: "But why would you be curious about something like *that?*" I didn't know why; I just was.

Of course I had never been curious about the square root of seven or what a Bible verse really meant.

I opened a can of tuna fish for my cats, Raj and Miss T, a consolation prize for being left alone all day, and then left immediately for Planet Java and the largest coffee they sold. But I did not reach full alertness until I was on the Northern State Parkway, almost to Nassau County. I live in Suffolk, the wilder of the two counties that comprise Long Island. If Nassau is a jaded matron sucking on an ivory cigarette holder, Suffolk is her teenage daughter, still experimenting with purple hair and navel rings. There is one nail salon for every two people in Suffolk and an attraction to lawlessness and danger, which spawns bars like Goodfellas and the Bada-Bing Cafe.

Lawlessness and danger. I thought about Amil and his violent outburst, and then forgot him as an SUV entering from Greenlawn cut me off. He could have waited five seconds and entered an emptiness as big as Montana. I guessed it was his way of saying "Howdy." One of his bumper stickers read I EAT TOYOTAS FOR BREAKFAST.

By the time I turned my decrepit white van north to Oyster Bay he was safely miles ahead of me. I was approaching an historic area of Nassau County, closing in on Teddy Roosevelt's Sagamore Hill estate and expensive waterfront properties. Most of the side roads were labeled PRIVATE, but at the corner of one was a discreet yellow TAG SALE TODAY sign.

My stomach jumped the way it always did, and my fantasies soared: Despite the extensive advertising for this sale, I imagined myself as the only book dealer there. Maybe the proprietors would decide to open at six A.M. instead of waiting until the scheduled time of nine, catching everyone else off guard. Despite Margaret's skepticism that such things existed, I would stumble on the find of a lifetime. After all, Teddy Roosevelt and his family were buried here on the quiet green slope of Young's Cemetery. Was an inscribed first edition of *The Rough Riders* too much to ask?

I tried to decide which dedicatee would make the book the most valuable—Teddy's controversial daughter Alice Longworth, or his friend, Mark Twain—and reached the estate sale shaky with dreams and fatigue. As were all the other dealers who had gotten there ahead of me. Headlights shone along the road like predatory eyes. I identified a Town Car and a Lexus as well as a Ford Escort, an ancient brown Cadillac, and several other vans in various states of rust. Mine was easy to identify. Both front doors had GOT BOOKS? and my phone number painted on them in bright blue.

I headed for the Town Car, which had the driver's side window rolled down. The man inside, a dealer who specialized in antique silver, silently tore the next number off a calendar and handed it to me. I squinted at it in the dawning light.

"Thirteen," I complained. "It's not even six yet!" Then I remembered Margaret. "I'll need a number for my partner."

He shook his head. "He's gotta be here. That's the rule."

"She. She'll be here any minute." Who made up these rules anyway?

He actually took the trouble to smile, though not in a way I appreciated. "Then I'll give her a number in a minute, won't I?"

"I guess."

Instead of whining, why hadn't I tried charm? Despite my lack of sleep, my hair was brushed and I was dressed in clean clothes. On my good days, I fit the book cataloguer's description, "slightly foxed, but still desirable"—a few age creases, but nothing serious. On my bad days, when my light hair hangs lank instead of curling, and my eyes are circled like edited mistakes, I am "a reading copy only."

Now that I had a number for the sale, I drifted back to my van to go find more coffee. It was still too early to call Amil.

No one tells people when it is time to line up at a sale. One minute they are dozing in their cars or showing each other yesterday's bargains, and then suddenly everyone is rushing the front door. As soon as I sensed motion, I was out of the van, transferring a slab of bills to my pocket to keep my hands free. I shoved my cell phone in my other pocket, but almost forgot to pick up my vinyl boat bag. Some buyers bring cardboard cartons, but I find a flexible giant-sized bag works better. With boxes you have to bring scarves to drape over them so no one thinks they are part of the sale. Anyone removing books from a green-and-white bag knows it's stealing.

In the shadow cast by the white stucco hacienda, I edged my way around ceramic planters of geraniums and found my place in line. The positive side of having rules is that most people obey them.

I stood with my back to the red-tiled mansion, facing the road so that I could see Margaret when she arrived. I rehearsed my apology for not getting her a low number.

"Delhi?"

I spun around quickly, though it was a man's voice. Jack Hemingway, brawny and white-bearded in denim overalls, was two places behind me in line. Although Jack might remind you of Papa if you hadn't seen a photograph of Ernest Hemingway in a while, he always said immediately that they were not related—as if that somehow gave him equal claim to the last name. I imagined he had spent years when he was teaching literature at Hofstra University making that distinction for people. During that time he had actually been writing too, turning out hard-boiled adventure stories that no one seemed to want to publish. He had much more success with critical analyses of contemporary fiction.

"I read your article on California pulps," I told him politely. It had been in one of the university quarterlies, and Margaret had shown it to me. "Very impressive!"

Jack smiled and swayed a little. "In this business you've got to share what you know. Life's too short for one person to know everything. Unless you're Marty, of course. You hear about his latest adventure?"

"No. What?" With any luck he had been hit by a bus.

Jack set down his empty cardboard carton. "Seems there was this dealer who closed up shop around 1975, but held onto his books. Probably sold some occasionally through *AB Bookman,* answering people's want ads. You know about *AB Bookman?*"

What kind of amateur did he think I was? Though it had folded its covers for good, the *Antiquarian Booksellers Magazine* had been the leading publication of the rare book trade for decades. "Sure."

"Anyway, after this dealer died, the Neanderthals—his family—came in and started throwing the books in a dumpster. Fortunately someone called Marty."

Why Marty? *Why not me?*

"Lots of thirties and forties novels with dust jackets, Long Island history. Marty knows his books, of course; he researches constantly. But even before he knew anything, he could find books." Pressing his wide arm against his forehead to capture sweat dots, he chuckled fondly at the memory. We were all Jack's protégés, but Marty was the standout. "First time he ever went out looking for books, he picked up something called *The Town and the City* by a John Kerouac. Who's John Kerouac? But inside it's inscribed, *Keep 'em hanging. Jack.*"

Jack Kerouac's first book. *Signed.* I always loved this story. "And he bought it."

"What's not to buy at twenty-five cents? Even you—"

"Marty's also all over the place," I reminded him quickly. "God couldn't be at every tag sale, so he created Marty."

"Isn't that the truth."

Marty definitely possessed *Finger-Spitzengefuhl*, that electric current that makes your fingertips tingle every time you are near something rare.

As if we had conjured him up, Marty Campagna appeared, crossing the driveway as he talked into a cell phone. He had cronies at sales all around the Island and called them constantly to talk strategy. The first time I met Marty with his shock of black hair, heavy-rimmed glasses and longshoreman's physique, I was not impressed. But gradually he and his tingling fingers made their way into my nighttime fantasies. I wasn't surprised; I'm rarely attracted to men who can do me any good.

"Hey," I said, as he passed us on his way to the front of the line.

"Hey, Blondie."

"I hear you struck it rich in the dumpsters."

"What?"

I started to repeat Jack's story, but Marty waved it away. "The books were *in* the house and we had to buy all nine thousand. Paid way too much, and threw half of them out."

"You should have called me for the throwaways."

He laughed at that. "Nothing there you'd want."

"Try me." I felt absurdly pleased that he was treating me as an equal.

Someone in the front called a warning to him to line up, and Marty moved swiftly into place. He was always first or second in line. The rumor was that he paid someone to wait in line for him overnight. It was a rumor I believed.

But where was Margaret? If she didn't get here soon, she'd never get in! But maybe something had come up about Lily. Or maybe, when faced with driving here, she just hadn't felt up to it. Taking out my cell phone, I speed-dialed her house and got her answering machine. I hoped it meant she was on her way.

"Delhi!"

Now what? I turned back around. Jack wasn't finished with me. "What did Margaret find?"

The words didn't compute. "Nothing. She's not even here."

He blinked with impatience, reminding me that, of his "students," I was sailing steerage. "I don't mean today. According to Marty, she found something very important. Something rare. I thought if anyone would know, it would be you."

"Well, I don't." I was about to say that Margaret didn't believe in great finds, when something dark red and hot, something that in my past had been linked with betrayal, crept up the back of my neck. Marty wouldn't be mistaken about something like that; he had been sure enough to pass it on to Jack. But Margaret had refused to tell me. *She must think you're a complete amateur,* my inner cynic jeered.

"When did she find this?"

"Dunno. I heard about it Thursday."

And then the hacienda door swung open, killing all conversation. A woman stepped through the carved door and waved an arm at us. She was thin, blond, and fretful, with red-framed reading glasses on the edge of her bony nose. "Listen to the rules," she announced in a reedy New York voice. "The first fifteen get in. Work it out among yourselves. I'm not getting involved. Work it out like adults or no one gets in!"

It had the effect of turning us into children. Eyes down, we formed a single straight line and shuffled along meekly as she counted us off. But we were the winners! The rest of the line would have to wait until we came out again. One out, one more in.

Inside the marble-tiled hall, I resisted the temptation to follow Marty and his *Finger-Spitzengefuhl*—he had leaped over to a built-in bookcase in the living room and was yanking large art books off the shelves. Probably wonderful books too. But I ran up the wide staircase and, in the first room, a wonderful assortment was laid out on a bed. I snatched up *From Edinburgh to India and Burmah, Arctic,* and a beautifully illustrated original of *Egyptian Mummies.*

In a smaller bedroom that had the mustiness of summers past, I came upon a collection of children's books, one of my specialties. After picking out Thornton Burgess, Clare Turley Newberry, and Noel Streatfeild, I saw that the shelf below held vintage mysteries. I was reaching for a Charlie Chan novel with a colorful dust jacket, my index finger pulling it toward me, when a larger hand snaked in below mine and gripped the spine. I held on and twisted around, outraged.

It was Jack Hemingway, his white-bearded face smiling at me. He took advantage of my shock to yank the novel free. "Sorry, but this one's mine," he said firmly. "I saw it first." What was he talking about? I opened my mouth to protest when I saw he was rapidly emptying the other mysteries into his carton. Furiously, I started grabbing books at random too.

When the shelf was bare, Jack disappeared. I dragged my vinyl bag back to the master bedroom to see what I had amassed. Charlie Chan had been the prize. Most of the other books had unfamiliar authors or were lacking dust jackets, their wartime-printed pages badly yellowed. I shoved the pile under the bed in case I came back to the sale later when they would be cheaper.

But I couldn't forget what had happened. By the time I clumped down the stairs with my heavy boat bag, the Charlie Chan mystery had attained mythical proportions. A fireplace set caught my eye, and I fantasized about grabbing the poker and attacking Jack. I wouldn't kill him—just teach him not to steal books from me again.

It wasn't until I started to unload my books onto the card table to pay for them that the image of an angry bookseller beating a Hemingway namesake to death made me laugh.

But I jumped when Marty Campagna stepped forward. He must have been in the shadows watching, checking out everyone's buys. When the cashier put *Arctic* on top of my paid pile, he reached for it. Flipping the cover back and forth appraisingly, he asked, "Where'd you get *this?*"

"Upstairs." But I felt my stomach tense. At one sale, Marty had accused another dealer of stealing his stash. There might have been a fight. But the other dealer had apologized, admitting he had found the books in a carton and didn't know they belonged to anyone.

What would I say if Marty accused me?

But he didn't, only looked skeptical, and then said, "What do you want for it? I have a guy who collects North Pole stuff."

When I hesitated, he added, "I'll give you seventy-five."

It would have almost paid for my other books, and I wanted to be his friend. I said, "I kind of like it myself. I'll get back to you."

He gave an impatient shrug, indicating that keeping a book for yourself was an amateur failing. Or maybe it was just recognition that when I found out what *Arctic* was worth, I wouldn't sell it to him so cheaply.

Before he could step away, I said, "You know what Jack did? He grabbed a book right out of my hand!"

If I was expecting commiseration, I didn't get it. Marty cocked his head, and then grinned. "Well, he's da Man."

Yours, maybe. On Long Island, despite women neurosurgeons and mayors, buying and selling books was still a boys' club. At many sales, I was the only woman in the first group in. There were bookstore owners like Margaret, of course, and a few women who were part of a couple, but I was an oddity at sales. They treated me as a novelty, but I was outside the circle.

As I waited for my change, I stared through the empty living room out the picture window. The people who once lived here had had a perfect view. A handful of sailboats bobbed whitely against the jade water of Long Island Sound. Connecticut's far shore was a mistier green. Beautiful and appealing waters—and filled with sharks.

Chapter Four

Back at the van I tried calling The Old Frigate, but got the after-hours message.

"Hi Margaret, it's Delhi," I said. "I'm just leaving Oyster Bay. It was a good sale, but not worth coming to now. Anyway, we have to talk." Those words always sound ominous when I hear them, but this time I didn't care. Despite the nice books I had collected, I felt upset. Angry with Jack for grabbing a book from me, annoyed at Marty for defending him and trying to steal a book from me another way. And furious with Margaret for lying to me—*if* Jack was telling the truth. I would give her a chance to explain before I embarrassed myself with accusations that weren't true.

I tried her home number next, listened to that machine, then left the same message, giving her my cell phone number again. She probably had many things to do involving Lily. I was only surprised that she had not called me since she said she would.

Next I wriggled out Amil's card from my depleted wallet, a stunning contrast to the way his had been.

After four rings, just as I was mentally composing a message, an American male voice bawled, *"What?"*

I jumped, startled. "Is Amil there?"

The receiver crashed against my ear.

Wrong number. I dialed again, this time very carefully.

The call was answered on the first ring. A woman's voice, accented and lilting, said, "Yes, hello please?"

Who was this? "Uh—is Amil there?" I realized I didn't even know his last name.

"No, he's not here! He never came—" She faltered, as the disagreeable male voice from the first call yelled something in the background with "Shut up" and "Bitch" in it. It was louder at the end.

This time I moved the phone away from my ear, so that I heard the crash rather than felt it. What did a boor like that have to do with a poetry graduate student with a cultivated British accent? Obviously they knew Amil. But I couldn't put anything else together.

Still, I was not going to call again, at least not today. Instead I retrieved the messages from my home phone.

The first was from my sister Patsy, reminding me that her beach party started at three this afternoon and not to bring anything.

The other call was, mercifully, from someone who wanted to buy a book.

I had no messages from my children, which meant that no one was having a crisis this morning.

And nothing from Margaret.

I drove home quickly, stashed my books, and decided to stop by The Old Frigate on my way to Patsy's party. Now I had the sense that Margaret was actively avoiding me. Maybe she was afraid I would ask why Amil *really* thought she had ruined his life. Maybe she was afraid that I had learned about her find at the book sale and would demand to know why she hadn't told *me*. Maybe she was afraid I would ask her questions about Lily and the suicide. There were actually a lot of reasons that she might not want to talk to me right now.

After changing into my newest thrift shop outfit, a gauzy soft-gold blouse and an Indian skirt printed with llamas, I headed into the chaos that was Port Lewis on a summer weekend. When we first moved to the village years earlier, staying in the university house between Colin's digs and guest lectureships, the town had been financially challenged. There had been a supermarket with wooden floors, an old-fashioned hardware emporium, and a Salvation Army store. These have been replaced by an Irish gift shop and many cappuccino bars. Port Lewis now has two Tarot card readers, four art galleries, and a pet store, The Yuppie Puppy, for impulse poodle purchases.

When I drove along High Street past the bookshop, the windows were lit up. So the shop *was* open. And Margaret hadn't bothered to return my calls. Still, if a parking place hadn't opened up just then I might have kept going. Dealing with my sister took a lot of energy, and I wasn't looking forward to weakening myself confronting Margaret. When I saw a Jeep pulling out, I slid the van in quickly and grabbed my woven bag. I would stay calm and nonjudgmental. And I wouldn't leave until I had some answers.

One of the two front windows of The Old Frigate had a vacation theme, with colorful children's books and old sand toys. The other held a patriotic display for the Fourth of July—red, white, and blue bunting, presidential biographies, and campaign buttons. Stepping into the alcove between the windows, I pressed down on the door latch. To my surprise, nothing happened. I pressed harder. Locked. Had Margaret forgotten to unlock the door when she went in? Putting my hand up to shade my eyes, I looked in as I knocked on the glass. Nothing stirred. But in the distance I saw something odd on the floor.

I pressed my face against the glass, straining to bring the white object into focus. It looked like the toe of a tennis shoe, lying in the aisle just inside the entrance to the second room of books. If it was a shoe, it was balanced on its side with the sole facing me. Soft canvas would have flopped over, so it had to be made of leather—or have a foot inside. I felt a chill in the humid summer afternoon. *Margaret's?* That would explain why I hadn't heard back from her. I had a sudden, terrible image of Amil returning before she had a chance to close the shop and gunning her down. It would explain why he hadn't returned home.

But I shook the idea away. I had never seen her wearing sneakers. She would *never* put on a pair of sneakers, let alone white ones. Her shoes were always a soft, polished leather, black or chestnut brown, either with a bow or tiny covered button. I squeezed my eyes nearly shut to try and see the object more accurately, the way I tried to decipher a signature in an old book. But this object was twenty feet away, floating in the dimness like the taunt of a ghost. Kneeling down in the alcove, I pried open the brass mail slot in the lower half of the door and yelled, "Margaret?" At the same time I rattled the doorknob, as if it would yield in the face of my need. But it remained unmoved.

I knew I had a key to the bookstore door at home, left over from the times I had helped out, but I wasn't sure where it was stashed. And I had no time to look for it; as it was, I would just make it to the Hamptons in time.

Yet, as I started back to the van, I couldn't shake the idea that someone was lying on the bookshop floor. Maybe it was Amil. Maybe when he came back with a gun, Margaret had struck out at him in self-defense and was now lying low. *Right.* That was about as likely as Lily's ghost coming back for her sister and carrying her off into another dimension.

Still, it wouldn't take that long to check. I turned and started back down the hill, dodging clumps of families eating ice cream. I almost knocked over a little girl covered in chocolate and sprinkles. But I knew I would find a constable in the "Residents Only" parking lot, punishing outsiders with a hundred-dollar fine. Because Port Lewis is a small seaport town with steep hills and only a few spaces in town, illegally parked vehicles are a main source of revenue.

I found the older officer in the parking lot, zestfully writing out a summons, his foot up on the bumper of a red Saab from New Jersey. As I rushed up to him, he mistook me for a scofflaw and pinioned me with a stern look. The Lecture was about to begin.

I shook my head. "No, no, I'm Delhi Laine. I *live* here. But I think there's a problem at the bookstore."

"You mean Margaret's?" His blue eyes took me in alertly, though his white hair and drooping mustache reminded me of a Civil War portrait.

"Yes! Someone's lying on the floor and the door's locked."

I began to jog toward High Street as he lumbered along beside me.

"Nice lady, Margaret," he puffed. "A real village idol."

I guessed he meant icon, but did not correct him.

When we reached The Old Frigate, he peered in, shading his eyes as I had, then turned to me. "The body's gone!"

"What?" I jammed my face against the glass. The toe of the white shoe—if it was a shoe—was still in place. I pointed. "There. See that sneaker?"

He looked in again, and then back at me doubtfully.

My heart dropped, but I reminded myself that he didn't know the situation the way I did. "I haven't been able to reach Margaret all day. Maybe the back door's open," I added.

"Where?"

"Through there." I pointed to a narrow passageway separating the bookstore from the nautical arts gallery on the other side. I had never been through it. Now, looking at it closely, I doubted that anyone could fit.

"Show me," he ordered.

Obediently I turned sideways and slipped inside. But I began breathing hard. What if it narrowed even more in the middle and I found myself stuck? What if the constable got stuck just behind me and neither of us could move? This was as narrow as some of the passageways in the Sangre de Cristo mountains that I had explored with Colin; more than once we had had to back out. But he had always gone first. Here the ground sloped down precariously as well. Catching his toe on a jutting rock, the constable grabbed at my shoulder, scraping my chin against the brick wall. *Never again.* Finally, after too many heart-stopping minutes, I burst free onto the small concrete stoop, the constable's hand embedded in my back.

I imagined making a funny story of it for Margaret—and then remembered why I was doing it.

I shook out my arms as if they had gotten compressed in the passageway, and then turned the metal door knob. Locked. *Great.* I was not about to back out the way I had come. Shoulder to shoulder, the constable and I peered through the panes of glass. From this distance, we could see even less. And then, while I was wondering what to do, he knelt and picked up a chunk of discarded brick. With no hesitation, he crashed it through one of the lower window squares. The tinkle of glass hung in the air like a wind chime. What would Margaret *say?* If this were just my delusion, I would have to offer to have the glass replaced with money I didn't really have.

"Don't get cut," I warned the constable, as he reached in boldly to turn the small button lock. But he managed to get the door safely open and we went inside.

Moving ahead of him through the dusky light, I ran to where I had seen the white sneaker. It *was* a shoe, a men's Nike trainer—but it was empty. Yet that was worse—it was like seeing a severed foot.

"Margaret?" And then I saw her. She was sprawled in the aisle to my right as if the shoe had been pointing at her. She lay on her back, her feet twisted under the bottom rung of a rolling library ladder.

"Margaret, it's me!" I dropped to my knees beside her head, conscious of the acrid odor of urine, mixed with a strange sweetness. Her face was an underbelly white, her lipstick and blusher like a separate artificial layer. Her mouth was open, as if she had been gasping for air, but her eyes were tightly shut. The India-shaped coffee burn on her cheek glowed even more, but now she was wearing a deep gold silk blouse and beige linen slacks, dark at the crotch.

I grasped her arm, shocked by its iciness. But the whole room was freezing, I realized, with the air conditioning running unchecked. Margaret, always worried about costs, would never have put it on this high.

"How's she doing?" the constable asked, though he could see exactly what I could. "I'm calling 911." Behind me I heard the click of keys on a portable phone and his muffled voice.

I kept my eyes on Margaret. The silky fabric *seemed* to be moving under my anxious palm, shifting just slightly, but it was impossible to be sure. "Margaret?" I whispered. "Don't give up; we're getting help!"

Then I looked up at the library ladder, at the riser that had splintered halfway up the wooden steps. Evidently it had thrown her off balance and pitched her backward. I hated those vertical ladders and avoided them whenever I could. Now I added them to my list of things to avoid, along with dark basements, open heights, and running out of money.

"Don't touch her!"

I jumped with fright at the voice.

As the cop knelt at Margaret's other side, I stared at his broad face and tight light brown curls. He had the bland look of a boxer outside the ring. And he was no more than twenty-four, my daughter Jane's age.

"You see it happen?"

"No. We found her like this. I tried to reach her by phone and couldn't and was afraid something had happened."

It was the abridged version.

Scooping up Margaret's wrist, he pressed his thumb against it expertly. Then he lowered his ear to her chest and listened. Straightening back up, still absently holding her arm like a plank of wood, he said, "Ambulance is on the way."

"Oh, good. Then she's not—is she. I mean, she's alive, don't you think? Or what . . ." I was babbling.

"I didn't order a body bag, did I?"

My God.

"She have a history of dizziness? Heart problems?"

"I don't think so. But her sister—"

He shook his head. "Those ladders, they're dangerous. Go straight up, and—" With unexpected gentleness, he turned her head to the right. "Nasty gash! Look at that."

I didn't want to. "What's that under her head?" I pointed to a piece of tan cloth that I'd noticed when he moved her head.

"Looks like some kind of rag." But he was fixated on her wound. "She must've hit something on the way down. Old people, their skulls get thin."

"Old people! She's in her fifties."

He nodded as if I had just confirmed his thesis.

I sighed. Even at forty-three, I could have been his mother.

Time held us tautly; hours passed before I heard the sirens outside the shop. When I checked my watch, it had been three minutes.

I heard the constable open the front door and slam it again, then the murmur of voices. Two women in loose blue cotton tops and pants hurried over to us. The lanky redhead was carrying a large metal box. The smaller woman held a contraption that I realized was a folding stretcher, a long board under her other arm. As the policeman and I scrambled out of their way, one of them pressed an oxygen mask to Margaret's face. The other started an IV in the crook of her elbow. Then they unfolded the stretcher and laid it down beside her. As they started to ease her onto the board gently, coddling her loose limbs, I pressed my hand over my mouth. No one could be that limp and still be alive.

They carried Margaret through to the front room, and I saw the policeman hand a leather purse with its familiar Celtic brass clasp to the red-haired EMT. It seemed incongruous—like she would need to freshen her lipstick on the way to the hospital. But in the next minute, I realized that, of course, they would need her identification and medical insurance. Some days I was a few chapters short of a book.

The village constable held the door for them, and then turned back to me. "Poor lady," he intoned. "A very bad fall."

"I should go with her!"

The young policeman ignored both of us. When he finished making notes in a cramped black notebook, he motioned us onto the paisley loveseat by the fireplace. Then he sat down in the brown suede wing chair across from us, and prepared to write. "Names, addresses, phone numbers."

As the constable gave his information proudly, "Officer Randolph W. MacWharton," and a Port Lewis address, I noticed a brown streak along the tan marble hearth. It looked like coffee; but there was no way the latte could have flown four or five yards and landed there.

"How long will this *take?* I need to get to the hospital. I'm Delhi Laine." I didn't offer to spell my name, though I knew he would probably write it as Deli—or Delly—Lane. I mumbled my phone number and address. I hadn't forgiven him for his body bag comment.

"Okay." He looked down at his brass nameplate bar. "I'm Officer Alexander Kazazian."

He hadn't done it to be funny, but a laugh clogged my throat. It came out as a snort and he stared at me. "The victim is Margaret Weller?"

Victim? But I suppose she was considered to be the victim of an accident. "Yes."

"Next of kin?"

"I don't—she has a younger sister—had, but she died Thursday night."

"*This* Thursday? Of what?"

"Well—it's probably suicide. She was hit by a train and—"

"Oh, that one," he interrupted. "And this here is her sister?" He shook his head at the coincidence of it. "So you work here?"

"No! She has—had—a regular assistant. But I don't know his last name."

"Indian fella," Randolph MacWharton said brightly. "Didn't wear a turban or anything, but he had that dark skin and hair. Popular with the ladies."

"So why isn't he here?" Officer Kazazian spoke with a native Long Island twang, he-yer for *here*.

I shrugged.

"He live around here?"

"Probably near the university; he's a graduate student." I remembered the weird phone calls and added, "I think he lives with other people."

"Never gave him a ticket that I remember," MacWharton added regretfully.

"He may not work here anymore," I added. "He got angry and threw coffee in Margaret's face."

"Yeah? Nice guy." He wrote something down. But then he added, "That was some fall she took. Old people and babies, they got soft skulls."

Why did he keep saying that? "But what about the shoe that was pointing at her? And who put the cloth under her head?"

Both men stared at me. I sounded like Nancy Drew. "I mean, it's like someone was here afterwards. Maybe Amil came back and found her, but he ran off so he wouldn't be blamed." *Leaving his glass Nike behind.*

"Yeah, he should have reported it," Officer Kazazian conceded.

"But isn't leaving the scene of an accident a crime?"

He actually smiled at me, his eyes crinkling in his broad face. "Only if you've caused it, Mrs.—" he looked down at his notes, "Mrs. Lang."

"Laine. And maybe he did cause it," I said stubbornly.

"How?"

"I don't know. Maybe he yelled something and startled her. Or got on the underside and pushed her off."

"You can see where the step split. I'm writing it up as a Domestic."

A domestic accident. The words Margaret had used when she pointed to the coffee burn on her face.

"But the rag under her head," I persisted.

"Yeah," he intoned piously. "Landing on it probably saved her life."

Give me a break. My father, a Methodist minister, had had an arsenal of stories about World War II soldiers whose pocket New Testaments had deflected enemy bullets over their hearts, saving their lives.

"She was probably on the ladder dusting," Randolph MacWharton explained. "My wife uses my old undershirts."

There was no arguing with these two.

"I'll talk to this guy, okay?" Alex Kazazian conceded. "What's his name again?"

"Amil. A-M-I-L. Pronounced like, well, 'a meal.' No last name."

Randolph MacWharton chuckled. "Like Dagmar," he said, earning a startled look from Alex Kazazian.

"Like Madonna," I translated. "Except he probably does have a last name. We just don't know it."

"And you don't know where he lives."

"I can find out. I know people at the university."

"It's probably in her office papers."

Of course. "Do you know where they took her? Port Lewis General?"

"With that head injury? Nah, she'll go to University Hospital, the Trauma Center. They've got the best stuff." He said it admiringly, as if it were a state-of-the-art sports store, and then snapped his black notebook shut.

"That's all?" MacWharton's mustache seemed to droop—an extra whose scene has just landed on the floor.

"You can keep an eye out for this Amil," the policeman promised, and handed him a business card. "Let me know if he comes back to work."

"Will do!"

As an obvious afterthought, he gave me a card too.

I glanced around The Old Frigate. Its wonderful atmosphere had disappeared; the room now had the flatness of a set created for the movies, unable to come alive until the actors stepped in. "So you think it was only an accident?"

"Someone falling off a ladder? Sure. I knew of a guy, he was cleaning out his gutters, and he missed a step coming down. Gone in an hour." Kazazian said it with satisfaction; not that the careless homeowner was dead, I hoped, but that it proved his point so nicely.

But as I left The Old Frigate, I still could not think of it as an accident. Two sisters, one dead, the other left for dead, within two days? What were the odds?

Chapter Five

I wanted to go straight to the hospital, but I was already late for Patsy's party. And this was nothing she would understand. Even though we were sisters—okay, twins, but only fraternal—our lines of communication had come down in a long ago storm. If we had talked to each other more, she might have understood my concern about Margaret. If we had been truly distant, she wouldn't have cared if I made it to her annual party or not. But she had always taken it personally, even when Colin and I were in New Mexico or Peru for July, acting as if we had deliberately planned to be away.

My twin's full name was Patience Faith, christened when our parents were hoping to be missionaries to India and were encountering delays because of partitioning. I was named Delhi Agra after their chosen destinations. By the time my brother, David Livingstone, was born they had changed their focus to Africa. But they somehow never got there either. They remained in Princeton, my father a minister who was never paid what he was worth, my mother busy with good works. Except for their fanciful children's names, they were exactly what you'd expect. Actually, they probably would have done well in a foreign culture. They spoke bravely of David Livingstone's "alternative lifestyle" after he went to Los Angeles to make satiric horror movies and introduced them to a string of Tiffanys, Ambers, and Lee Anns.

I decided to make a quick appearance at the party, and then go to the hospital. But before turning the key in the ignition, I pulled out my phone and called the emergency room. They could tell me nothing about Margaret's condition, only that she had been admitted, and that I couldn't see her until she was out of the ER.

I had forgotten that there is no quick way through the Hamptons in the summer. Mired in traffic in Hampton Bays, I considered how I would tell Patsy about Colin. But there was really no way to make her understand. I barely understood myself.

Last October he had come into the kitchen where I was reading and handed me a copy of *The Shenandoah Review*. It was open to his latest poem; he leaned against the refrigerator, watching me read it. Despite myself, despite the fact that our relationship had fallen on some hard times, I felt flattered that he still valued my opinion. After all, he was adored by thousands—a large, bearded, hero-poet, a kindly Santa Claus to his classes, and an intrepid archaeologist.

This poem was in his usual style. Except that it was called "Separation," and the last line lamented, *A man can't dance with a wife who hides his shoes.*

I was wedged tightly into the wooden breakfast nook, with two burnt cake pans soaking in the sink. Hannah, the forgetful baker, was home from Cornell. Closing the magazine, I tried to calculate the time between his writing the poem and its publication. At least a year. Had he been planning this moment for a *year?*

I glanced over at his muscular arms and paunchy stomach. "You can't dance anyway."

It was mean. But what about the line about hiding his shoes?

A long-suffering sigh. "You take everything so literally, Delhi. It's childish."

But I understood the symbolism. "You could have discussed how you felt with me before announcing it to the world."

"You think I haven't tried? How many times have I complained that I was being buried alive? That I needed air to break free and find my voice again? My poetry is far more significant than just you or me. It's a gift I'm responsible to protect." He went on to lecture me about the fatal domesticity of his days, how being squeezed into the small-minded routines I created meant he could no longer soar.

It didn't make sense. His pathetic life consisted of archaeological digs, poetry awards, and home valet service. And whatever adoring graduate student barnacled herself to him for the semester.

"There's a reason Walt Whitman never married."

"Yeah. He was gay."

He glared at me. "You know what I mean."

"Right. What *you* mean. It's always about you, isn't it? It's never been about me. What about *my* voice?"

We stared at each other. I didn't have one. My role had been to follow Colin around the world on his sabbaticals and guest lectureships, providing healthy food, fresh clothing, and emotional support for four children and a media star.

As if he were reading my thoughts, he said, "It's not like you were ever Susie Homemaker. As far as your performance in the past year, I'd give you a three out of ten. I even have to iron my own shirts!"

Poor baby. "In case you haven't noticed, I'm working too."

"You mean trying to sell books?" He rolled his eyes. "Not that you have a lot of options."

"Oh, right—I forgot to go to law school."

But he was shaking his head at me sadly. "You could have at least finished your B.A. You always were too undisciplined."

I could have pointed out to him that in those days we weren't ever in the same place for a year, but I chose another direction. "As I remember, I *was* working on my B.A. when you threw a little roadblock in my way. Several of them, as a matter of fact." I knew he hated to have me bring up the facts of our courtship: the charismatic teaching assistant and the pretty sophomore enamored of archaeology and undiscovered places; my fear that if I didn't marry him before he went off to New Mexico for two years, I would never see him again. It wasn't his fault that I got pregnant before the ink on the thank-you notes had dried. But it ended my academic career.

"I'm not going there," he said firmly.

"You know what, Colin? Here's another metaphor. You're like an elephant who sat on a tulip and then got up and complained that it was squashed."

I knew he would not like the elephant comparison, and he didn't.

Blue eyes narrowed, he stared at me for a long time, thinking. "I'll say this plainly, Delhi. I'm moving out. It's over."

I crossed my arms, as if trying to keep myself from flying apart. I felt the same dizzy unreality as the afternoon I was twelve and skidded on wet leaves on my bike. I was thrown over the handlebars onto the concrete, badly scraped and my arm broken, but for a moment, I didn't realize that it was me lying on the ground.

"I'll pay the rent and utilities for the next year, although I won't be living here." He straightened up, back in professional mode. "I'll come over when the kids are home for the holidays. There's no reason for *them* to suffer."

"What happens after a year?" I had barely enough breath to ask.

"I'll decide then. It could go either way."

"Will you be getting another place?"

He shook his head with pity at my naiveté. "I already have one."

And that was that.

Or so I remembered.

As always, the food at Patsy and Ben's party was spectacular. Although my nieces, Tara and Annie Laurie, complained that there was nothing to *eat*, I knew better. Endive leaves wrapped around garlicky goat cheese, golden passion fruit stuffed with crabmeat, and tiny brown quail quarters like mummified baby arms. Caviar-decorated smoked salmon on black bread—I went from table to table, sipping white wine and unashamedly sampling everything.

When I was finally satiated, I went looking for Patsy. I found her kneeling in her all-white kitchen pulling bottles of champagne out of the refrigerator. Her blond hair was pulled back in an impeccable French braid that dramatized her beautiful profile. Ingrid Bergman. Did that make me Goldie Hawn?

She turned as I came in, thinking I was Ben, her face furious. "Can you believe it?" she cried. "Those idiots didn't chill enough champagne! Oh—Delhi. You finally got here."

"I was outside talking to people." I tried to make it sound like it had been hours instead of fifteen minutes.

She peered behind me. "Colin's still outside?"

"No. It's just me. Colin and I are no longer an item."

She put down the green-gold bottles. "What are you talking about?"

"He's taken his business elsewhere."

"Del!" Ben came up behind me, crushing me in a strong hug. No air kisses for this man. Tanned and muscular with black curls and a bony face, he was a man to whom life had kept its promises.

Now he ran his hand down the length of my hair. "Gorgeous, as always. How's business?"

"Fine. Believe it or not, people still buy books."

"Ben, I *need* you—"

Instead of responding to his wife, he kept his eyes on me. "Terrific! Give me your card. I know some people who are interested in buying. One guy, a friend of my partner's, has a temperature-controlled library in his brownstone. All original manuscripts of Poe and Melville. Letters signed by Abraham Lincoln, stuff like that."

I doubted I would ever have anything to offer that kind of collector, but I reached into my woven bag and pulled out several of the cards I had designed and printed up myself. They showed Raj, my seal-point Siamese, sniffing at a pile of classics, with the message *Got Books?* My information was on the back of the card.

Ben grimaced. "What's this? If you're going to be in business, you need something *professional*. Something that says—"

"Oh, don't waste your breath." Patsy was finally standing up, a row of Piper Heidsieck bottles behind her like obedient ducklings. "Delhi, are you saying that Colin *left?* Who's the woman?"

"No woman."

She raised her eyes to heaven. "There's always a woman. And if you don't believe it, you're just as bad as Mama was about David Livingstone."

When one of my brother's girlfriends, Jennifer or Tiffany, answered the phone, my mother clung to his assurances that she was just the maid.

Ben winked at me. "It's *his* loss."

"I'm sure it is, but we've got to get this champagne outside. Did the Mellons get here? Or the Krikjmas?"

"No idea." He bent to help her lift the dark green bottles. I was sure that Patsy saw it as one more failure. No degree, no career, and now no husband. And, of course, the thing that no one ever talked about.

Patsy's money came both from her own accounting firm and Ben's holdings. He had gambled on the gentrification of Park Slope, Brooklyn, years earlier, buying up buildings cheaply, then doing the same in underrated parts of Manhattan. David Livingstone had made a fortune with his movies, which had titles like *The Tomato That Ate Akron* and *Plant You Now, Dig You [Up] Later*. I was the only one who had inherited my parents' talent for hand-to-mouth living.

"But you know what?" I said to their backs. "I'm happy. For the first time, I'm doing what *I* want."

By the time I reached Stony Brook and University Hospital, visiting hours had ended. But it wouldn't have mattered. Margaret was in Intensive Care. Her prognosis was guarded, and only family members were allowed up to see her. The fact that she *had* no family members didn't sway the receptionist. I left, determined to try again on Sunday.

My last thought before sleep was of the pointing sneaker. It had to be more than a random piece of the scene's kaleidoscope. And most probably, it belonged to Amil. But where he was and why his shoe had been left in the bookstore aisle, I couldn't guess.

The next morning I dressed more carefully than usual, in a navy T-shirt and khaki skirt. I tamed my hair into a tight French braid and traded my woven bag for a leather Coach purse, a gift from my oldest daughter, Jane. It wasn't until I was closing the front door that I realized I had turned myself into my twin, Patience. But why not? One look from her chilly eyes and empires fell. By the time I parked in the multilevel garage and crossed the path to the hospital, I was convinced I had a moral imperative to visit Margaret.

The receptionist at the information desk had a froth of white hair and a happy face pin on her pink smock.

I made my case.

She didn't agree.

"But she has no family," I argued. "I'm the same thing." While she pondered that, my identity slipped and I whispered, "You don't even have to give me a pass. Just tell me which room."

At her outraged look, Patience came back. "I have to speak to somebody then."

"But—it's Sunday! The Fourth of July." Inspiration. "Come back tomorrow!"

"This can't wait. Who's her doctor?"

"I'll check." Bending away from me, she crouched and punched in numbers; I stepped back to let her know I wouldn't try and eavesdrop. After a minute, she looked up, relieved. "Dr. Gallagher will be down. She has some questions anyway."

Patience and Delhi both thanked her.

Ten minutes later, a large-boned young woman approached us, giving me a puzzled look. No doubt she was expecting a deranged lunatic, instead of a woman holding a Coach bag.

She was almost six feet tall in blue scrubs, with a scraped-back ponytail and a friendly face. "Uh—I'm Dr. Gallagher?"

"Hi! I'm Delhi Laine. Sorry to trouble you but, how's Margaret doing?"

She nodded at the question. "The good news—if there is any—is that her vital signs are steady."

"What's the bad news?"

She sighed. "She's not responsive. There's a test we use—and she's not scoring well on it. The police report said she fell off a ladder?"

I nodded. "A library ladder."

"You mean she was inside? I was picturing her like, falling from a roof. What could she have landed on? You don't get a wound that deep just by hitting the floor."

"Could she have hit her head on the corner of another bookcase?" It seemed unlikely.

"Wrong angle."

"Could someone have come up from behind and hit her?"

"Only if he was ten feet tall." She grinned. "No, she was definitely hit from above. But I probably shouldn't be speculating anyway."

"When do you think she'll be conscious?"

"Well." She looked troubled. "She should have been already, if she's ever going to be."

"Really?" I felt the blow to my stomach. I hadn't realized there was a time limit. "But don't people sometimes stay in comas for a long time?"

"Yes, but this isn't a coma. We don't know what the problem is."

"When can I see her?"

"Really, there's nothing to *see*." She was edging away.

"Could you at least call me if there's any change? She really doesn't have any family." My voice choked and I had to stop.

Dr. Gallagher gave me a smile redolent of wheat fields. "Sure."

When I handed her the Raj card, *she* looked at my cat and said, "Cute!"

Chapter Six

Since the university was just across the road, I decided to take a chance and see if Bruce Adair was in his office. Most faculty wouldn't be. Even those who stayed to teach summer school would be on chaise lounges somewhere. But Bruce was not exactly a beach bum. And if anyone knew how I could find Amil, he would.

Bruce has the nicest office in the Literature Department. His full name, Bruce Malcolm Adair, Ph.D., glows in gold letters on the frosted glass door—he paid to have it painted himself—and he has a window overlooking the Quad. It is the lair of a powerful Scottish warrior. But although Bruce has the necessary intellect, severe scoliosis kept him under five feet tall; he is primarily interested in combat of the mind. As I knocked on the fancy door, I had a vivid memory of Bruce standing next to Colin at a Christmas party, shaking a finger far up at him to make a point. It was one of the few times Bruce was not surrounded by a bevy of fawning young women. I wondered again what his secret was.

Bruce no longer writes poetry himself, if he ever did. What he likes to do is mentor a deserving but obscure poet, and write brilliantly about him or her, starting them on the road to Pulitzers and MacArthurs. He is happy in his kingmaker role. He has also published essays in journals that Jack Hemingway can only dream about. Bruce would never grab a book out of a colleague's hand.

"Come in!"

Bruce was positioned at his large walnut desk, the prized window to his left. Because of his height, bookshelves lined only the lower half of the walls. On the painted upper half were portraits of Keats, Shelley, and Yeats, holograph pages of their poetry, and soft color photographs of misty English landscapes. Two of the photographs had been taken and hand-tinted by me. It had been during my artistic phase, when I was casting around for something meaningful to do—besides ironing. It had come after the painting on china, but before the macramé.

"Delhi?" Bruce has intense blue eyes that bulge when he is excited. They are the most noticeable feature in his pleasant rosy face. I saw that he had clipped his white beard short for the summer. "My God, it *is* you. What have you done with your amazing hair?"

"It's here." I turned to show him. "Just subdued."

"Sit, missy." He indicated a shellacked blond wooden chair with a slatted back that faced his desk.

I sat. "Is this where you grill students?"

"I grill no one. These days they grill me. Mostly about the A that I 'forgot' to give them, which they really *really* need, Dr. Adair!"

I smiled and he grinned back. He could have asked me how Colin and the children were, or gestured at my photographs to show he still appreciated them. But Bruce does not believe in normalizing chatter; he prefers to keep people off-balance. So he gave me an interested look and waited.

"I'm looking for a grad student," I began, not knowing how much of the story I needed to tell him. "He's specializing in Irish poets."

"Which poets?" But he dismissed his question immediately. "Doesn't matter. What's his name?"

"Amil. That's all I know," I apologized. I had no idea if it was a common male name in India. "A-M-I-L."

"Amil? No Amil here."

"But—slender, very good looking? From India. He has—"

"Delhi." He said my name to stop the flow of words, looking amused. "I have my limitations, but a deficient memory isn't one of them."

"I'm just surprised."

"We did have one Indian student, Raphael Singh, but he left the program in April."

Not Amil then. But I asked, "Why did he drop out?"

"Well, let's see." It was his way of buying time while he decided whether or not to tell me.

"Do you have a lot of students from India?"

"Rarely. They go to the sciences and tech. More than half the engineering grad students are foreign."

I thought. "Would you consider this Raphael attractive?"

He grinned. "And you're looking for him because . . . ?"

"Not because of that. He works at The Old Frigate, the bookshop. But he said he needed to tell me something, then Margaret came in and he threw coffee in her face. So I never found out what it was."

"Quite the gentleman. But it could be Raphael."

"Why? Why do you say that?"

His blue eyes probed mine. "This stays between you and me, Delhi."

"Of course!"

"Raphael had an altercation with an instructor in the department. She said he shoved her and raised his hand to her; *he* said she was blocking the door and he was only trying to get out. It got very messy." Bruce chewed his lower lip contentedly. He has never been above enjoying other people's failings. "Specifically—according to Ruth, my colleague—it was over a paper he wrote that she had criticized. She felt that his conclusions were illogical and told him so. He became furious and accused her of trying to force him out of the program."

"Was she?"

"Oh, I doubt it. He was gifted enough. But he always had reasons for not completing the work and wanted exceptions made for him. You know the type, bright but with his own agenda. He got upset when you tried to keep him on task."

"But isn't that a sign of creativity?"

"It can be. In a doctoral program there are certain standards to be met. You don't need *us* if you want to go off and do your own thing."

"But you might need some structure to push against."

He grinned. "What are we talking about, Delhi?"

"Probably not Amil," I admitted.

"There's more. When Raphael was interviewed privately, he claimed she had been coming on to him all semester and was trying to embrace him when he pushed her away."

"Yikes. The sexual harassment defense?"

Bruce spread his pudgy hands. "Maybe. But he *was* attractive. Ruth isn't. The tendency is to back staff, but his version was persuasive enough to keep her from any hopes of tenure. It didn't mitigate the fact that he grabbed her and almost hit her, but it muddied the waters some. What Raphael didn't know was that he wasn't the first male student to accuse her of impropriety."

"Really? And nobody told him? That's not fair! If he had known that, he might have been able to fight the charges."

Bruce laughed. "Before you get all avenging angel, he did *what* to Margaret?"

"I know. But I still want to find him."

"Okay. But you didn't get it from me. And don't give it to anyone named Ruth."

But as soon as he looked up the address in his computer, he started to worry about my safety.

"Can't you just call him?" He indicated the sleek red phone on his desk.

"I've tried, but he's never there. And weird people answer the phone and hang up on me."

"And you want to go somewhere like that?"

"Showing up has the element of surprise."

He groaned. "You used to be so bright. You want to 'surprise' some-one who has a reputation for attacking women?"

"He has no reason to attack me. I'll be careful." But I didn't tell him about Margaret's accident. I doubted that it would reassure him.

Chapter Seven

This is how you recognize a house rented to college students: blankets and beach towels hang over the windows instead of curtains, cars parked where grass should be. The house inside is bare except for stained mattresses, clothes draped over banisters, and more dirty dishes than a college cafeteria. In summer, you can find it by the music blaring into the neighborhood and the lights left on all night.

Which was why I drove past Amil's house the first time. I had to check the number, turn around, and drive back slowly until I reached a neat brown-shingled ranch. It was a common Long Island style, the kind you saw and forgot immediately, but I had to admire the tidy mounds of red impatiens and the very green lawn.

There were no cars in the driveway and I doubted that anyone was home. But I parked by the curb, walked between the flowers and rang a small bell in a brass holder. It chimed far inside the house and nothing happened. But as I was turning to leave, a young South Asian woman, baby on her hip, pulled open the door. The red dot between her brows enhanced her deep brown eyes. She was wearing a blue denim jumper as if it was a sundress. Her baby was more festive in red overalls.

"Hi," I said. "I called yesterday about Amil."

Her face stayed a beautiful walnut carving.

"Is he here yet? You said he hadn't been home. But he gave me a message to call him on Saturday."

It convinced her to step back and let me come into the beige-tiled hall.

"Is he here now?"

She shook her head and I realized she had not said anything.

"I'm sorry. Do—you—speak—English?"

Her delicate lids lowered, so I could not see her eyes at all, but her lips seemed to be twitching. "Yes, I do."

Stupid American. "Is he here?"

"No." She moved as if she were going to close the door, but I smiled at the baby whose huge golden brown eyes were watching my face. "Hello, sweetheart." I put my hand out to allow him to grab my finger. "What's your name?"

She answered reluctantly. "Billy."

Billy? "Hi, Billy," I said, "What a good boy you are!" I turned to his mother. "He's beautiful!"

It sounded contrived though it was true, as clumsy as my question about speaking English. But she beamed suddenly. "You have children too?"

"Only big ones. Not so cute." *Sorry, Jason, Jane, and Hannah. And Caitlyn.* I pushed that sadness away. "Amil wanted to tell me something."

"But he never came back! Where could he be?" She had gone from aloofness to trust, with no stops in between.

"Is he your—" I tilted my head at the gold ring on her finger.

"No, no, *Russell* is my husband."

"Was he the one on the phone yesterday?"

Our eyes met in rueful understanding. "But you know Amil," she said quickly. "Can you find where he is?"

"I'll try. But—" Reaching into my wallet, I extracted the card with Raj and my phone number. "Tell him to call me if he comes back. Actually—what's your name?"

"Shara." She looked at the card and then back at me. Billy, who had been remarkably good all this time, made a grab for its bright colors. Touching him playfully on the nose with one corner, she slipped it into her jumper pocket.

"Was Amil upset when he left?"

Billy gave a sudden outraged squawk, his small face reddening before breaking into furious sobs. Shara turned deftly away to comfort him, and I saw that her black hair went past her waist. I was left to open the door and let myself out.

Walking down the path past the vivid red flowers, I wondered about mothers who pinched their babies to make them cry.

And now it was time to go home and upload the best of yesterday's books to the bookselling Web sites I used. Selling books during the summer is slow, August the worst, but once they were listed on the book sites, they stayed searchable until they sold.

Driving through a neighborhood of white Cape Cods and saltboxes, I began to have black thoughts about Margaret. What if she *never* regained consciousness? Would they move her to a nursing home? From my mother's experience, I knew how expensive that could be. What would happen to The Old Frigate? Maybe I should try to keep the shop open for her. It would give her some income and keep up the momentum that was lost when a business closed, even temporarily. During slow times, I could price and upload my own books.

When I called Alex Kazazian to give him Amil's address, I would ask him if it was okay to reopen the shop.

Back in the barn, I found the business card he had given me and dialed his number. But it was a holiday and I was shunted to voice mail. I left him a long message, spelling everything, including Christian Avenue.

Then I settled in. The barn where I shelve my books dates back to the days when this area was farmland. But it is in better shape than the house. When we first moved in, the university was renting the barn separately to an actor who taught performing arts. Unexpectedly he won a part in a long-running musical on Broadway, and never looked back. Colin quickly offered to pay more to use the barn as a study.

But he was seduced back to the university where there was always an admiring audience. Jane, Hannah, and Jason took it over in turn, but when the last one left for college, I moved in.

I love it more than any place I've ever lived. On the rough walls I hung posters by René Magritte, Maurice Sendak, and Frida Kahlo. The floors are covered by worn-out oriental rugs from my parents' home, and the brass banker's lamp from my father's study graces the scarred library table. I store the books waiting to be described in the loft; those already for sale are on tall bookshelves downstairs, grouped by subject and alphabetized. Because a kitchenette and tiny bathroom are hidden in the back, I sometimes fantasize about abandoning the house altogether and moving in here.

I wrapped a few book orders and packed them in bubble envelopes to mail out, and then picked up some signed art catalogs I had bought from a gallery owner's estate. He had been friends with everyone, from Thomas Hart Benton and Georgia O'Keefe to John Marin and Jackson Pollock. Signed books and catalogs have a magic all their own. They have been physically touched by the artists and the sense of greatness still lingers around them.

Yet before I settled down to work, I went to the *Newsday* Web site to see if there had been any story about Lily. There was. A photograph showed her standing in front of a display case of small carved netsuke figurines at the Met; her arm was out, head tilted, as if she had whipped them up herself. The story again described how she died. But this time the reporting hinted at discrepancies in the scenario which the police would not disclose until the autopsy was complete. Discrepancies in the way she had died? Or whether she had done it herself?

Now I was intrigued. What actor had she been married to, anyway?

I made an espresso in the kitchenette, and then settled back down at the computer.

I typed *actor* and *Carlyle* into Google, and the usual thousands of references materialized. The one obvious choice was Robert Carlyle from *Trainspotting*. He was the right age. But as far as I could see, he had never left Scotland and London for very long, and his one ongoing marriage was to someone else. Next I tracked down the actors Francis Carlyle and Jack Carlyle, both of whom had died before Lily was born. A John Carlyle seemed more promising, though thirty years older than Lily. But he had died in 2002, and my sense from Margaret was that he was still alive.

Lily, I knew, had been born in 1964, and I seemed to remember that her birthday was sometime in the fall. If Carlyle was her married name, then she had been born Lily Weller. Possibly Lillian, but that name seemed too old-fashioned. *Try Lily first.*

Going back to the Google search, I typed in *Lily Weller 1964,* using quotation marks to screen out other information. Nothing. I removed the date and the quotation marks and found a Lily Weller born in July 1893 in Adams, Massachusetts, and one registered to vote in London in 1945. I had even less luck with Margaret Weller, though in the Mormon genealogical database I found a Margaret Joyce Weller born May 4, 1953. But she had died on December 14, 1979 in Nebraska.

Google also listed a number of the articles Lily had written on her specialty of Oriental art. But I did not think they would tell me anything and most were viewable only by paid subscription. I recognized that I was avoiding the most tedious part of my bookselling job; checking the number of pages of each book, deciding whether their condition could be called "Fine" or only "Good" or even "Fair," and listing their faults in detail. Then I had to skim them to write a quick synopsis of what they were about.

When the phone rang at 6:45 P.M. I looked over at the caller ID display, and then let the machine in the house pick up. This was a holiday, after all; no one would expect me to be home working.

At eight o'clock, I returned to the house to heat up a Lean Cuisine pizza and listen to my message.

"Delhi? This is Patsy. I want to know what you meant when you said that Colin had moved out. What do you mean, he moved out? Is he on sabbatical somewhere, or is this permanent? I looked for you, but you had already gone. Call me back!"

Cutting the pizza circle into four pieces, I thought about the different ways you can say the same words. You can express sympathy and concern. You can sound excited, hoping for the inside dirt. Or you can demand answers in a tone that suggests that the person you are calling has, once again, screwed up.

Even if Patsy had sounded as compassionate as Florence Nightingale, I didn't feel equal to a conversation with my sister. Instead I poured a glass of Chardonnay, ate my pizza, and read the rest of the Sunday *Times.*

Chapter Eight

The phone woke me at 4:25 A.M.

After four or five rings, when I realized it was not the dismissal bell for the exam I was failing, I pawed at the bed table frantically. In my panic, I grasped the receiver by the wrong end and had to twist it around. *"Hello?"*

"Hello?" The voice was soft and male. "I have something you might be interested in."

Wonderful. An obscene phone call. I was about to slam down the receiver when the enticing voice continued. "A signed copy of Emily Dickinson poems?"

Was this the mystery bookseller? I struggled into confused consciousness. "But—Emily, she never published any books, did she? Just a few poems in a local newspaper. So what did she—"

The answer was the smash of his receiver in my ear, jangling me awake.

I lay back in the fading darkness, breathing as hard as if I had just finished a 10K race. Raj, my aging Siamese, gave a little mew and I stroked him. It actually hadn't sounded like the yokel who had called me Friday morning. This voice, though disguised, was more cultured. Could it have been Amil? Maybe it was a joke, that he had hoped I would recognize his voice and let him explain what had happened to Margaret. If Margaret's find *was* a lost book of Dickinson poems, printed privately during her lifetime, what a treasure that would be!

Moving my face to the cooler side of the pillow, I pictured the block-long lines of bibliophiles, Emily Dickinson fans, and university curators who would batter down the doors of The Old Frigate.

50

But damn! For the second time in a week, a potential treasure had slipped from my grasp. Then I remembered Jack Hemingway grabbing Charlie Chan. *Make that three.*

I was too agitated, my thoughts too wild, to get back to sleep. At five A.M. I went downstairs, made coffee, and started the day.

At 8:10, I dialed the precinct.

Second ring. "Alexander Kazazian here."

I had a quick, mean image of him checking his name bar before answering.

"Hi, this is Delhi Laine. We met at the bookstore Saturday?"

"Roger."

"Did you get the information I left you about Amil Singh?"

"Yeah, thanks. I'll get a statement from him. But there was nothing in her office records about him. You're sure he worked there?"

I wanted to laugh. "He worked there. Do you know how she is?"

"Nah. Domestic accidents, we don't follow up."

I took a breath. "Would it be a problem if I kept the shop open for her?"

"The shop?"

Maybe he hadn't had his coffee yet, I thought charitably. Or his daily brain transplant.

"The bookstore. Margaret will need the income." But as soon as I said that, I wondered if it were true. Although she was always complaining about money and how much everything cost, Margaret never looked as if she wanted for anything. She and Lily owned one of the most beautiful houses in Port Lewis and both drove silver Volvos.

"It's not like it's a crime scene or anything," he pointed out. "We don't condemn houses when people fall off ladders."

Good point. "Well, I just wanted to make sure it was okay. I have the key," I added. I had finally unearthed it at the bottom of a kitchen drawer, under packets of soy sauce and used birthday candles. This time I made sure to put it on my key ring.

"Okay. Just let me know if that Indian guy shows up. And stay off those ladders!"

"Hah."

Next I called the hospital and found that Margaret was still in intensive care, her condition critical.

By 9:50 I was standing inside The Old Frigate, fantasizing that the beautiful store belonged to me. At Christmas I would preside over a wassail bowl by the fireplace. Tom Wolfe and Toni Morrison would exchange witticisms, and Colin and Patsy would stop by to apologize for ever doubting my success.

Quickly I walked through the shop, switching on the lights in each of the three book rooms. The shop was laid out railroad-car style, with one room opening onto the next and no side windows. Every volume was neatly categorized and shelved. I glanced over at the ladder with the broken rung. If you had an armload of books to shelve and were not really holding on, I could see how you could be thrown backward if the step under your foot gave way. But where were the books?

I looked at the Nike that had been kicked to one side by the ambulance squad. The crumpled rag was still laying in the aisle where Margaret had been, and made me feel squeamish. But I couldn't leave them on the floor looking like the debris of a car crash.

I moved toward the rag, expecting that it would be blood-caked from Margaret's head wound. But when I lifted it gingerly by a clean edge and shook it out, the rag became a tan golf shirt with a small blue-embroidered polo player on the pocket and no stains at all. *My God! Amil's?* It looked familiar. If he had returned to the shop, crept up behind her, and hit her harder than he intended, he might have pulled off his own shirt to stem the flow of blood. Except—there was no blood. And Dr. Gallagher had said Margaret was struck from a different angle.

Was it possible Amil had come into the shop *after* Margaret had fallen and found her on the floor? He might have cushioned her head, and left a shoe pointing toward her so she would be found, but not wanted to implicate himself by calling for help.

Picking up the Nike by a shoelace, I pulled down the tongue to look for the size. It was a U.S. men's 8, which might fit Amil. I carried both items to the back door and out onto the cement stoop to the small silver garbage can. Removing the top, I looked in. The can was filled with shredded papers. I hesitated about putting the shoe and shirt on top of them and in the end left them neatly against the wall.

Back inside, I noticed the wooden door in the left-hand corner that led to the basement. I considered going down, but my curiosity about the books Margaret had stored there was dampened by old terrors. I was afraid of basements. As a child I refused to go into our dirt-floored 1790 cellar in Princeton by myself. Only one faint bulb hung from the ceiling and did not reach into the dark corners where my brother David Livingstone liked to hide and jump out.

Basement scenes in fiction haunted me too. The most terrifying was from *Salem's Lot,* in which all but the top two steps had been removed, plunging visitors into the darkness to be impaled on a row of upended knives. Every horror story writer, from Edgar Allan Poe to Stephen King, seemed to have a favorite cellar scene.

This basement had the faint sweetish odor that I associated with thrift store clothes and books. But I closed the door firmly and walked back to the front.

My first customer came in at 10:25. All I saw was a puff of dyed black hair and red harlequin sunglasses before she disappeared into the paperback section. When she emerged carrying a paperback historical romance that I was surprised she had found in The Old Frigate, I saw she was wearing a red-checked playsuit. Everything from her cheeks to her upper arms drooped softly.

"Good morning!" I said. Glancing at the price I halved it and gave her the penny. "That's two ninety-nine plus tax."

"How can that be?"

"The cover price is five ninety-nine and it's half off."

"But I never pay more than fifty cents for a romance novel. My store at home sells them for a quarter!"

"All paperbacks are half the cover price."

"But it's just a romance!"

That triggered several thoughts: *Why don't you wait until you get home and buy twelve of them for three dollars? If it's "only a romance," why bother reading it at all?*

Reading part of my mind, she whined, "I left *my* book on the ferry. I have nothing to read on the trip home."

When that didn't move me to lower the price, she demanded, "Is this the only bookstore in town?"

"No. There's another one just up the street. Howard Riggs Books."

"Where up the street?"

I gave her directions. I was happy to send here there. Howard Riggs and I had a history, and it wasn't *War and Peace.*

I first met Howard years earlier when I entered his shop to sell him some books. The shop had had a military outpost feel, with dusty wooden floors, books on metal shelves like you'd expect in a Pentagon office, and others imprisoned in glass cases. The front window read *Fine First Editions and Rare Art Titles,* and the window display showed them attractively. But when you stepped inside, you were in front of a rickety sale table of mistakes labeled FUTURE TREASURES.

In those days, Howard Riggs had been a wiry man in his early thirties, with sandy hair that was rapidly decamping. He surveyed the world sourly through gold-rimmed glasses.

I entered the shop hesitantly and asked if he was buying books. It was before I was selling books myself.

He waved an arm. "Show me what you've got." So I brought in three boxes from my car and put them on the floor in front of his sale table. I realize now that they were not books *any* dealer would be thrilled to see. But even so . . .

After slipping on a pair of thin white vinyl gloves, Howard knelt and poked at the books like a proctologist, burrowing in with one finger to see the spines beneath. I expected him to tell me they had hemorrhoids. But his diagnosis was worse. Straightening up and peeling off the gloves, he gave me a scathing look. "Don't ever waste my time like this again." As he was heading back behind the counter, he added, "And take this dreck with you!"

As if I would try to sneak a few onto his sale table.

I didn't know then that we were far from finished with each other.

I ordered lunch from the deli three doors down, and a few other customers came in and bought books. None of them questioned the price. I found several books under the counter with credit card slips inside, mail order purchases waiting to be sent out and, after locating the packing supplies in the side room, wrapped them quickly. Margaret had foam peanuts for filler, which I disliked but used anyway.

At four thirty P.M. Marty Campagna, *Finger-Spitzengefuhl* in tow, bustled through the door.

His black eyes rapidly scanned the locked glass cases behind me, taking in the better books, and then came to rest on mine. "Someone told me about Margaret. Bummer. She going to be okay?"

"I don't know. I hope so. She's still in intensive care."

"Jeez." He moved a powerful shoulder in a red T-shirt, which had the cuffs tightly rolled. I could imagine a pack of cigarettes in one. But Marty also gave the impression of being involved in the most exciting venture in the world. Books were his life, but not for the money. His grandfather had invented the first waste-dissolving process on Long Island. You still saw Campagna cesspool trucks prowling the roads with their old slogan, YOUR WASTE IS OUR GOLD—but it was the patent for the process that had secured the family fortune.

"Jack told me Margaret had made a big find," I said immediately. "That *you* knew about."

He blinked at the change of subject. "I knew she was researching something. She called to ask me about source books."

"She called *you?*" It sounded more insulting than I intended.

But he only laughed, running his hand along the bristly edge of his black hair. "Hey, Blondie, I research everything. I have a ton of reference books."

"Margaret didn't ask you to look anything up for her?"

A curiously tense moment.

He shook his head. "You didn't find it in here?"

"I didn't look."

He made a disbelieving face, eyebrows raised above the frames of his black glasses, a knowing smile.

"Why would I look? It doesn't belong to me." Yet as I said it, I felt the stirring of book fever, those glowing coals ready to flare up at any gust of information. I doubted though that she would leave it in the store anyway. "She didn't tell you *anything?*"

"It's American. I think."

Emily Dickinson. But I said, "Gee, *that* narrows it down."

"Hey, kid, it's a big world out there. Could have been Rackham or T. S. Eliot."

"Tell me honestly: did you ever read T. S. Eliot—or any other poets—before you got into the business? Do you read them now?"

His smile disappeared; he actually looked annoyed.

Why had I said that? Was it my way of showing that I had an equal, though different, claim to books? But before I could apologize, the bell over the door tinkled again. We both looked over and saw Howard Riggs. Today he wasn't wearing his white vinyl gloves and had actually gotten a summer tan. But the receding hairline and petulant expression were unmistakable.

I thought he had come to yell at me for sending the romance reader to his shop.

Instead, he and Marty eyed each other with an enmity I found chilling. Finally Howard turned to me. "Where's *Margaret?*"

I started to explain about the accident, but Howard waved that aside. "I know all that; I don't live in a bubble! I thought she'd be back by now. Where's that assistant?"

"Margaret's still in the hospital. Amil's not here."

His eyes slitted. "And she asked *you* to run the shop?"

"How could she? She's not even conscious! I'm doing it as a favor."

His eyes raised to heaven put me in the class of little old ladies who arrived with casseroles and hand-crocheted afghans. People who screwed things up and ended with a plaintive, "But I was only trying to help!"

"And you've been *eating* in here." His small nose wrinkled in disgust. "I smell tuna fish!"

"No, I haven't," I lied. It had been turkey with honey mustard and Swiss cheese.

"Well, you can leave now." As I stared at Howard, he added, "Margaret and I have an understanding to look out for each other. I'll lock up for her."

I didn't know what to say. Marty gave him a mulish glare.

"Will you be here tomorrow?" I asked.

"Of course not! I have my own shop to run. I just stopped by when I saw The Frigate was open. I'll stay until six o'clock."

I didn't like it, but what could I say? He and Margaret had the only bookshops in town and might well have had such an agreement. Technically he was the only one of us with retail experience.

I moved into the side office to get my purse. At least if I left now I would have a chance to mail Margaret's books. But when I came out with an armload of Priority Mail boxes, Howard glowered. "Where are you going with those?"

"I thought I'd try the post office."

"Leave them! You don't know what she wants done."

"Who do you think wrapped them—the book fairy?" As soon as I said it, Marty chortled, at something I'd never meant. "I mean, *I* wrapped these books. They've got to be mailed." The trouble was that now I didn't dare take the money for postage out of the cash register; Howard would accuse me of stealing. I would just have to charge it on my business credit card and get reimbursed.

Marty helped me carry the boxes outside. "He could care less about Margaret. He just wants a chance to search the place," he said grimly.

Don't all of you?

We stopped at my van and I slid the side door open. I was tempted to reassure him that Margaret would never leave such a valuable book in the shop. Yet as soon as I thought it, I remembered her talking once about a closet she had had installed during the renovations. It was state-of-the-art, fire-walled and dehumidified with its own temperature control, to keep truly rare books safe from sunlight, insects, and mildew. "Not that I have anything to put in it," she had joked. "Talk about overly optimistic!"

I didn't mention the rare-book closet to Marty.

Chapter Nine

I stopped at the post office to mail Margaret's books and then, on impulse, went to Wild by Nature to buy ingredients for a healthy dinner. But by the time I pulled into the driveway after a day that had started at four thirty A.M., I was in no mood to husk corn or broil salmon. Even lifting the lid off the container of salad bar greens seemed like too much work. Opening a can of Senior Friskies for Miss T and Raj, I listened to my messages instead. The second was from my older daughter, Jane.

"Hey, Mom. I'm calling because the cappuccino maker at our rental broke? And I know you have one you never use? Our ferry leaves from Sayville for Fire Island around five thirty and if you could meet us there with it, I'd appreciate it."

It was not what I wanted to hear. How like Jane to expect me to drive an hour round trip to deliver a coffeemaker! I glanced up at the schoolhouse clock. Thankfully, it was after six. How did she *know* I never used it, anyway?

But I had been a mother too long not to hear the marching band of guilt, its drumbeats in the distance. *Jane never begs you for money the way Jason and Hannah do. She's entitled to a favor once in a while. And shouldn't you be happy to see your own child, even if it's only to hand off an appliance? Think of all those young professionals who will be caffeine-deprived in the morning.*

The voice was relentless, even as I yanked out the bottle of Chardonnay. *You can spend a whole day doing a favor for a friend and not even spare an hour for your child? Even if her sense of entitlement does remind you of your sister Patsy?*

58

Would Jane still be waiting on the pier, looking the way she used to when I was late to pick her up from Brownies?

The final message told me. "Hey, Mom, I guess you're not home. So don't come! We won't be here. We have Lance's car, and we'll come over sometime to pick it up."

Her cheerful acceptance intensified my guilt, but I managed to pour a glass of wine and carry it out to the backyard chaise. I lay there drinking in the mellow summer night. Stella d'Oro lilies bloomed all around me and the hostas were sprouting antennae. As I watched the goldfish in the small pond to my left, I caught sight of a delicate creature, a tadpole, pressing up through the tiny green circles of duckweed. His brave new legs were stretched out behind him. The enchantment of the start of new life gave me the energy to make dinner.

When I finished eating, I called University Hospital again and insisted on being connected with the Intensive Care Unit. The floor nurse told me that Margaret was still unresponsive, but her condition had been downgraded to "Serious."

I supposed that was something to be thankful for.

I went out to the barn to catalog books, but couldn't concentrate. An annoying tape starring Howard Riggs began an endless loop. Why had I let him order me out of The Old Frigate? Margaret trusted me to work in the shop when she wasn't there; why hadn't I stood up to him? Marty would have backed me up. But instead we'd slunk off like two cats who had peed on the rug—leaving Howard to search the shop.

I jerked awake. It wasn't just Howard who could search the shop. All anyone needed to do was reach through the broken back door window and turn the lock. The outside passageway was so narrow that no sane person would use it. But sane people did not include book dealers. I had thought about getting the glass replaced, had even located the Yellow Pages in the office, but as the day got busier, I had forgotten it. But I could at least cover the window with cardboard temporarily and call the glass company in the morning. Maybe I would have to check what was in the climate-controlled book closet too, to make sure no one had gotten in.

In my line of work, cardboard and masking tape are easy to come by. I dropped a utility knife into my woven bag as well, and minutes later was behind the wheel of the van, fueled by my fury at Howard Riggs. Not only had he made off with Margaret's find, he had probably helped himself to the money in the till as well.

At the top of the hill, the sight of Port Lewis calmed me momentarily. It was a fairyland. Paper lanterns had been hung around the harbor and reflected soft colors in the water. Music floated into the street. Even the teenagers that were crouched at the base of the Unknown Lobsterman looked more wholesome than usual. Rolling down my window, I breathed in the sweetness of cotton candy, the salt tang of seawater, the pungency of fried shrimp.

Yet High Street, two blocks away, was as dark as any basement. I parked the van in front of The Old Frigate with no trouble. I wondered why The Whaler's Arms was deserted at this hour, and then remembered that it was closed on Monday. For a moment, I sat looking at the darkened windows along the street. Then I found the key to the shop's door on my ring and was starting to climb out of the van, when a flash of light shone from the fireplace area in the store. The next gleam was closer to the counter, and then the light disappeared.

I felt unable to move. Someone was in the shop *now*. I waited for another flash of light, but next there was a more diffuse glow that seemed to be coming from the middle room. Two different flashlights? Immediately I thought of the Hoovers. Paul and Susie's last name was actually Pevney, but people called them the Hoovers because of their habit of arriving at the end of sales when prices had dropped, and vacuuming up everything that was left.

I had talked to Susie two weeks ago after a sale, as she was leaning against their ancient station wagon that was already crammed with books. Paul was bringing out the last of the cartons.

"Looks like you did okay," I said.

"This morning? *Not*." She brushed dusty hands against a blue and orange Mets shirt that was starting to unravel at the bottom, her brown eyes sardonic behind round glasses. "All we can afford to do now is buy on the cheap. Paul thinks books are this wonderful investment. *I'm* the one who has to list them all on eBay."

"How's that going?" To have to describe each book and upload a photograph had to be tedious.

"It would be fine if I could do it twenty-four/seven. No, make that forty-eight/seven. Paul does the packing, and he's good about that. But we can't even pay the mortgage! Do you want our books if we end up on the street?"

"If you need some money . . ."

But what was I saying? I had exactly three months before Colin made a final decision. If he decided to stop paying rent on the house, even a small reserve inherited from my parents would not get me a place for all my books. I could probably move into the barn, but not if I started lending people money. It was the kind of offer my father would have made back in the days when he had very little himself.

"No. But thanks. All we need is one good find. Something that's been overlooked by everyone else. It happens to other people—why not *us?*" She had been near tears.

I thought about Susie now, fortified by huge bags of M&Ms, working way past midnight to upload book descriptions. Why did we torture ourselves this way? Why not just get a job at Walmart or buy lottery tickets? The truth was, we were addicts. Addicted to the heft of a book under our fingers, the wonderful mystery of where it had been. And we were addicted to the hope that one of these days a book, a scrap of paper, a tattered pamphlet, would pay back our devotion by being worth more than we could have imagined.

I prayed that it wasn't the Hoovers inside, looking for a windfall to save them. But other booksellers had secrets too, stresses I did not know about. Howard Riggs couldn't be making a living in that barracks of a shop. Marty had a craving for important books that was close to an illness. His good friend Roger Morris, known professionally as The Bookie, was a dealer in black Americana. Who knew what *he* had to do to survive in a cutthroat world?

I commanded myself to calm down. None of the dealers I knew would steal books from an injured colleague. No, my cynic countered, but they might search the shop for the find that everyone else knows about. *Wake up, Goldilocks, the bears are here.*

Even though the July air was still muggy, I felt chilled. If people were in the front of the shop, I could not risk unlocking the door and stepping inside. Not with Margaret's head injury that seemed to have been caused by more than a simple fall. Much as I dreaded it, I would have to use the alleyway again and go in the back door.

Slipping the cardboard and tape into my woven bag, I climbed down, and then looked right and left on High Street. No one. Unfortunately.

The passageway between the bookstore and the gallery looked even narrower than before. Who would leave an opening between buildings only two feet wide? Reminding myself that at least this time I would not be pushed down by a nervous constable, I turned sideways and started through the tunnel, feeling rather than seeing the rough brick. Once, I stumbled where the ground sloped more steeply than I remembered, and caught myself, scraping my arm against the wall.

Reminding myself to breathe, I kept going.

When I burst onto the patio, I realized I had been picturing a small overhead light beside the door. But this area was nearly as dark as the alley. To my right, the ground dropped to a public parking area far below, planted in between with dense evergreens. In the brief headlights of a car that was leaving, I saw that the back door was partly open, the broken-out window like a missing eye.

I was infuriated. Who would have the gall to not even hide what they were doing? Moving across the cement apron, I pushed the door open all the way, stepped just over the threshold, and stopped. I strained to hear a sound, any noise at all, as my fingers skimmed the wall beside me. Where was that light switch? I remembered lighting the room from the opposite wall when I opened the shop yesterday, but I assumed there would be a switch by the back door as well. My fingers scrabbled nervously across the plaster.

It felt like the darkness was filled with people listening. Then, from the middle room there was a creaking sound: a shoe on a wooden plank.

"Hello," I called out. "Who's there?"

For a moment there was absolute silence. Then I heard feet again and the unmistakable tinkle of the bell above Margaret's front door.

They were getting away! Still, if I ran through the shop quickly enough, I might get a look at the car driving away. I started to run and had nearly reached the middle room when an arm snaked around my waist and a forearm crushed my throat. The arms held me fast, dragging me back toward the basement.

Chapter Ten

Years of terror made me fight back, twisting and kicking like a furious delinquent. The utility knife in my bag glowed in my mind like an icon, but my arms were pinned tightly to my sides. We danced toward the basement door and toward the reality of my hurtling head-first down the stairs. Would it break my neck? Out of habit, my left hand was still inside my woven shoulder bag, grasping my keys; I let go of them and felt around for the textured handle of the knife.

I sensed that my attacker was trying to get a hand free to turn the doorknob, but could not risk letting go of my neck *or* my arms. By then I had found the utility knife with its sharp narrow point. But there was no way I could pull it out of my bag. Desperately I clenched the handle, and then shoved the blade through the woven cloth into his thigh.

It was little more than a pinprick, probably did not even break the skin, but he grunted with surprise. He loosened his hold just long enough for me to pull away from him. But then he gripped my shoulders and pushed. I tripped over the leg he extended and went sprawling between two bookcases. He gave me a kick in the ankle, out of pure meanness, and was gone.

Dazed and shaken, I could not even move for a minute or two. Then I pushed painfully up from the bare wood floor and gingerly balanced on my knees. Everything ached, but I knew I was not seriously hurt. I wondered if he was still in the bookstore, lying in wait. Yet he could have killed me if he had wanted to when I was lying facedown on the floor. Perhaps the attack had been more of a sense of pique at a plan foiled than murderous rage.

Using the bookshelf to my right, I pulled myself slowly to my feet, and rubbed my throat, checking for any damage. My cheek was friction-burned from sliding against the floor. But I would live to fight over books another day.

Limping from my kicked ankle, I switched on the lights in each room, ending up at the front counter. One of the doors of the glass cases was standing open; the lock had been forced. But what was missing? *The Tin Man of Oz* was still there, as was *Poems of a Long Island Farmer* by Cutler Bloodgood, a traveler on whom Mark Twain had based a character in *Innocents Abroad.* The two volumes of *The Apples of New York,* with their beautiful color plates, still stood together with a copy of *The Razor's Edge* that I hadn't even noticed before. There were no gaps and I couldn't honestly see that any books were gone. While these were all books you would not want to have stolen, books for which, on the right day and with the right buyer, you might get up to several hundred dollars, they were not exactly firsts of *The Catcher in the Rye* or *The Great Gatsby.*

I stared at the cash register, unwilling to open it. I could not bear to see that it had been emptied, that all my work on Margaret's behalf had been wiped out—as well as the money left in there from Friday. But when I rang up the NO SALE sign, the drawer bounced open. All of yesterday's cash was still in place, singles, fives, tens, and twenties, curling up neatly from under metal prongs.

So: whoever it was who had been in here had been after the book.

Time to call Alex Kazazian. I moved toward the phone, and then realized that his card was still in the book barn. Hanging around here was not a good idea anyway. Without bothering to tape up the back window or even turn out the lights in the other rooms, I opened the front door, locked it, and got into my van.

Alex Kazazian didn't call me back until 7:40 the next morning. I was already up and at work in the book barn, wrapping orders.

As soon as he identified himself, I said, "There was a break-in at the bookstore last night. The Old Frigate."

"What did they take?"

"I'm not sure. But they attacked me! One held me from behind and was trying to push me down the basement steps."

"Big guy?"

"Bigger than me!"

"Anything special about him? He smell like anything? Could you feel what he was wearing?"

"I think just a T-shirt. Maybe jeans. It happened so fast."

"You go to the emergency room?"

"No. I mean, I wasn't really hurt. I'm just stiff today."

"Get it checked out anyway. Go to the ER. Look, my tour starts at four. I'll stop by the shop and take a statement from you."

"You want me to go to the *shop?*"

"I thought you worked there."

"Can't you come any earlier?"

"I'll see what I can do."

My next call was to Port Glass and Mirror; they promised to get to The Old Frigate before noon to replace the window. I guessed I could stay there that long.

When I got to High Street, it was hard to recall last night's terror. Galvanized pails of Gerber daisies stood outside Love in Blooms; just beyond the flower shop the antiques' dealer was sweeping his sidewalk clean as a waitress sponged off outdoor tables at Wrap Wrap! It really was a charming street. Before unlocking The Old Frigate, I went next door to The Whaler's Arms to pick up coffee.

Derek, the silver-haired owner, handed me the Styrofoam cup. "How's Margaret?"

"Hanging on."

"A damn shame," he pronounced. "Especially after all she's put into that shop. They say a boat's a hole in the ocean you pour money into, but retail's just as bad." He glanced around ironically at his nautical restaurant.

"It can get expensive," I agreed.

"When she took that balloon loan, I couldn't believe what she was spending. New wood floors, the fireplace in, new everything. Gorgeous."

"It is." I tried to remember what the shop had looked like before the renovations, but in those days we were on the road a lot.

"You gotta keep your interest in something fresh, you know? You lose interest, customers can tell. Anyway, give her my best."

"I will."

Walking the short distance between shops I wondered if Margaret had also bought new ladders during the renovation. A five-year-old library ladder step should *not* break.

The first person through the door was Susie Pevney, aka Hoover, cheerful in denim shorts and a black SUBWAY SERIES T-shirt. She was as interested in baseball as in books.

"Hey Delhi! Margaret's not back?"

"Not yet."

"How is she?"

"She's still in the hospital." I could have told her more. But after last night I was no longer sure who I could trust. Why was Susie here *now?*

She made a commiserating face about Margaret, and then added, "I thought that other guy would be here."

Perhaps because with Amil, less knowledgeable, she could have continued her search?

"Amil? No."

"Is something *wrong,* Delhi?" Her brown eyes blinked earnestly behind her glasses. "Did I do anything?"

I leaned forward on the stool behind the counter. "I'm just upset. Did you know that Margaret found something important?"

"No. What?"

"I don't know. Jack Hemingway told me. I thought you might have heard."

Susie made a disbelieving face. "You're kidding, right? You think anyone tells *us* anything? We're the pariahs, didn't you know? You're the only friendly one. And Margaret's okay." But then she laughed. "But Paul's always reminding me that it's a business—not my mom's book club."

"How's he doing?" I asked. Paul Pevney, tall and very thin, with granny glasses and untidy colorless curls, was one of the gentlest men I knew. Absurd to even imagine him attacking me.

"Oh, he's fine. He's started working at Home Depot now—six nights a week. We decided it's the only way for us to get out of the hole. But he's on the four-to-midnight shift, so that it doesn't inter-fere with book buying." Her lips tilted with irony and sweetness.

"I'm not so sure that's a good thing. His night off is even Friday, so he can get to bed early for weekend sales!"

"But he likes it?"

She considered that solemnly. "Actually, he does. Paul's very handy with tools, how they work and all. He can explain to people what they need to do."

"Great." Of *course* it hadn't been the Hoovers last night. "So can I interest you in a signed first of *To Kill a Mockingbird?*"

"I wish! Actually I came to sell Margaret some stuff. Good enough books, you know, but the kind that do better in stores."

"You could try Howard Riggs."

"Oh, right. Do I look like I need to be beat up?"

At that moment the glass man arrived, a baby-faced teenager with a continuous smile. He grinned at me, smiled again when he saw the broken-out window, and beamed as he extracted a metal tape measure from his pocket.

Whatever he was on, I wanted some.

I left him to his work and, as I entered the second room, looked more closely at the ladder.

The broken rung was halfway up, probably the highest step you'd stand on to shelve a book at the top. But wasn't it higher than Margaret would need? Tentatively, I climbed to the step just below it and stretched out my arm. I could reach the books on the top shelf easily, and she was taller than I was. On my way down, I also saw that although the ladder of thick blond wood looked new, the top of the broken step had splintered unevenly as it cracked.

Back on the floor, I pushed the step into place. But as soon as I took my hand away, it flopped down. Something was wrong. Shouldn't the splinters catch? I tried again, watching as the wood dropped, then knelt down and looked up from beneath. Someone had sawed the rung almost all the way through, so that the surface of the step would have broken naturally from the weight.

I looked for sawdust on the floor but saw none, and then ran my finger lightly over the grooved step below it. Several tiny beige flakes clung to my skin and I quickly rubbed my thumb against my finger to return the specks. I was handling *evidence*.

Yet it made no sense. No one could have gotten into the shop and pulled out a saw without Margaret knowing. Except, possibly, Amil, when we were next door having coffee. Had he been replacing the saw in the office Friday when I came in and surprised him? He knew Margaret would be the only one to climb that ladder. There were signs at the top of each warning FOR STAFF USE ONLY! PLEASE REQUEST HELP.

Now I had something to show Alex Kazazian, though I still wasn't sure what it meant. Where was he, anyway? I paid the smiling glazier, and rang up a steady stream of sales. With people always in the shop, I felt safe. And I was collecting a nice amount of money for Margaret.

At half past two, just when I thought things were slowing down enough to think about lunch, my daughter Jane walked through the door, accompanied by her new friend. He had short fair hair and a squared-off jaw with a deep cleft. His face had angles like a comic book hero and his shoulders were boxy in the same way.

After Jane and I hugged, she announced, "This is Lance! He's pre-med at NYU, plays tennis, and scuba dives." She pushed him forward as if showing off a Prada bag. But pre-med meant he was still an undergraduate, several years younger than Jane. This was a recent development. Throughout college, she had dated much older men, as if trying to copy me. But since starting her career in finance in Manhattan, she seemed more interested in finding a playmate.

"Nice to meet you, Mrs. Fitzhugh," he said heartily, thrusting out a tanned arm. He was as pleasant as a Boy Scout, and I did not bother to explain that I used my maiden name.

They made an attractive couple. Jane had dark blond hair the color of mine, but wore it short; that day she had it clipped with colored barrettes, creating several odd but attractive waterspouts. Her outfit was the unattractive style of the sophisticated young—baggy khaki travel shorts and a crisp white camp shirt.

"How did you know I was here?"

They looked at each other and burst out laughing. "Janie was just showing me the town and spotted your van. She said you wouldn't be anywhere but the bookstore."

"Mom, that van's a mess! All those McDonald's wrappers. You never let *us* eat fast food."

"And see how beautifully you turned out."

"Why are you behind the counter? Where's Margaret?"

"Long story."

"And what's that smell?" Jane crinkled her perfect nose. "How can you *stand* it?"

I considered. The faint aftershave odor I associated with thrift shop books had gotten stronger in the last hour, and taken on a meaty undertone. I had noticed it more since the back window glass had been replaced.

"*Tell* her, Lance," she commanded.

He gave me an apologetic smile. "It is kind of ripe."

"Mom, it's like when Jason's guinea pig got inside the wall and died? And we could smell him, but we couldn't find him?"

I was sorry she had said that. Looking over at a very tall man who was sitting in the tan wing chair, a mound of books in his lap, I called, "We have to close now. I'm sorry."

He sighed. "You mean I have to decide?" He shuffled through the pile, and then brought over two Eyewitness Guides, one for France and one for Italy. I looked at them longingly. I wished *I* were back in Sorrento. Or Nice. Or even on my chaise lounge by the fish pond with a cup of espresso.

As soon as the man was out the door, I said to Lance, "Snap that lock, will you?"

Jane gave me a wary look.

"We have to find out what it is," I said.

"Lance and I can wait outside."

Oh, no you don't. "C'mon, Jane. You've got the best nose."

"Mom!"

"It's true."

When she was growing up, Jane drove Colin crazy by sniffing out milk that was just beginning to think about turning and refusing to drink it; she knew instantly where a cat had done something naughty. "You know I get sick," she warned. "I don't have a cast-iron stomach like you."

"Lead on, McJane."

Now I can't remember why I had insisted, why I thought it was up to us to find whatever it was.

Taking Lance's hand, Jane stepped cautiously into the next room of books, and into the next. Then we were in the last room. For a moment I hoped we were smelling something from outside, a dead raccoon or a possum that had collapsed on the patio. But Jane was turning toward the closed basement door. The odor was now a presence.

"What's down *there?*" she asked me nervously, waving her scarlet-tipped hand at the door.

"Just the basement." Every cell in my body was on alert, ready to stop me.

Slowly I reached in front of her, turned the knob, and snapped on the light. "I think Margaret keeps books down here."

"Smells like she cures hams too," Lance said cheerfully.

I shivered.

When neither Jane nor I moved, he edged around us and started down the stairs. I followed with Jane at my heels. The smell reached out with ghostly arms to welcome us. Finally standing on the cement floor, I saw that the whole downstairs was lit by a single bare bulb; I prayed that it would not burn out. Or that a malevolent hand would not switch it off at the top of the stairs.

But I was just as shocked by the chaos around me. As perfectly as the books were arranged upstairs, this looked like a dumpster explosion. Books crashed out of broken cartons or were tossed on the cement. A few shaky towers had collapsed.

I stared down at the books as we edged past. Danielle Steel and Judith Krantz jostled James Patterson. Most looked like book club editions, good reads but with no resale value. There were multiple copies of fad diets and celebrity biographies, mass market paperbacks and dog-eared travel guides. None of us could avoid these when we bought books in bulk. But I quickly donated mine to library sales and trashed any dangerously out-of-date.

But why did Margaret have so many? And then I understood her sad secret. Not wanting to offend the community that revered her as a village icon—or idol—she must have accepted them in trade, knowing she would never be able to resell them. A few, maybe, to walk-in customers, but never the hundreds and hundreds abandoned down here. This was a book graveyard.

Following Jane, trying to breathe through my mouth, I was sure Margaret would never have left the basement in such a mess. These books had been tossed with a vengeance, as if someone had been in-furiated at finding Irving Wallace instead of Shakespeare.

Jane moved like a sleepwalker toward the barely ajar metal door at the end of the room. Margaret's climate-controlled closet.

"It's in there," Jane shrilled, then pressed her hand over her mouth and buried her face against Lance's strong shoulder.

"Why don't you go back upstairs?" I said.

"No! I'm fine!"

"You don't have to be here."

"I'm not going back upstairs by myself!"

"Well . . ." I stepped forward and gave the door a push. And then I was gagging, hand across my stomach. The smell was like a blast from the devil's oven, a liquid heat pouring over us. And yet the air from inside was cool. I moved my hand up to cover my mouth and nose.

We had to get out of there. This was beyond anything we should be doing.

The overhead light moved like exploring fingers into the small rectangular space.

I knew what we'd find. But the vision of the figure sitting sideways, brown feet bare and khaki legs pushed up to his chest went through me like uncontrolled electricity. I stared at the side of his bent head, now a map of bloody lines. Something about his skin seemed to be melting.

Behind me Jane moaned, though I was not sure she could see anything.

Spinning around, I pushed her across the cement floor toward the stairs. Lance was right behind us. "Yikes," he kept saying, then added a few other words.

The odor chased us up the stairs like an angry ghost.

When we got to the front counter, I realized I was saying out loud what had been repeating in my head. "My God, my God, my God!" It was more a plea for help than anything else.

Without taking another breath I reached around the counter and pulled out my bag by its yarn handle. Then we tumbled onto the sidewalk, crashing into a group of vacationers.

"Where's your phone?" I begged Jane, when we were on the sidewalk in front of The Whaler's Arms. Mine was on the desk in the barn, getting charged.

"Here. Right here. Mom, you look terrible! What *was* it?"

So she hadn't seen.

"You don't want to know," Lance assured her.

Shaking, I fished Alex Kazazian's card out of the bottom of my bag. "Dial this number for me?" I had no idea how to use the lime green toy she was holding, and was not capable of learning now.

The phone rang four times before his voice mail came on. When the tone beeped, I gasped, "This is Delhi Laine. I found Amil. In the basement closet behind a lot of books. I'll be at—" Then I stupidly gave him my home phone.

"What's a mil?" Jane asked, puzzled. "Some kind of animal?"

"Mrs. Fitzhugh, you okay?"

He asked because I had leaned back against the restaurant wall, eyes closed, and was laughing as tears blurred my eyes. "Amil is not a pet," I gasped. "He's Margaret's assistant."

"You mean it was a person in there? And he's dead?"

"Yes. Oh yes. Look, I've got to call the real police." I waited, and then realized I was still clutching the cell phone. "Do I just dial 911?"

"I'll do it." Jane retrieved the phone and pressed in a series of numbers.

"There's a special access code," Lance explained. "So if she loses the phone, someone can't start making calls."

Jane pressed the phone into my hand.

"Police emergency," a voice intoned. "Your call will be answered by the next operator. Do *not* hang up." In less than thirty seconds, I was speaking to a calm voice.

"We found—someone's been killed." My voice shook.

"Where are you now?"

"The Old Frigate Bookshop. High Street. I don't know the number but they'll see it."

"Town?" She was patient with me.

"Oh. Port Lewis."

"Just a minute."

I imagined her relaying that information to the police.

Then she was back. "Your name?"

For a second I blanked it out. "Uh—Delhi Laine." I spelled it for her.

"Did you call an ambulance?"

"No. Look, he's been dead for . . ."

"Stay right there, Ms. Laine. A police officer will be with you shortly."

I handed the phone back to Jane and she wrapped her arms around me, her hair soft against my face. The scent of vanilla creme rinse made me gag, but I didn't want to let go of her. I swallowed down hard as Lance moved in for a group hug, his larger arms enfolding us both.

We held on to each other, swaying as people eddied curiously around us. When we finally pulled apart, Jane demanded, "Mom, *what's* going on? I find you working in the bookstore instead of Margaret. Then we find someone *dead* . . ."

In a series of choppy sentences I told them about everything, including my mistaken belief that Amil might have attacked Margaret.

"I was wrong," I wailed. "And he's the one who's dead."

"But it's not your fault," she said, puzzled.

Lance and Jane looked at each other. What could they say to me?

Chapter Eleven

It seemed no time at all for the wail of sirens to begin, all in different frequencies. Two squad cars, an ambulance, and an off-duty EMT van stopped just short of each other, blocking in a row of hapless cars. Three officers in navy uniforms leaped out, racing as if there were still a life to save.

I ran toward them. "In there," I heard myself saying. "All the way to the back and down the stairs."

But the third policeman stayed with me instead. He had black hair in a buzz cut and blue eyes with amazingly dark lashes. I found I couldn't stop looking at his eyes.

"Can you tell me what happened?" he asked.

We told him, in stops and starts.

"Do you know who he is?"

"Yes." My voice died and I had to swallow. "Amil Singh. He worked here."

"Okay. I'm Matt McLand. Why don't I take your statement first?"

Leading me to the blue and white car, he settled me on the leather seat. It felt wonderfully cool, but I was dazzled by the array of lights and devices. The radio crackled to life, but he ignored it.

"Are you okay?" he asked.

I shook my head.

"Do you feel sick?"

But I could not even answer. I was afraid that moving would shake loose what I was trying to keep inside.

"If you get sick, don't worry. Just open the door. Otherwise, try and relax. No, don't close your eyes!"

I did what he said, and after a minute my system was calmer.

"Can you talk now?"

"Yes," I whispered.

I gave him Amil's full name and address and told him everything, starting with the discovery in the basement and continuing with Margaret's accident, the ladder that had been tampered with, even the attack on me. I talked without stopping, even bringing in Lily. When I mentioned that Amil's family was in India and didn't know what had happened to him, my eyes overflowed.

"So he doesn't have family here?"

I shook my head. "Just housemates."

Handing me a clutch of tissues, Matt McLand said kindly, "Suffolk Homicide will be picking this up. I'll tell them what you told me, but you'll have to make a statement to them."

"You won't be handling this? I want you to handle this!"

He patted my hand. "Homicide is specially trained."

"But why can't you do it? I want you to do it!" *Woman behaving badly.*

"Trust me. It will be fine."

Still blinking away tears as I eased out of the cruiser, I saw that the bookstore door had been Xed with yellow plastic crime tape. I leaned wearily against the window as Officer McLand interviewed Lance and then Jane. While I waited with Lance, two unmarked cars pulled up, the men inside quickly allowed in the building by the cop at the door. Alex Kazazian never appeared.

When Jane climbed out of the police cruiser, we loitered on the sidewalk, not knowing what to do next. "Let's walk," I suggested finally.

We drifted down the High Street in the direction of the harbor. At the corner we could see the waterfront hotels festively outlined by tiny white lights in the summer dusk. We were pulled toward the lights, drawn as insects.

Crossing Anchor Road and making our way onto the long pier, we stared at the boats moored around us. People were sitting in the open sterns of larger crafts, enjoying drinks. Silvery collisions of laughter hung in the air. How had it gotten so late? Soon people would be *eating*. The smell of the salt water made me think of raw clams, and from a hotel kitchen came the nauseating sizzle of beef.

It had a different effect on Lance. "I'm starved," he said brightly.

Jane shuddered, but said, "Mom?"

My stomach was pitching in small waves like the ripples beneath us, but I wanted to keep them with me. "Maybe something to drink."

We walked back into the village, to a small Mexican restaurant that Lance chose. I meant to order a Diet Coke, something that would settle my stomach, but when I next looked there was a large blue Margarita in front of me, a specialty of Cafe Rio.

Lance plunged his fork into his burrito and did most of the talking. There had been an altercation at their group rental on Fire Island that morning with two women who refused to wash any dishes or clean up after themselves. Unpleasantries had been exchanged, and Lance and Jane decided it would be prudent to spend the day on the mainland.

"We weren't *that* insulting," Jane said plaintively, poking at the dish of nacho chips but not eating any. "But Susan is really gross." A shudder. "She left squirts of toothpaste all over the sink!"

I grabbed a chip to calm my stomach and changed the subject. "What's new at work?" Jane had earned an MBA right after college and was now an investment counselor. She was also earning as much as Colin ever had. I listened now to the murmur of her stories as to a comforting brook just out of sight.

Yet every few minutes the image of Amil—Amil bloody and *dead*—crashed in, shocking me all over again. Finally I did something I used to tell the children to do when something had frightened them. I placed a soft midnight blue velvet cloth over his body and told myself I couldn't see him anymore. It actually worked—or worked well enough for me to think about other things.

Jane and Lance followed me back to the house in his Hyundai to pick up the espresso machine. After Jane's phone message, I had set it out on the counter, scrubbed and ready to travel, though its carton had been discarded long ago. Colin and I had bought it after our first summer in Italy to prolong the feeling of Sorrento. While the warm weather lasted, we made cappuccino at ten at night and sat in the back garden, pretending we were still on the Amalfi coast. Had we been as happy then as I remembered now? I had loved each new place we washed up in, each desert or college town or foreign city. And I had loved Colin too.

Jane frowned. "It's littler than I remembered."

"What?"

"The coffeemaker."

"You were expecting one of those copper steamers?" I teased.

"What do you think, Lance?"

"We could buy one, Janie. Since we have to leave it there anyway."

The conversation was taking on the unreality of one of my beloved Magritte paintings, a surrealistic juxtaposition of people chatting while a corpse lay at their feet. Someone Jane's age *was* a corpse, never again to joke about wanting a triple latte, never again to return to his home in India. The time he had been given on earth was over, snatched away, while Lance and Janie debated the merits of an appliance. But why not? They hadn't even known Amil.

"You could pick out a book." I gestured in the direction of the barn, hoping to keep them with me a little longer.

Jane frowned. "Why would I want a *book?*"

"That's right. You already have one."

She rolled her eyes at me. "You and Daddy, still pushing me to read! How do you think I got where I am?"

"That's not the kind of reading I was thinking of."

"*I've* seen her reading a book," Lance said protectively.

It was so sweet and so absurd that Jane and I looked at each other and burst out laughing. Then we hugged each other hard. I begged them to stay for the night.

She looked as if she wanted to, but Lance said, "We'd better get back. All our *stuff* is there." His tone implied that their warring housemates could not be trusted not to destroy their socks and bathing suits if left alone with them overnight.

It was the right thing to say to Jane, though she still looked torn.

"What do you think will happen now, Mom?"

"I don't know, Babe." I tweaked one of her hair spouts as if she were nine years old. An irony: I hadn't loved her this much when she *was* nine years old. It wasn't that I hadn't loved her, but I had been too overwhelmed by the needs of everyone to think about relationships. I had loved each new place we ended up, but it was my responsibility to make sure everyone else was happy and had everything they needed. Another irony: Growing up I had never fantasized about being a mother or played with dolls. I was too busy exploring secret places, imagining everything *I* would do when I was grown.

"I mean, what will happen to you? You're here all alone. What if *you're* in danger? Maybe Dad can come over and stay with you."

"He's back from Peru?" I had a sudden image of Colin, arms crossed, protecting me the way he did his students from Shining Path guerillas. "Look, I'll be fine. This has nothing to do with me."

"Look, you're connected with that bookstore. Keep all the doors locked! Keep your cell phone right next to you. And *charged.*"

"I will."

They left quickly for Sayville to catch the ferry to Fire Island, not even taking the cappuccino maker. It stood forlorn on the empty counter, all cleaned up and nowhere to go.

Lifting Raj from where he was purring against my leg, I cuddled him against my face. My stomach bumped. *No.* I had made it this far, past blue drinks and the smell of sizzling *carne.* I had covered Amil's body so that I could not see it anymore. I focused on the Siamese, shifting him up to my shoulder where he liked to cling. But with a groan that startled him and made him leap gracefully to the floor, I rushed down the hall to the bathroom. I did not pause to switch on the light.

Kneeling beside the cool porcelain, I waited. Nothing else happened. But feeling nauseous was worse than getting sick. I opened memory's door just a little and forced myself to smell again the sweet aftershave odor of rancid meat. It worked very well. Afterward, I lay with my face on the cool tile for what seemed an hour. It wasn't only my stomach that needed the rest; my shoulders and ankle still ached from being attacked the night before.

But I couldn't lie on the bathroom floor all night. I pushed myself up in slow stages and was finally back in the kitchen feeding the cats. Then I walked out to the large black mailbox by the road. I pulled out appeals from charities, too many bills, a few checks in payment for books, and a Priority Mail box from Akron, Ohio. It joined the pile on the oak table from yesterday. I knew I should check my e-mail messages, but that took a level of initiative I didn't possess. Instead I pressed the button to retrieve a single phone message.

After the machine announced that the call had been received at 2:37 P.M. a woman's voice said clearly, "This is Shara Patterson. You came here about Amil? Can you please come and see me again?" Her lilting voice was agitated.

Shara! So the police had already told her the grim news. Except—at 2:37, Jane and Lance and I had still been upstairs in the shop, wondering about the strange smell. The police hadn't even been called.

Maybe she didn't even know that he was dead! He wasn't her husband or the baby's father, but she seemed to have a close relationship with him, worried when he never came home. I had told the police that his only family was in India, minimizing the idea of housemates. I had given Matt McLand Amil's home address, and they would go there in their investigations—but when?

Ignoring Raj pushing at my legs for attention, I listened to her message again. She had asked me to stop by, not to call. And did I really want to tell her what had happened to him over the phone?

Leave it to the police. Go to bed.

But death is a funny thing. Although it is news that will never change, there is a fearsome urgency to letting people know once it has happened. In an odd way it seems unfair to let them continue to live their lives without knowing. Once *you* know, it is a lit match you have to pass along or risk getting burned yourself.

When I arrived at the student house, cars were zigzagged along the road and against the lawn. So they did know and were already gathered in grief. I would leave quietly without even knocking. But when I walked curiously up the neat path of impatiens, just for a quick look through the picture window, I saw that this was no wake.

When I knocked, the door was pulled back by a young man in white slacks and a paisley shirt. Behind him, music I did not recognize rocked a room lit only by candles. People who weren't dancing were talking and laughing in expansive groups, and at the far end of an ell was a table of colorful food. Near my elbow several couples gyrated, the women in tight-wrapped floral saris. The spicy odor of food blended with incense and made me press my hand to my stomach.

I tried to see Shara Patterson among the dancers, but the room was too dim. All I remembered anyway was that she was beautiful and had long black hair. Would I know her in party clothes, her hair swept up? For all I knew, she was working hard in the kitchen. I shouldn't have come.

"How about some Sex on the Beach?" The young man in white was anxious to make me welcome. His smile was not unlike Amil's, but his face, dotted with several moles, was broader and less attractive. He laughed at my expression, before I remembered it was the name of a cocktail. Something lethal with vodka and two kinds of liqueur that would have me in a heap on the tile floor.

"Not tonight," I told him with a smile. "I just need to talk to Shara."

A quizzical smile. "You're friends?"

"She asked me to come." Although we were still standing in the foyer, we had to shout to hear each other.

He surprised me by spinning around agilely and catching the arm of a short, well-muscled American. A bruiser with curly red hair and a good number of freckles, holding two dark bottles of Sam Adams.

"Roosell! This lady needs your assistance."

It took me several seconds to process the name: Russell.

Russell gave me a wink. "You need a Sam?"

"No, I need to talk to Shara."

He raised light eyebrows in surprise. "Shara invited you? I didn't know she *had* any friends."

How insulting was that? "She called me this afternoon."

"What about?"

"Amil? Raphael Singh?"

"What the *hell?*" He squinted at me. "Wait—you're the one who sent the police!"

"They've been here?" *And you're celebrating?*

Someone had changed the music to a song I recognized, "Can't Get Enough of You, Baby," by a group called the Smashed Mouths or the Smashed Pumpkins. More people started dancing.

We moved into a sheltered pocket beside the front door.

"So Shara knows?"

"Knows?"

"About Amil. That he's dead?"

"That he's—yeah, right." He rolled his eyes. "I *wish*."

"He is. Didn't the police come here tonight?"

"Tonight?"

The music, the gyrations, stopped then. From the living room a circle of uneasy faces moved closer, although they could not possibly have heard what we had said.

But then Shara was coming toward us, the group parting for her. Why had I been afraid I wouldn't recognize her? She was wearing a midnight-blue and gold sheath, a red hibiscus behind one ear, and was the prettiest girl in the room. But her eyes grew wide when she saw me.

"This a friend of yours, Shara?" Russell indicated me with a Sam Adams, ignoring the foam that splashed on the tile. "She says she is. You've been holding out on me. Again."

Shara gave me a blank look, and then shook her head.

I didn't blame her. If I'd been married to this idiot I would have done the same. I moved toward the door.

"Ya know what she told me? Wait!" he cried, as the door opened onto a night of stars. "Tell her what you told me."

But I wasn't going to tell anybody anything. My foot caught on the metal door strip and I almost fell, saving myself only by grabbing for the black iron railing.

Russell gave a sharp laugh, and then I felt the vibration of the slammed door.

I didn't look back.

The phone was ringing as I turned my key in the lock. I knew who it would be. Picking up the receiver, I expected to hear music and a babble of conversation. But all was quiet.

"Hello, Shara," I said wearily.

"You came here? To tell me about Amil?"

"Russell didn't tell you?"

"No . . . But he said I could call you." She made it into a concession.

"Listen, something bad happened. Amil—got hurt."

"He's in the *hospital?*" It must have explained a lot of things to her. I wished I could say yes.

"No. I'm sorry. He died."

"No!" Her voice barricaded the truth. "You said he was hurt."

"Well, sometimes hurt means—too bad to get better. I'm really sorry."

And then she dropped the phone. I heard it bounce and listened to the background voices, some murmuring, some shrill. I was about to hang up, when a familiar male voice demanded, "You told her what you told me? He's dead? Like, he's not alive anymore?"

Which word don't you understand?

"But I thought you were—"

"That's why I asked if the police had been to tell you."

"He's dead, really? So what about his stuff?"

That pushed me over the edge. *Sell it on eBay.* But I hung up before I could say anything I would regret.

Chapter Twelve

My body was screaming for sleep, demanding to lie down on any available surface. But fatigue is an old familiar friend who has watched me nod off on Laundromat chairs and playground benches. I've slept through poetry readings, Montessori programs, Disney cartoons, and memorial services. I can sleep anywhere. So I was tempted to stretch out on the couch in the living room. But I made myself climb the stairs and strip off my clothes before falling onto the wide brass bed.

I dropped into a black hole. But thirty minutes later I was awake again, alert and panting, drowning in air too wet to breathe. The thud of insects hitting the screen felt like I was under attack. I shifted around on the sheet, trying to find a cool patch of cotton. But when that didn't help, I pictured myself getting up, dressing, and going downstairs. I played the scene again and again in my head, as if preparing for a role. But I finally roused myself, pulling on a fresh T-shirt and wandering down into the dining room.

The bottle of cabernet sauvignon was in the sideboard. Pulling out the cork, I sniffed it; finding no unusual effects from its sitting two months in the heat, I took a juice glass from the kitchen and poured wine to the brim.

Then I went into the living room and curled up, legs crossed, in Colin's wing chair. It was tan velour, similar to the leather chair my father had had in his study. Men needed chairs like this to think important thoughts. Now I could see why. Its high back and soft body were comforting. When Raj jumped into my lap, jostling the wine, I removed him gently with my free hand. I needed to think hard thoughts.

Lily's suicide, Margaret's attack, and Amil's murder had to be connected in some way. Yet I couldn't see how. As far as I knew, Lily and Amil hadn't really known each other. Could it be connected with Margaret's mysterious find? What if it was not a book at all, but something Lily had stolen from the museum? Maybe she could not live with herself afterward. Or maybe she realized someone else knew about it, someone who would attack Margaret to get it. Maybe Amil had overheard bits and pieces in the bookshop and put it all together Friday morning! He had been going to tell me Margaret was a thief. But then he was silenced.

Except . . . that Margaret had called Marty for information about a book. And if it were stolen property, she wouldn't have really talked about it.

Sipping a fruitiness just this side of spoiled, I turned the puzzle around. Perhaps Amil had been the real target and Margaret had been the one in the way. If so, knocking her out temporarily and pointing to where she was lying so she could be rescued made sense. Amil's wallet had been bulging with cash. Perhaps he had been commissioned to score a drug deal for his housemates.

To die in a drug deal gone wrong was too boring, too mundane. But I knew that it happened, even in Suffolk County.

The headlights of a passing car played out their own drama on the ceiling. Had Margaret seen Amil die? Was that part of the trauma that was keeping her unconscious?

My eyes were starting to feel grainy and I imagined myself moving over to the couch. But then other thoughts shook me awake again. Why hadn't that mystery bookseller ever called me back? Maybe after selling a book to Margaret, he had found out how truly valuable it was. He had met her at the shop Friday night to demand more money. She had refused and, as he was attacking her, Amil walked in and tried to intervene. Probably the seller hadn't meant to kill either of them; he just wanted his book back. So he had searched frantically, creating the chaos in the basement. Maybe he had found it.

End of story.

Except that why couldn't Margaret and Amil between them fend him off? Unless he had an accomplice with him. Or a gun. But neither of them had been shot.

When I woke up again the room was shimmering with morning light; the striped couch seemed to be dancing up and down. I lifted my arm and pain radiated along my back, the payoff for having slept upright for five hours. Raj had crept back and was creating a warm spot in my lap. Reflexively, I reached down and petted him. He gave his usual yelp, and then looked at me anxiously with his crossed blue eyes. Spending the night in a living room chair meant something was amiss.

"It's okay, baby," I crooned. "Want some coffee?"

Coffee. Despite the pain I knew I would feel, I leaned forward and pushed myself up. I had dreamed about Amil's parents in India, something drawn-out and melancholy. I had been trying to explain to them that I had gone to the beach with Amil and he disappeared, something that they refused to understand.

In the kitchen I gave the cappuccino maker a longing look, but did not remember how to froth the milk. The directions were somewhere under a furl of cheesecloth, and appliance warranties. But even if I found the instructions, I would have to try and figure them out. Instead I measured coffee into the French press, and went upstairs to take a bath.

By the time I was sitting on the stone bench beside the fish pond, clean and sipping coffee, it was still only six thirty A.M. For several minutes I watched the flashes of orange and black, the languorous silky fins, but I couldn't stop thinking about Amil. I was also becoming obsessed by the mystery seller. Had something I said made him think I was only an amateur, that I wouldn't bid high enough on what he had? Truth be told, I probably wouldn't have been able to, but how did *he* know? In the old days the phone company kept records of incoming local calls, but with unlimited calling plans I wasn't sure they bothered anymore. I supposed I could try to find out.

But why even bother? I needed money myself. I'd fallen behind in my work the last few days. I had a pile of packages to open, checks to log in and cash, and new books to catalog.

Reluctantly I picked up my coffee cup and went back into the house. Although I tried to keep the business confined to the barn, I now had a stack of Media Mail packages and envelopes on the dining room table. It was not Christmas in July; most of the packages were either books I had ordered for customers or found as sleepers on eBay. Carrying the armload over to the wing chair, I sat down and picked up the first box. It was a package I had mailed out myself; across the front was scrawled, "No such street number." Sighing, I put it to one side to investigate. The second package held *The Pop-Up Book of Phobias,* which I had bought on eBay and hoped to briefly enjoy before I sold it. The third package had a Port Lewis postmark and a post office box for the return address. It was the smallest of the Priority Mail boxes used to mail books, designated by the post office as Large Video. Modern novels and children's chapter books fit compactly inside. I saw that it had not gone through the postage meter. Instead, someone had created a colorful train of stamps that nearly ran off the right-hand corner.

But—had they forgotten to put something inside? The box felt too light to hold anything at all.

Prying open the sticky flap, I wondered if I would need my utility knife. But the cardboard fold yielded to pressure. I pulled out a crumpled *New York Times* page and a small package of bubble wrap. But there was no book inside. I ripped off the clear mailing tape and retrieved a piece of white paper wrapped around a small brass key. On the inside of the paper Margaret had written in her distinct angular script: *Delhi, please keep this safe. If something happens,* you'll *know where to look.*

I stared at the postmark. It had been stamped in Port Lewis on Friday and probably been delivered Saturday. But that was the only thing that was clear. Keep *what* safe for her? Surely not the key. *If anything happens*—and something had—*you'll know where to look.* But I didn't. I hadn't a clue. Her house was the logical place to start. But maybe there was a locked desk drawer or file cabinet in the bookstore.

Shakily, I went to the kitchen for the coffee I had stashed in the thermos. I had just started pouring a cup when there was a sharp rapping on the front door. It turned me to cement. The key! I had to hide the key! Darting back into the living room, I stuffed the note and key under the cushion of the wing chair. Then I went to the door.

I did not know the man on the porch. He looked about my age,
perhaps forty-five, with a colorless buzz cut and hazel eyes that indicated they had seen everything and didn't like most of it. His
mouth pursed with the same sentiment. Even at this hour he had on
a tan suit that contrasted nicely with his olive skin. A political can-
didate? But no. Candidates smiled at you and didn't show up at
seven A.M.

He took out a black leather case and flipped the top down. It
showed a silver badge. "I'm Detective Marselli, Suffolk Homicide.
You're Mrs. Laine?"

"Uh—yes. Delhi Laine. Come in." I unlocked the screen door and
extended it all the way, and then led him into the living room. Thank
God I had not brought my pillow and sheet downstairs and left them
on the sofa like a derelict bunking down. I sat in the wing chair, on
top of Margaret's key, and watched him settle himself on the striped
couch across from me.

"Too early for you?" He sounded as if he hoped it was.

"No, I get up early. Want coffee?"

"No."

We stared at each other.

"You found Mr. Singh when you were working at the bookstore?"

So I explained. I told him about how I had found Margaret and
even mentioned Lily. But when I explained about deciding to keep
the bookstore open, his head jerked up.

"You don't *work* there?"

"No. But I thought Margaret would need the money, so I kept it
open."

"You aren't employed there?"

"No, we're just friends. I'd fill in sometimes when she needed
help. I'm a bookseller too."

"Do you know if she kept a lot of money in the store? Or removed
it at night?"

"I don't. Sorry."

"How about security: Was the shop alarmed?"

"Alarmed?" For a moment I pictured the leather couches and oriental rugs upset at the goings-on. "Oh. No. At least I never saw any
keypad."

And then he erupted. "Let me understand this: You didn't really work there, you don't know squat about how she handled the money or locked up at night. Yet you suddenly decided to play store, totally screwing up a crime scene!"

I jumped. Who did he think he was talking to? "I wasn't 'playing store'! I'd worked there before. Many times. I even checked with Officer Kazazian and he said to go ahead!"

"Maybe because you didn't tell him about the ladder being tampered with. That didn't set off any alarms?"

I was almost too shocked to answer. "I called him as soon as I saw it! He should have checked it anyway. *He's* the policeman."

"Allegedly." But he was calming down. "Okay. You were in the shop, you smelled something bad and went downstairs and found Mr. Singh."

"Actually my daughter noticed the smell. I have allergies this time of year; her nose is much better. I mean, I did smell something, but it seemed sweet like, you know, aftershave." I was babbling, no doubt relieved that he was no longer furious.

He eyed me curiously, as if the men I knew had strange tastes in toiletries. "But you knew Mr. Singh was in there."

"Of course not! How could I?"

"What was your relationship with him?"

"Amil? We didn't really have a relationship. I saw him when I went to visit Margaret."

"Oh please, Ms. Laine. You went to his *house*."

"But—that was after he disappeared! I was trying to find him."

He leaned toward me, his thighs muscular in his tan suit pants. An attractive man, I realized, though exhaustion was making his eyelids droopy. "Why were you looking for him?"

"Because I told Alex Kazazian I would. He told me he wanted to talk to him."

This detective said everything with his eyes. Now they slanted skeptically. "So as a good citizen, helping out the police. How did you know where he lived?"

"I didn't. Until I found out from the university. Amil was, had been, a grad student there." Before he could ask why the university would tell *me,* I added, "My husband teaches at Stony Brook.

Dr. Colin Fitzhugh. They weren't sure Amil was still at that address, so I went to the house. But I called the police as soon as I found out!"

He seemed to accept that. Or perhaps the fact that I had a husband who was a professor made it less likely that Amil and I had been dancing cheek-to-cheek. "Was Mr. Singh involved romantically with anyone? Did he have a girlfriend?"

"I don't know. He *was* very attractive." *Uh-oh.* "On the other hand, he got into a lot of fights," I added quickly.

"Fights? What kind of fights?"

I explained what had happened with Margaret. "And there was the instructor at Stony Brook. He cost her her tenure."

"Would you like to tell me what you're talking about?"

I did. He made more notes.

"Who else did he have altercations with?"

"His housemates, I think. At least one of them, Russell Patterson; he seems to hate him. I don't know why," I added, to forestall more sarcastic questions.

He shifted against the striped sofa back, which was a little too low to support his shoulders comfortably. "Did you have fights with Mr. Singh?"

"Me? Of course not! Why would I have fights with him? I hardly knew him. Everyone thought he was charming. Margaret certainly liked him. And Shara Patterson. And that woman at the university. I don't think it was a woman anyway. More like an angry husband. Or a drug deal gone wrong."

That head jerk again. "Why a drug deal?"

I hesitated. "When Amil took out his wallet on Friday to write down his phone number, the wallet seemed stuffed with money. A lot of bills."

He held up a callused palm—a home do-it-yourselfer? "Stop. Right. There." He enunciated very slowly, as if speaking to someone who was mentally challenged. "Why was this man you 'hardly know' giving you his phone number?"

Damn. "I don't know! When I saw him in the shop Friday, he seemed upset and wanted to tell me something about Margaret. Then he saw someone out the window and stopped. I don't know who. Then he wrote down his number on a card and said to call him Saturday."

His head found the wall behind him and he leaned against it, eyes closed. "How long, Ms. Laine?"

I shivered. "How long what?"

"How long would it have taken you to realize that this is information that the police needs to know?"

I accepted the question as rhetorical.

"So he was carrying a lot of money and was upset with Margaret Weller. And for some reason he wanted to confide in you."

I shrugged. "I have kids."

He accepted the shorthand of my being a mother figure. "Any idea at all what he wanted to tell you? Problems on the job?"

"I asked Margaret after he pushed the coffee back at her, and she said that she was going to have to let him go. But—mostly she was acting like it was just an accident, that he hadn't meant anything. When I said she should call the police, she thought that was silly." I could not tell if he thought it was silly too. "But it burned her face! It could have blinded her. To me that's assault."

"Battery," he corrected absently.

Whatever.

"Anything else you've forgotten to tell me?"

"Actually, there is," I confessed. "When I reopened the shop, I moved the shirt that had been under Margaret's head and the Nike, and put them out next to the trash. I didn't want customers to fall over them. I didn't know they were *evidence.*"

I expected a tirade, but he only looked interested. "So you did that." Then he flipped back several pages in his notebook. "So you don't know if Ms. Weller kept a lot of cash in the shop."

I almost laughed. "There's not that much cash in a used book business. Any big sales would be by credit card. But Margaret can tell you that when she's conscious."

He stood up. "Ms. Weller won't be telling anybody anything."

"*What?*" My hand flew to my throat. In all yesterday's craziness, I hadn't called the hospital.

"She's in a coma. And as far as you're concerned, the shop's closed."

"Don't worry! You couldn't *pay* me to go back there. Not after finding Amil. The smell alone. Not after two people I know were attacked there!"

He watched me with a small smile that was not heartwarming.

Shut up, Delhi.

"You have the key?"

For a horrible second I thought he meant the one she had sent me in the mail. How did he even know? Then I realized he meant the key to the bookshop.

He held out his hand.

I found my woven bag on the kitchen table and fished out my knot of keys. I wasn't sure why my fingers were shaking, but it took a long time to untwist the silver key from the double ring.

I dropped it into his outstretched palm.

"I'll be back," he warned. "There's too much that doesn't make sense." He handed me a card with a raised line drawing of a bull inside a circle, the Suffolk County logo. I saw that his full name was Francis X. Marselli. With his hand on the front doorjamb, he added, "Thank you, Ms. Laine. You've been a veritable fount of information."

I knew he was referencing my academic connections, ironically. But it sounded more teasing than mean-spirited. And I felt happy that a *real* policeman was finally in charge.

It wasn't until he was halfway down the front path of bobbing hosta wands and daylilies that I remembered that Margaret's key might unlock a drawer in the bookshop that I was now banned from.

Stupid, stupid, stupid.

Chapter Thirteen

I didn't go down to The Old Frigate. How could I? Instead I reminded myself that it was more likely that Margaret would hide
something valuable in her house. She would have remembered that I
had a house key from the times I had watered her plants when she
and Lily were traveling. Leaving something in a public place like
the bookshop was just too risky.

Rather than park outside her house, I drove to the residents' lot
and got the last parking space. Or, rather, I created it. A car was
waiting, signal on, as a motorcycle backed out of the only vacancy.
Although the car pulling in had a New York license plate, I could see
that it did not have a village sticker.

As the family started unloading, I slid out of my van and approached them. "If you don't have a permit to park here, it's a
hundred-dollar fine."

The father, pale behind blue sunglasses, gave me a doubtful stare.
"They really ticket you?"

I thought of Randolph MacWharton. "All the time. I bet some of
these cars already have fines."

He didn't stop to look. I heard some expletive about my town as
he climbed back in the driver's side and slammed the door. Under-
standable. But he would just have to look harder.

I parked and walked the several blocks up the hill to Margaret's
house. It was one of Port Lewis' original Victorians and had been
on the annual house tour several times. Rising behind an ornate
wrought-iron fence, it would have been equally at home in San Fran-
cisco. Margaret and Lily had turned it into a Painted Lady, with the
body a light coffee, and the gingerbread trim painted a deep pink,

sky blue, and mauve. Unlike many of the Port Lewis Victorians, it had not been built by a sea captain but by the town doctor.

As I reached the walkway, I saw that the ancient tin bathtub planter was bursting with red Everblooming begonias. Several days' worth of the *New York Times* in blue plastic wrappers crowded the door, a bad signal to give. I would try to call and have delivery suspended. Unlocking the beveled glass door, I scooped up the newspapers, and stepped in. The ornate hall, a perfect recreation of a Victorian entrance with a large armoire of mirrors and brass hooks, had not had time to develop any stale odors. But there was an eerie stillness, as if the house had sensed what happened to its owners.

The hallway was a bit of whimsy. You expected to enter a parlor of carved oak, marble-topped tables, and stuffed pheasants behind convex glass. Instead you found yourself in the living room of a sophisticated collector of art and artifacts, a room in which the off-white furniture seemed to disappear as the walls of glass cases sparkled instead. But today something was wrong. Several of the cases that at Christmas had held exquisite masks, antique Balinese puppets and the eighteenth-century stoneware that Margaret loved were now empty. It looked like a museum where the display was being changed. Had they had to sell some of their collection? Had someone broken in? I was relieved to see that the more traditional dining room with its cabinets of early Wedgwood and Staffordshire looked complete.

At the back of the first floor was Margaret's office. Books that she would never keep in the shop, her personal collection, were shelved here. Surely the lock that fit the key would be there.

Pushing open the white-painted door, I reared back in shock. Like the keys on a derelict piano, books had been pulled from the shelves, and then stuffed unevenly back. A precarious stack tilted on the cherry coffee table. Two wooden file drawers stood open.

I was too late! I cursed myself for not paying attention to the mail. If I had opened the package Saturday, I could have gotten here first. But by now, Wednesday, everyone knew that Margaret was in the hospital. Someone had searched the bookshop—of course they would look here!

Disheartened, I moved over to the beautiful cherrywood desk, noting a disarray of papers that Margaret would never have left.

Then I stared into the hanging files. They had been pushed back and forth, but not pulled out. The lock to one side, a silver oval, was unscratched. Experimentally, I removed the key from the coin section of my wallet and brought it to the lock. Wrong color, wrong brand. The cabinet had probably not even been locked.

Rapidly, I checked the desk drawers and opened a closet. I looked for another piece of furniture with a keyhole, and anywhere a locked box might be hidden. Nothing. Maybe I wasn't too late after all.

There was still the upstairs. I had never been anywhere but on the ground floor, and felt hesitant about invading Margaret's privacy. Would she have even left me a key to somewhere in her bedroom? But as I was debating it, I heard the creaking of steps on the porch outside. The mailman? No, Margaret had a post office box. Then I froze at the brisk tapping of metal against metal. I pictured the brass door knocker in the shape of a woman's hand being lifted and dropped, lifted and dropped.

Finally the rapping stopped and there were more creaking sounds from the steps. Edging into the living room I looked out and saw with relief that a brown truck was pulling away. Sometimes an intruder is only the UPS man.

But it made me conscious of where I was and what I was doing. I would run up the wide staircase, scan the rooms for anything with a lock, and then get out.

At first I wasn't sure that Margaret's bedroom was hers. There was a brass bed with a crazy quilt made of dark velvet pieces that I could imagine her sleeping in. But the rest of the furniture was haphazard, the kind of modern wooden dressers that companies like IKEA sold and lamps that could have come from any thrift store. Still, the room held the now-muffled fruity scent of Shalimar, her perfume. I opened the narrow closet and, reassured, saw her silk blouses and long, old-fashioned skirts. Of course this was Margaret's room, Margaret my friend!

And yet—I was surprised by the paintings on the walls. The most striking, over the brass bed, was of a younger Margaret in a checked western shirt, with flowing chestnut hair and an enigmatic smile. She looked beautiful and wild. I checked to see if it was a self-portrait, but the artist was a W. Weston. Two small seascapes next to the door had rocky cliffs that reminded me of the Pacific coastline; both had been done by an artist named Becca Pym. I was disappointed not to see any of Margaret's own artwork, but she had said she knew a lot of artists.

Quickly I checked the back of the closet, under the bed, and any-where else a box using a key might be stored. A large jewelry box stood on one of the dressers. It was beautifully handcrafted of wal-nut and looked expensive, but it didn't have a lock.

I looked into the other rooms on my way out. Except for Lily's, they had the impersonal hospitality of bedrooms created for overnight guests. But Lily's room troubled me. It was decorated the way I would have expected, with heavy dark green velvet drapes, a matching lustrous bedspread and heavy brass candle sconces. But when I pulled open the closet door, it was completely bare inside. A scent of cedar lingered, but not one piece of clothing, not one purse or shoe, remained.

It made my head spin. Had Margaret spent Friday afternoon packing up every single thing Lily owned? Was she that upset by her death? And if she had, where were the cartons?

I made a very quick tour of the basement—not a happy experience—and found a padlocked shed out near the garage. But the key did not come close to fitting the lock. I realized reluctantly that the answer to my search must lay in the bookshop after all.

Chapter Fourteen

Walking back down into the village, I tried to think how I could search inside The Old Frigate without disobeying Detective Marselli's directive. Perhaps when he told me the shop was closed to me, he meant I could not work there anymore. Maybe I could use the excuse of putting a sign, CLOSED UNTIL FURTHER NOTICE, on the inside of the door, and have a rapid look around while I was installing it. Then I remembered that the yellow crime scene tape was all the message people would need. Some days I wasn't the coldest beer in the fridge.

When I reached The Old Frigate, the tape still hung across the door, but it had a morning-after-the-party droop; one of its corners was even trailing to the sidewalk. There was no guard posted outside.

I glanced through the glass of the front door, just as any curious tourist might. No lights were on and no one was moving around inside. Looking up and down the street, I could not see any police cars. Evidently their investigation was finished. While watching the street, I pushed down on the front door lever with my thumb. The shop was locked.

Still trying to seem nonchalant, I walked away from the door until I was facing the narrow alley. I had vowed never to go through it again. But at least the sun was out, I reminded myself, and I could see the sky.

After another check for watching eyes, I slipped into the passage sideways and began edging my way down. By now I was used to the scrapes and bruises the alley liked to inflict, and I was reassured by the tiny ribbon of blue sky above me. But I was relieved to stumble onto the tiny cement square.

There was no tape around the back door, nothing to indicate that this was a crime scene. Still, what was I *thinking?* No way was I going to defy Detective Marselli's order and go inside, and then have to face those angry slitted eyes. After all, he was a police officer. Even if all I wanted to do was run in and check for a lockbox or file cabinet, and run right out again. Even if Margaret had *asked* me to do it.

Rotating casually, I scanned the patios behind the back doors of several other shops and examined the parking lot below the evergreens. No one was looking back at me, and yet I had the sense that I was being watched.

Well, fine. I was not going to do anything anyway.

I just have to check one thing, I informed the watcher. I'm not here to *steal* anything. After all, if I hadn't told the police about Amil, I'd still be working here. *I'm doing this for Margaret.* Reaching behind me, I tried the handle. It gave easily and a second later I was turning around and slipping inside, not closing the door completely. My heart banged like a fire alarm. Then it stopped dead. For several seconds I felt nothing at all. Finally there was a feeble blip. If I was having a heart attack and Detective Marselli found me, I hoped by then I would be dead.

I pushed on despite my arrhythmia. But when I passed the slightly ajar basement door, I thought I heard someone talking. A trace of the sauerbraten smell remained, and now the trouble was lodged in my stomach and was creeping up my throat. I wasn't made for this.

The front room had enough light coming in from the windows to see where I was going, but the side room office was dim. I felt my way clumsily over to the metal file cabinets, past the plain oak teacher's desk, and stacks of unassembled shipping cartons. Somewhere in here, there was an old wooden box with a brass keyhole. The key did not fit the newer file cabinets or the oak desk's center drawer. There had to be something else.

But I did not find it.

Could there be a box I never noticed stashed on the shelf below the sales counter? I retraced my steps to look. Crouching down, I had just swept my arm across its expanse when I heard the creak of the back door being opened and rapid footsteps.

No! This couldn't be happening! My heart, which had returned to normal, began lurching against my chest like a drunken dancer. I pressed my palm against it, and made myself breath deeply. It was too late to dart around the counter and run out the door without being recognized. All I could do was pray that it was a technician headed for the basement. Even if it were someone else, they might just walk through here and not search the area where I was hiding.

How could this *happen?* I hated scenes in mysteries where the protagonist was illegally searching someone's home or office and heard them coming back. Even though I knew I was reading a story someone had written, even though I knew they would get out without being discovered, I always skipped ahead to where they were safely somewhere else. And now it was happening to me. *Be sure your sin will find you out.* Hunching down further, I knew I would be caught. Because the footsteps had continued past the basement door and were now entering the middle room.

If I were caught, could I actually be arrested? Would Colin put up money for bail? Perhaps he would, but only after a lot of lectures and a promise that I would get a day job where I could be closely watched.

The creaking footsteps kept coming. It was not exactly the assertive tread of a person who had a right to be there, the sure steps of a cop. But it was someone moving rapidly nevertheless, someone with a purpose.

And then I could feel the pressure of another person in the room with me.

"Delhi?"

The voice was soft, but when I heard my name my whole body twanged.

"Delhi, are you in here?"

The footsteps approached the counter and were moving around behind it as if to get to the glassed-in cases . . . I gave a soft scream as someone stumbled over me and yelped too. He had me pinned to the floor.

"God! This is how people die!" he croaked.

Twisting my head, I stared into the large liquid eyes of Roger Morris. *The Bookie.*

For a moment, pressed together, we did not move. It felt like an embrace and perhaps it was. Then he righted himself awkwardly, pulling up by the counter and then putting out his hand to me. Getting up was a slow process; I had stiffened with terror. Finally we were eye to eye.

"I didn't plan to die in here," I whispered.

"Not you, *me*. This is how people get heart attacks! When you didn't answer, I thought you'd gone out the front."

"How did you know I was in here? No one is supposed to be in here. But I thought I had left my cell phone here."

He gave me a penetrating look.

"Really. I've been keeping the shop open for Margaret. I'm not here to *take* anything." That was almost true.

He nodded slowly.

"Let's get out," I begged. "The police are in the basement."

Instead of moving, he gave the glass cases a longing look.

"Roger, there's nothing in there! Believe me. I know exactly what books are there. I'll tell you. Let's just get out of here—then we can talk."

We could talk about why he was so far out of his territory, for one thing. Roger was one of my favorite book people, but he was an enigma. He lived in Brooklyn, but spent a lot of time scouting books on the Island. He was West Indian, but his pink-tinted prescription glasses and sculpted dark curls gave him the look of a dandy. From his professional name, The Bookie, you might assume he was some poor schlep peddling books out of the trunk of his Toyota, when he wasn't running bets on the side. But if you assumed that, you would be wrong. Roger had a lucrative business selling black literature and Americana to a sophisticated Manhattan clientele.

As we moved rapidly around the counter to the front door, another flash of yellow caught my attention. The police had draped crime scene tape around the fireplace area. I remembered the streak of brown I had seen on the hearth, and then forgotten. Had Amil been killed there? My stomach flipped over again. Opening the door and making a rapid check of the street, I led Roger out, ducking, then holding the yellow tape up for him. By now I was sure no one was guarding the shop. Whoever was working in the basement probably thought they had heard their colleagues walking around upstairs. They counted on the crime scene tape to deter people from entering and stealing a bunch of used books. Normally it would.

But book people are a little crazy. Or a lot crazy. At a book sale, if someone yelled, "Fire!" the dealers would have to be dragged out. Even as they were being pulled toward the exit, they would be grabbing at any good book they passed.

I started to take Roger into The Whaler's Arms. But it held Derek and too many other memories. Instead I turned us in the opposite direction. There was yet another new espresso bar near the harbor, with outdoor tables on the deck, and I bought cappuccinos for both of us. We sat under a blue-and-white-striped umbrella, facing the water, watching the gently bobbing boats.

"That was wild, you coming in right after I did," I said.

He gave a soft chuckle, playing with his spoon. "Not so wild. I'd been watching the shop from those benches for a while. Then I saw you go in."

"I didn't see you."

"I didn't want to be seen."

I sluiced a mouthful of foam. "But what are you doing way out here?"

"Oh, who knows. It was a long shot. I saw Marty in Wantagh yesterday, and he told me that Margaret had something of black interest. Something important. So I thought I could make her an offer."

Black interest? Marty had told me Americana, but said nothing about black interest. Maybe he was feeding everyone misinformation. "He didn't tell you about her accident?"

"Sure. But he thought she might be back."

That wouldn't convince anyone. "He didn't say anything about Amil?"

"Amil? Who's Amil? Another buyer? It figures. I'm always too late." It was his standard line of self-deprecation, and totally untrue.

"He was Margaret's assistant." I gestured in the direction of the shop. "But he was killed. It must have been in *Newsday*."

"Who reads newspapers?"

"The yellow crime tape?"

"Jeez! I knew there had been a robbery, but I thought it was only Margaret."

"Wait. Who told you there was a robbery?"

"I thought that's what Marty said."

More misinformation? "What did he tell you about this book of Margaret's?"

He shook his head, but the curls didn't even move. "Not much. Just a book, something unique. Black Americana. But when I saw the crime tape, I *knew* it wouldn't still be there."

Then why were you hanging around?

"Unless the robbery was only about money," he continued hopefully.

"Except that used bookstores aren't known for tons of cash. You'd be better off robbing a nail salon." Then something struck me and I laughed. Too much nervous laughter these days.

"What?"

"There were probably so many book dealers in the shop Monday night that someone should have given out numbers."

He looked gloomy. And then happier. "But if it's black Americana, they might overlook it."

"Marty wouldn't."

"No. Marty sure wouldn't!"

We both laughed at that.

He sighed. "Why wasn't *I* here Monday night?"

"Because Marty didn't tell you. And he lied to me. How obsessed is that?"

Roger held up his hand as if considering numbers. "On a scale of one to ten? At least a fifteen. But so is that pompous ass up the street, Howard Riggs." He laughed. "And a few other people I could name."

I hoped he didn't mean me.

He gestured at my cup. "Want another one?"

"No. I've got stuff to do."

He stood up. "Let me know if you come across the book, okay? Or hear anything."

"I will."

Back at my van, as I started to climb in, he reached out and held my arm gently. Gently, but I would not have been able to pull away. His face was so close to mine, I could see myself reflected in his rosy glasses. "What's going on, Delhi?"

"Nothing! I mean, you know as much as I do."

"But you'll keep me posted?"

"Uh-huh."

He moved in then and kissed me on the mouth. I kissed him back, and we clutched each other as if we were lovers about to be separated by war. Finally he let me go. Was it only a kiss to seal a promise? We searched each other's faces for the meaning of what had happened. I felt shaken, the backs of my hands prickling. Had it been *that* long?

He studied me. "Want to hang out sometime?"

Hang out? I laughed. "I think I'm too old for you."

"Not."

"Roger? If you go back in the shop, be careful!"

"I'm always careful. We darkies have learned *something*."

But had he learned enough? I watched with concern as he ambled toward the benches at the end of the parking lot again. Despite what I had told him, I knew he would wait and search the shop thoroughly when he felt it was safe. Part of him would not be able to shake the belief that, like pulling the sword out of the stone, only *he* would be able to identify the treasure.

Driving away, I thought of something that troubled me more. Although Roger pretended to arrive places late, after everyone else had come and gone, that wasn't true. He liked to say things like, "I got there late, as usual" or "I waited for three hours and the sale never opened." He accused books of leaping off the shelves into my bag instead of his. But most of the time, he was ahead of me in line at sales. There was no reason to believe that he had not been here Monday night with the others. Or even last Friday night, for that matter.

Chapter Fifteen

I drove home. I could not think of anywhere else to go with Margaret's key and had to wrap books and list others for sale. But I worked steadily and, finally, with a stack of bubble-wrapped packages in addressed boxes ready to go, I could spend a few minutes on the part of bookselling I liked best. I reached for the stack of children's books at my feet. There were some treasures inside: *Mousekin* and *Freddy the Pig,* several Noel Streatfeild *Shoes* books, a first edition of *A Little Princess* by Frances Hodgson Burnett. Classics that were hard not to reread on the spot.

I was opening the flaps of the carton when the phone rang. I jumped, still shaky from the bookshop experience, but it was only Colin.

He wasted no time. "Are you okay? Jane just called me. She was very upset."

"You mean about the fight at her rental?" Of course I knew he didn't mean that. But I could not talk yet about finding Amil.

Still, it threw him off. "What fight?"

I told him.

"No, it wasn't that. They didn't even go *back* to Fire Island; she was too spooked to stay out here after what happened in that bookshop." Then the parent-to-parent reproof. "She may seem mature on the surface, Delhi, but she's still very impressionable. She was frantic about you; she wants me to come over and stand guard."

"That's silly. It had nothing to do with me."

"She said the stench was *overpowering*."

"Well, you know Jane. She's got a great nose."

"Delhi, she's not a hunting dog!"

He said it reproachfully, but in a moment we were both laughing. Then he moved on to what was really bothering him. Not my safety. Not Jane's sensitive nerves. "You went out to dinner. I'm supposed to be involved whenever the children are out here."

"It wasn't dinner. Lance was the only one who ate anything. You would have been holding my head while I was throwing up."

"I'll come over if you want."

I hesitated. Did that mean he wanted to come home? Or was he just trying to placate Jane?

"Nobody's about to murder me," I told him honestly. "But—thanks."

"By the way," he said, "I ran into Loretta Hawn yesterday on campus. She's still running the university day care center."

"That's good. How's Loretta?" Asking after her was on a par with wondering if we were getting enough rain. Humorless Loretta wore Birkenstocks with white socks and printed smocks. When she talked about "fantasy builders," she did not mean Victoria's Secret.

"Oh, she's fine. But she's short a helper again. So I told her you might be interested."

"*What?*"

"Come on, Delhi, it's good respectable work. The pay's not great, but there are a lot of benefits. It's even part of the retirement system now."

"Colin, what makes you think I'm looking for a new *job?* And with little kids?" I had a nightmarish image of myself spending eight hours a day singing "I'm a Little Teapot" and mopping up "accidents." Why not just kill myself right now? "Why do you keep coming up with these menial jobs for me? Last month they needed someone to pass out samples at Trader Joe's. It's not like you're encouraging me to go to medical school. Anyway, I love bookselling!"

"And that's not menial?"

I was squeezing the receiver in a death grip. "No. It's fascinating. And it's all mine."

"That's for sure. You have no pension, no social security, no guarantees for the future. You'll have to make some decisions in October."

October. What if he wanted me out of the house? Could he? If he wanted to live here by himself, I could still move into the barn. As long as I could do what I wanted.

"What should I tell Loretta?"

I slammed down the phone.

Then I turned to my new books to console me. Some of them were very collectible and could bring an infusion of cash. People were always looking for *Mousekin's Golden House* by Edna Miller with its adorable illustrations of the white-tailed little rodent. I had *Movie Shoes* and *Family Shoes* in dust jackets. The quirky illustrations in M. Sasek's *This Is Venice* always made it desirable. There were other favorites in the box too, a *Nurse Nancy* Golden Book, a *Freddy the Pig* first edition, and *Big Susan*.

Yet as I price-checked the books with those listed by other dealers, I was alarmed to see that, although some of the prices had held since the last time I sold these books, others had dipped. Marcel Sasek had taken a beating because his books were being reprinted. A bad omen. Books should be getting more rare, more expensive as they aged, not less. Colin's predictions trembled on the edge of my consciousness like cobwebs high in the corners of the barn.

If I had to give up books, I would die. No, scratch that. Lily and Amil had died; I would survive. Then, remembering Margaret, I made my daily call to the Intensive Care Unit. To my surprise, the desk nurse with whom I had become almost friendly told me that Margaret was about to be transferred to a regular ward. I would actually be able to see her tomorrow after ten A.M. She warned me, however, that my friend was still comatose.

Around seven, I did what any bookseller who had slept too little the night before and had had a frustrating day, what any bookseller with low standards and no self-discipline would do. After locking the barn, I drove to the take-out window of my favorite fast food restaurant, ordered dark meat chicken original style, with mashed potatoes, coleslaw, and gravy. Then I raced home before my dinner could get cold, skimping on two stop signs. I poured a large glass of Chardonnay, pulled my signed first edition of *Breakfast at Tiffany's* out of the bookshelf and settled on the den couch. All comforts in place, I abandoned myself to the enchanted world of 1950s New York.

At eighteen, I had discovered the movie, a blueprint of freedom for an earlier generation of young women. Trying to live an authentic life and be as true to myself as Holly, I met Colin my sophomore year at Douglass College and dreamed of a life of adventure. Colin married me quickly, as easily as claiming a book from the stacks. It was a whirlwind courtship, as they say. By the time my head cleared, I had four cranky babies and one self-absorbed poet, and I wasn't humming "Moon River" anymore.

Why did I love this book that had misled me about life? Why could I still recite my favorite paragraphs by heart? Go figure.

I finished reading a little before ten, closed my eyes and fell into a deep sleep.

By morning both Raj and Miss T had found body crevices and settled in. When I slitted my eyes open, I saw that the red and white cardboard box was shamefully overturned, like an empty wine bottle, on the floor. Next to the box was a chicken bone picked clean. I could not remember leaving much chicken the night before except for the skin, but undoubtedly both cats must have enjoyed that.

Sleeping in the wing chair, crashing in the den. I consoled myself with what my friend Gail had told her kids: "When I'm old, if I stand in front of the refrigerator eating ice cream out of the carton, or if I sleep in my clothes on the living room couch, just remember—I've been doing it all my life!"

Slowly I began to orient myself. It was time to mail books, and then see Margaret.

The Port Lewis Post Office, although dating back to the 1930s, is not particularly picturesque. There are no WPA murals or old oak counters. You enter through a vestibule lined with ornate brass mailboxes with tiny windows, and go into an office with a vinyl counter that was updated in the 1980s. Needless to say, I spend a lot of time here mailing books and chatting with the clerks.

As I stepped inside, I wondered what it would be like to have a post office box here. The smaller boxes had combination locks, something I was not particularly good at, but the larger ones looked like they had keyholes set in their elaborate brass designs.

Brass keyholes. As my son, Jason, would say, *Earth to Mom, calling Earth to Mom.*

No wonder Margaret had assumed I would know where the key belonged. She had written the box number in the return address.

It meant having to drive home again, but I knew the empty carton was still beside the wing chair. I raced to my house, left the engine in the van running, and was back at the post office in ten minutes.

Although mail had begun crowding in, I could see a small package in box 738. I turned the key and removed everything, discarding advertising circulars and catalogs. I put the rest of the mail back and dropped the unaddressed package into my woven bag.

My van was parked in front of the post office in a 15-minute zone, so I drove to Shore Road where I could sit by the water. The only homes there were set far back from the road, overlooking the Sound. I doubted that anyone would notice me.

I parked by a strip of low dunes and sand, turned off the engine, and opened the windows so I could smell the salt water. On a morning like this, you could see Connecticut clearly, although it was over an hour away by ferry. I decided that I was looking at Westport.

I reached into the envelope and pulled out a bubble-wrapped package. Through the plastic I could make out a small, pale green book with vertical stripes and a title in darker green. It was a thin book, light and comfortable in my hand. But when I unwrapped it and looked at the title I almost laughed: *The Story of Little Black Sambo.* My favorite childhood book.

Could this be Margaret's great discovery? *You're no Emily Dickinson,* I told the little volume. *You're just a kids' book that everyone already knows about.*

I pried the cover open gingerly, as if the contents might fall out. But they didn't. If any book could be called pristine, this one could. I would defend it as "Fine" to the severest critic. The corners were not even bumped and the binding was tight. I checked further. The book had been published in London in 1899 by Grant Richards.

So. At least a first edition?

I took in the book slowly, not allowing myself to look at the illustrations yet. As a child I had been giddy with excitement when the tigers chased each other so rapidly that they turned into butter. But I had also loved Sambo's green umbrella and purple shoes and his mother who made him as many pancakes as he could eat.

Finally I chose a page at random as if it would have a personal message for me. Patsy and I had done that with the Bible when we were thirteen, opening it blindly and jabbing a finger on a verse to tell our fortune, laughing hysterically when it was either uncannily accurate or wildly off-target. When had we stopped being friends and become rivals? Was it when we went off to different colleges? When I suddenly got married and became a mother when she was still immersed in pre-law at Barnard? I never realized how much difference it would make.

After opening the book I looked down, and then jerked back. Instead of the smooth-haired, brown-skinned child of India that I had been expecting, Sambo, with his thick mouth and prickly curly hair, was the worst kind of stereotype. Choosing another page, I found Black Mumbo flipping pancakes, the sure forerunner of Aunt Jemima.

What did it *mean?* These illustrations were close to caricature! Was this book some kind of joke, a cruel parody of the innocuous original? Or was memory playing me false? I went back to the front and looked at the opening pages, and then caught my breath. On a blank front leaf, across from an illustration of Sambo taking a bow, and so faint that you could almost miss it, was an inscription: *To JRK, One who has felt the tiger's pounce, Helen.*

A signed book, a detail that sent its value skyrocketing. This was no parody. I closed the book and pressed it between my palms. I had no idea who JRK was, but Helen was certainly Helen Bannerman. The browned ink had started out boldly, and then faded as she finished writing, but the inscription felt authentic. Having handled thousands of books, I could tell the difference between a facsimile edition, a Shackman reprint, and the real thing.

Talk to me, I whispered, closing my eyes. *Tell me your story.*

The book did not yield up its early history, did not tell me where it had spent the last hundred years, but it confided that Margaret had been fearful of someone stealing it from her. She had not even thought it would be safe in her house. But why hadn't she told me about it when we were having coffee and I brought up the mysterious seller? She must have bought it from him. But then something happened. Perhaps he had called her, threatening her and demanding the book back.

Something else was puzzling. This was certainly a first edition, inscribed by its author. So why would Margaret have contacted Marty for further information? Did she think it would help her discover who JRK was and how the book had traveled across several oceans to arrive here?

I rested my head against the back of the seat and watched a gull swoop down to the sand. How, in the mildewed, abandoned house I had been imagining, had this book remained so perfect? It must have been stolen from a collection. And if there was one stolen book, there had to be others. Perhaps it was one of the others that Margaret had been trying to research. Marty had said it was American, which this one wasn't, though he had told Roger it had "black interest"—which this one did.

I didn't like my next thought: that Margaret would buy stolen books and not tell me about them for that reason. I didn't believe it anyway. Margaret was a proper bookseller with a code of ethics even more stringent than mine.

In any case, my only responsibility now was to keep this book safe from harm.

But safe from who? Who was keeping Margaret's other books safe? As long as no one knew I had *Little Black Sambo,* it could stay in the barn. But what about fire? Then I remembered Colin's safe in the basement. Irreplaceable family pictures were stored inside, but he had actually bought it for his volumes of poetry. Wanting to make sure that *Bluer Mountains, Voices We Don't Want to Hear,* and *Earthworks* would survive him, he had researched safes and bought the finest, the one reputed to withstand the Devil's own flames. We never kept it locked—presumably no one would want to steal his poems or my New England ancestors—and I didn't even know the combination. But since no one knew that I had *Sambo,* fire was all I had to fear.

Yet I did not immediately drive home. Instead I opened the book again carefully and read it all the way through. There were about twenty-five illustrations that looked like hand-colored woodcuts, all charming, all stereotypes. Little Black Sambo lived with his parents, Black Mumbo and Black Jumbo. She was a loving mother and made him a red jacket, blue pants, and purple shoes. Dad gave him a green umbrella.

Dressed in his new clothes, Sambo went for a walk in the jungle where he encountered a series of tigers who threatened to eat him. Each time, he offered one a piece of his finery in exchange for his life. But as he sat weeping when his treasures were all gone, he heard a terrible growling and crept over to see what it was. The tigers, who had been arguing about which one was now the grandest in the jungle, had put aside their new accessories, gotten hold of each other by the tail, and started racing around a palm tree. They raced so fast that they eventually turned into butter.

Sambo retrieved his outfit, his father scooped up the tiger butter, and his mother made pancakes to celebrate. The little family ate a total of—I did the math—251 pancakes.

On the inside end page I discovered something else. A pale red stamp stated that it was an "Author's Copy." There had probably been only a handful, making the book even more valuable.

I pressed the book against my ribcage. Despite everything, I still loved the story. It spoke of familial love, plenty to eat, and a logical magic. There was the appeal of a frightening object turned into something benign. For little children, the thought of turning four mean tigers into something as harmless as butter was thrilling.

And who wouldn't want a beaming Mama who made you all the pancakes that you could eat?

I thought of the inscription again: *To one who has felt the tiger's pounce*—someone who has felt it, perhaps been scarred by it, but survived. Maybe, if Helen Bannerman were living in India, she might not have wanted to set her book there. By choosing African characters, she would not be giving offense. Why would she think that her tiny book would ever wash up on distant shores anyway?

Or maybe I was just making excuses for her.

Checking my watch, I saw that it was nearly ten. Time to see Margaret!

Chapter Sixteen

This time the pink-smocked volunteer at the desk downstairs gave me a pass for Margaret's room. I felt as anxious as someone meeting a friend after a long separation. When I joined a cluster of other visitors at the elevator, I saw, dismayed, that I was the only one who was empty-handed. The people around me were holding paper cones of flowers, gift bags, and magazines. Next time, I promised myself.

My next jolt came when I found that Margaret was not in a private room. Blame too many old movies, but I had expected to find her motionless in an all-white chamber, worried faces hovering over her like Raphael's angels; the whole hospital waiting for her to reclaim her life; classical music playing softly in the background in an effort to tempt her senses into waking and remembering.

But there were two names outside the door, Cassidy and Weller.

Margaret's roommate was in the bed closer to the door. She was plump, black-haired, and grimly jovial, flanked by what could only be her son and two teenage grandsons. They had identical pudgy faces and shiny blue-black hair, as if the woman in the bed had just cloned them.

I murmured hello, and moved toward the bed next to the window.

"You here for Margaret?" the son asked.

His knowing her name gave me hope. "Yes! How is she?"

"Still pretty out of it. They brought her in yesterday afternoon." He didn't seem to realize that she had been moved there from the ICU. "She must be important though."

I gave him a blank look.

"All those cops guarding her?"

"What cops?"

"They're probably using the remote camera now. But they've been in and out. Two guys came and tried to ask her questions last night."

"Really? What kind of questions?"

"They pulled that green curtain around the bed. I couldn't hear anything," he confessed.

"But he tried hard!" the woman in the bed called out, and they all laughed.

I moved quickly to Margaret. Against the white sheets, her face looked warm and healthy again. Her hair, loose around her face instead of pulled back, made her look younger, more like the girl in the painting in her bedroom. I wondered about her brief marriage and why she had never married again.

With her full lips parted, she looked peacefully asleep. Only the vinyl tubes doing her body's work told me that this was more than a nap. With a jolt, I thought about the prospect of brain damage; why had it not occurred to me before?

Moving aside a cart on wheels, I leaned in close. "Margaret? It's Delhi. I've been trying to see you for days, but they wouldn't let me."

"She can't hear you," the son advised.

I spun around, annoyed. "You don't know that. Why do you think they talk to people in comas and play their favorite music?"

His mouth drooped a little; to make amends, I said, "Look, her legs are moving!"

He gestured toward the end of her bed. "Look."

Tentatively I lifted the lower covers and saw that Margaret's calves were covered in furry gray legwarmers with bright orange trim. As I watched, first one and then the other inflated, squeezing her leg like a blood pressure sleeve.

"It's to prevent clots," he said. "You get them if you don't move around."

"They put them on *me* the first day," Mrs. Cassidy announced. "I ripped them right off!"

Her men laughed. I turned back to Margaret.

"It's Delhi," I whispered again, squeezing her hand. We stayed that way for several minutes as I told her about Jane and Lance and the travails of the young on Fire Island. She looked peaceful and unresponsive. The subjects we actually had in common, the people we knew, seemed too upsetting to mention. I started to tell her that I had kept The Old Frigate open, but remembering how everything had ended, I didn't. Did she know *anything* about Amil? I leaned close to her ear. "Margaret, I found the book. Don't worry, it's safe." As safe as it could be locked up in my basement.

The stiffening of her arm, her hand imprisoning mine, was so startling that I almost cried out. Then her grip dropped away.

"Margaret?" I gave her hand the slightest shake. But there was no response.

I talked on, skirting any mention of Amil, the shop, or *Little Black Sambo*.

Finally I stood up and bent over to kiss her forehead, promising that I would come back later. "Is there anything I can bring you?" I asked. "A triple latte?"

It was a silly comment, especially when I belatedly remembered who had said it, but it agitated her. "Police!" She said the word clearly. "Police!"

She was *talking* to me. Margaret was talking to me. She would come out of this after all.

"That's right, the police are protecting you. You're safe now. You're in the hospital and no one is going to hurt you." She must have thought she was going to die on the floor of the shop she loved so much. "They're here to keep you safe. You just concentrate on getting better." I gave her hand a squeeze.

She did not stir.

At the nurses' station, I asked them to page Dr. Gallagher and was told that she was enjoying a rare day off.

"Is Margaret Weller's nurse around?"

"She's in 617? I think that's Clarisse. Wait."

I waited.

Several minutes later, a young woman came over to where I stood near the elevator. She had the look and cadence of someone from the Caribbean, but a brisk efficiency I did not associate with the islands. Her overblouse of pale flowers hung crisply around navy pants, and she had a scent of oranges that I liked.

"You have a question about Miz Weller?"

"She said something to me!"

Clarisse did not look quite as excited as I felt. "What did she say?"

" 'Police.' Somehow she knows the police are protecting her."

"Yeah, they've been here. Anything else?"

"Not really," I admitted.

"Well, that's more than that detective got." She smiled. "She wouldn't say *anything* to him. Then he kept asking *me* questions. But I didn't tell him nothing either."

I didn't know what we were talking about.

"They're going to move her out, maybe even tomorrow," she added, as if she had just thought of it. "They can't keep her here."

"Oh, no," I cried. "You mean to a nursing home?"

"Maybe they should let her go home."

"She can't go home." Obviously Clarisse didn't know that Margaret was by herself now. "She'd just lie there and die!"

Clarisse gave me a polite but disappointed look. Somehow I had said the wrong thing.

"Gotta run," she told me, and did.

And I was lost. I hesitated, and then went back into Margaret's room

The Cassidy grandsons were teasing their grandmother about something to do with a fireman's picnic and too much free beer; I wished they would go away. Standing beside Margaret, watching the drip of pale gold nourishment that was keeping her alive, I felt my eyes blur. How could life be this unfair? To Margaret, of all people . . .

Taking her hand, I whispered. "Ve haf ways of making you talk."

There was not the response I had hoped for; there was no response at all.

Bending down, I kissed her warm forehead. "See you later!"

I said good-bye to the Cassidys, who responded with laconic waves, and started for the elevator. But as I passed the nurses' station, I was intercepted by a policewoman in official navy pants and short-sleeved shirt. She was young and very thin with straight blonde hair.

"Speak to you a moment?" she said.

"Uh—sure."

"You were visiting Margaret Weller."

"Yes."

"Name and address?"

I gave them to her.

"I need to see some identification."

Digging into my purse for my wallet, I brought out my driver's license. Why hadn't she checked me before I went into the room? By the time someone pulled out a stiletto and stabbed Margaret to death they would have it on tape, but be too late to save her. With my back to the camera, bending solicitously over her, I could have covered her mouth with my hand and pinched her nose shut. What kind of police protection was *that?*

Waiting for the elevator next to a gurney packed with supplies, I thought again of *Little Black Sambo*. There were, no doubt, *Sambo* aficionados as well as black memorabilia collectors who would be very interested in an inscribed original. Unlike a handwritten fragment of *Moby Dick,* which would need a provenance to help prove its authenticity, the book was what it was. Besides, as Margaret was fond of telling me, "The paper never lies." I would stake my bookseller's reputation, modest though it was, that the *Black Sambo* paper, printing, and binding were one hundred years old. And that the author's inscription was authentic too.

That still left the puzzle of JRK. John Keats? No, I had seen the small stone house next to the Spanish steps in Rome where he died, and I was sure he had succumbed around 1823. Just a friend? Jane Rebecca? Jasmine Rachel? Perversely, I could not think of one notable turn-of-the-century woman with the initials J. R. K. Famous men were not plentiful either.

Was I trying to make something from nothing? The odds were that the book was inscribed to a friend, not to anyone famous. The people I knew who signed books of poetry, Colin and his friends, were more than happy to write something memorable for any stranger who approached them with $12.95 for a volume the size of a brochure.

Outside on the path to the parking garage, I realized that I had forgotten something crucial. This was not my book. All I was supposed to do was keep it safe for Margaret. Still, what could it hurt to figure out to whom the book had been inscribed?

Back in the barn, I checked my e-mail and was happy to see that there were three new book sales. Two were quite modest, but the third was for a $55.00 copy of *Tarzan the Terrible,* complete with dust jacket. And there was a nice e-mail from a buyer in Pennsylvania telling me how thrilled her mother had been to receive the copy of *Skippack School* by Marguerite De Angeli.

When I finished responding to the buyers, I logged into my Internet dealers' site, BookEm. I enjoyed reading the rants of other booksellers, whether about customers or each other. As cantankerous as members could be, there were bookmen and women in the group whose experience took my breath away. Most of what I knew about bookselling I had learned on this list. As with the Oracle, if you asked a stupid question, you would be held up to ridicule. On the other hand, members vied with each other to tell you what they knew.

Again I ran through all the names I could think of beginning with J—James, Joshua, Jedadiah—but came up empty. Impulsively I clicked on the New Message icon, and then stopped. What was I *doing?* Wouldn't this advertise that I had something valuable—like Margaret's find? Yet as far as I knew, none of the Long Island dealers belonged to this list. They operated in parallel universes: selling to private collectors, issuing catalogs, auctioning books on eBay, running a brick-and-mortar shop. BookEm wasn't even the only site for Internet booksellers. My question was tangential to the book itself anyway. People asked questions like this every day. I just hoped that JRK was not a famous personality who every other bookseller would know instantly. In the headline, I put:

QUERY: Identifying Inscription Initials
   Good morning,
   Can anyone identify these initials from an inscription: JRK?
There is a connection with India ca. 1900.
   Thank you for your help!

As soon as I sent the e-mail off, framed that way, I had a nagging feeling that I already knew the answer. But it stayed stubbornly beneath the surface.

Reaching for a yellow-lined pad, I made a "To Do" list:

1. *Find out if local calls to your phone line can be traced.*
2. *Drive around the area and look for houses under renovation where caller might be working.*
3. *Call Marty and ask if he knows who the mystery seller is and if he thought Margaret was researching more than one book.*

But before I embarked on any of those activities I had to list some of my own books for sale.

There were fewer orders than I had hoped that day, none from Barnes & Noble or Amazon. Things slow down in the summer, but it is odd: Whenever you upload twenty-five or thirty new titles, there is a jump in orders—but not necessarily for the newly listed books. It is as if a psychic spotlight has been turned on your entire collection, making people notice titles that have been languishing for months.

On the other hand, online competition had increased even as the economy waned. As I climbed the stairs to the loft, I imagined myself wiping down tables at McDonald's. Yet better that than wiping little faces under Loretta's benign glare.

Chapter Seventeen

When describing books became as onerous as writing book reports in fourth grade, I turned to my to-do list and decided to call Marty. I pulled his card from a collection in my small file box.

Marty's was a real business card, the kind my brother-in-law Ben would approve of, with raised black printing on a cream surface. There were no cat photos or the perforated edges that came from making the cards yourself. The front was simplicity itself, with *CAMPAGNA ARTS LTD* in the center and *Fine Paintings and Literature* underneath. In the lower left-hand corner was a nod to his cesspool-business roots—*We pay cash!*—and in the right corner a phone number, a Web site, and an e-mail address.

Knowing how Marty roamed Long Island, I figured I would have to leave a message. As I dialed, I wondered if his restlessness had been inherited from his inventive grandfather, and if his grandfather had been as scornful of wealth's trappings as Marty was. He usually looked as if he was about to crawl under his old Caddy and work on the brakes. When I first met him, the bridge of his black glasses had been repaired with duct tape.

The call was picked up on the second ring. "Marty here."

"Hi, this is Delhi Laine. I'm the—"

"Right. Blondie. What's up? How's Margaret doing?"

"Better. She's out of intensive care, thank God."

"She say what happened?"

I hesitated. "Not yet."

"So what's up?" he repeated.

"This guy, this kind of strange guy who's renovating a house, called me last week. About some books he'd found."

119

"Oh, yeah. He was planning to take *bids?*" Marty gave a snort. "He hasn't got anything."

"Who is he?"

"I don't remember his last name. Shawn something."

"He'd mentioned something about a children's book I might be interested in. But I didn't get his phone number."

"I have it here somewhere. I don't even talk to people unless they give me their information first."

My first mistake.

After a moment he read the number off to me. "You're lucky you caught me at home."

"Yeah. Thanks." But before he could hang up, I asked, "Was Margaret trying to research more than one book?"

"Could be. Why?"

"I'm trying to figure out why she and Amil were attacked. If there were several valuable books, it might have been worth somebody's while."

"Didn't tell me anything." It was his usual dismissive tone.

"Did *you* smell anything when you were in the bookstore?"

"Only Howard."

I laughed.

When I hung up, I dialed the number Marty had given me and let it ring twelve times. Shawn was probably still at his day job, renovating houses—or stealing rare books. No answering machine came on. I checked for a reverse address at whitepages.com and got a *No Match.*

Too restless to sit at my desk any longer, I decided to head out to the university library. I could check the Coles Reverse Directory there for better information. The real reason, which I barely admitted to myself, was to see if they had a biography of Helen Bannerman with a clue to JRK in the index.

It was the kind of day outside that reminds people why they chose Long Island. A sky the Kodachrome blue of 1950s *National Geographics,* warm sunshine, and a breeze off the Sound to keep the air fresh. The dusky sweetness of a thousand flowers in bloom. And, as always, the tang of saltwater just out of view.

I drove to the university with the windows down and parked at the edge of the campus near the LIRR station, and then walked on past athletic fields and brick dormitories. A number of students were playing tennis, and another group was tossing a Frisbee across the grass, teasing a small red setter by sluicing the yellow disk just over his head. The metal glint off a window frame reminded me of Detective Marselli's badge on my porch yesterday when he flipped the holder open, but I quickly pushed it aside. On this perfect day I didn't want to think about all the things I had seen in the bookshop. I especially didn't want to relive my terror when I thought he was about to catch me there.

Climbing the wide library steps, I entered and hurried past the display cabinets to the Reference Room. Another bookseller had taught me about *Coles Reverse Directory*. When a promising sale was listed in *Newsday* with the address, he used it to find the phone number and call for a preview. I needed the opposite now. For no real reason, I trusted *Coles* more than the Internet. There didn't seem to be the same level of responsibility online that there was from a published book.

But today even *Coles* couldn't help me. Next to Shawn's number was *NP* for "not published." I wondered crossly why so many kids had unlisted phone numbers.

But now that I was here . . . Helen Bannerman.

I wasn't surprised to find that only one biography had been written about her. Unfortunately the library did not own it. The only thing they had was a booklet that was kept on reserve. Not just on reserve, but in a director's office. Not just in a director's office, but in a top-secret place. I had to sign for it and let them keep my driver's license as collateral.

The broad-beamed young woman with the honey-colored braid to her waist eyed me sternly. "Which department did you say you are in?"

"What department?"

"You're not on the faculty?"

"My husband is."

She shook her head as if I were a panhandler trying to pass myself off as a charity.

"The library isn't open to everyone?" I asked.

"The library is, but—this material can't leave the room. And you can't photocopy it!"

"What?"

"Those are the rules." She held the booklet close to her heavy denim thigh as if one misstatement would forever forfeit my chances of even a glimpse.

"Okay. Sure."

She paused, as if trying to come up with another condition, and then reluctantly handed it to me. I sensed her vigilant eyes on my back as I carried the booklet to a library table. Sitting down, I took out a pen and notebook to prove I was a serious scholar.

I saw immediately why Sambo was getting such restrictive treatment. Although the booklet had been published in 1976 by the Racism and Sexism Resource Center for Educators, it contained far more inflammatory images than Helen Bannerman's drawings. If photocopied, the illustrations could be enlarged and used in destructive ways.

Two of the worst offenders were illustrators whose other work I admired. John R. Neill, who did the charming illustrations for the *Wizard of Oz* books, portrayed Sambo's mother as a three-hundred-pound caricature in a polka-dotted apron and matching bandanna. Johnny Gruelle, best known for *Raggedy Ann and Andy,* put the family in minstrel blackface with exaggerated lips and eyes. There was even an unfortunate contrast of Helen Bannerman's drawing of Black Mumbo helping Sambo into his new jacket placed next to an illustration from her unfinished book, *Little White Squibba,* in which the child and her mother, standing in front of a mirror, looked like an illustration from *Dick and Jane*.

Quickly I scanned the text. It corrected misinformation about the author's nationality. Helen Bannerman, née Watson, was not English, but Scottish, and had lived in India with her physician husband between 1890 and 1917. In her thirties she gave birth to four children. It was for her two older daughters, not for publication, that she first created *Little Black Sambo*.

But *Sambo* was an immediate success in London, and reached the United States in 1900, courtesy of the publisher Frederick Stokes.

Once here, despite the copyright, it was treated as a folktale and fair game. Twenty-five different companies pounced on the story, each with their own illustrators. Sometimes the setting was Africa, sometimes the American South. Helen Bannerman's later books were largely ignored, though she caused a blip in 1936 with *Sambo and the Twins*. The twins, Little Black Woof and Little Black Moof, had been stolen by wicked monkeys and were rescued by Sambo and a friendly eagle.

Up through the 1960s *Little Black Sambo* was highly recommended on children's literature lists: many educators felt that Sambo's heroism created a positive image for black children. Yet even in the 1940s, a few black librarians were wondering about a Black Mumbo who had been fattened up like a Macy's balloon and given a red polka-dotted kerchief. Perhaps they also learned that Sambo had been a popular name for a doltish character in minstrel shows and that Black Jumbo's striped trousers were part of that traditional costume. The rationale that the story was set in India, not Africa, didn't appease them. It took place in "the Jungle," and who thought of India that way?

But how could the Scottish daughter of a Presbyterian clergyman be familiar with American blackface? Someone suggested that Helen Bannerman had based her drawings on those from a German book, *Der Struwwelpeter* (*Slovenly Peter*), a moralistic tome more likely to be found in religious Scottish homes.

One story had a "black-a-moor" with a green umbrella who is teased unmercifully by three young toughs. When they did not stop, they were snatched up by Saint Nicholas and doused in an inkstand. I caught my breath at the picture of the "black-a-moor" of 1846 striding with his umbrella, juxtaposed next to Sambo with his. The stiff-legged stride of both boys, their exaggerated features in profile, were too close to be an accident.

Borrowing, to put it kindly—but why not? When you are making up stories for your own children, you pull in elements from everywhere; you aren't worried about charges of plagiarism. If it were true that *Little Black Sambo* had been intended as a way of keeping in touch with her daughters when they were sent back to school in Scotland, she might not have even realized what she was doing.

But just as I was consoling myself with that thought, I imagined Bruce Adair's voice. "Really, Delhi, you can't fall for that old Victorian conceit. Do you really believe that *Alice in Wonderland* was written for one little girl or that *Winnie-the-Pooh* was intended only as a bedtime story for Christopher Robin?"

Yet no matter what its conception really was, I saw how the illustrations, even the name Little Black Sambo, could cause problems for black children. Again, publishers responded. By 1970, there was a red-haired and freckled Little Black Sambo, with a slim white Mama in a leopard-skin sarong. Other versions sent him back to India. Looking at both the politically correct illustrations and the ones that made me cringe, I felt that the original pictures were intrinsic to the story. Better banned than whitewashed.

When I turned the last page, I sat looking out the window at the leafy green campus. I was sure that this booklet would mysteriously "disappear" now that someone had shown an interest in it. I turned and saw that the moral guardian at the reference desk had been replaced by a Chinese student. But it didn't matter. I would never join the community of book thieves. Besides, I needed my driver's license back.

With a smile I returned *Little Black Sambo, A Closer Look* to the reference desk. "Make sure Brunhilda sees that it's back," I said.

Expecting puzzlement, I was gratified when he laughed.

But I still did not know who JRK was.

When I got back to the barn, I found out.

Clicking on my e-mail icon, I found I had thirteen new messages. Five of them had the heading *QUERY: Identifying Inscription Initials.* I opened the first, from a bookseller in Minnesota.

Hi Delhi,

Though I can think of several writers with those initials, with the date you suggest the most likely is Rudyard Kipling. Although he never used it, his first name was Joseph. Hence: JRK.

Cordially,
Steve Gunderson

Of course! I stared at the screen, quickly checking whether he had sent the message just to me. No. He had cc'd the entire BookEm list. And why not? It is more gratifying to have your expertise acknowledged by many. Yet nobody jeered at my ignorance. There were four similar messages, one also mentioning the remote possibility that it might be a John R. Kippax, best known for his book *Churchyard Literature: A Choice Collection of American Epitaphs,* which was published in London in 1877. Another added, *If you have Ruddy's monogrammed handkerchief, don't dry clean!*

Ha. But the implication that his initials could be found on something I owned bothered me. *Rudyard Kipling!* Kipling had his own devout following. Lawrence Block may have exaggerated their fanaticism in *The Burglar Who Liked to Quote Kipling,* but I knew there was an army of them out there. And this was a book that he had actually touched, one that had been inscribed to him.

Maybe. No wonder Margaret had been trying to research the book. *She* would have known the significance of the initials immediately. Had she had a chance to find out if Rudyard Kipling and Helen Bannerman had been friends? It should be easy enough to check their biographies. I reminded myself again that it was Margaret's book, not mine. But that didn't mean I couldn't find out about it.

I sent thank-you messages to the people who had responded and was about to leave the barn to nuke a Lean Cuisine pizza for dinner when the phone rang.

"Secondhand Prose!"

"Delhi? It's Jack Hemingway. I left a message earlier for you." The voice rolled on richly, leaving me no time to wonder why he had called. "I've been thinking about the Charlie Chan. I didn't mean to grab it from you; it was an automatic reflex. A *bad* one. As my wife often tells me, I can be a boor. It fit in with an article I was writing and I didn't think. But of course you can have it."

So it wasn't worth as much as he had thought, my inner cynic pointed out.

"No, that's okay," I said. "It's not in my area, and it was one you really wanted."

"Well . . ." He allowed that that might be so, but that he was still willing to sacrifice it for me. "I'd love to see *your* books sometime. I bet you have some interesting stuff!"

"Actually, you can go to my website on AbeBooks or Alibris and check my listings. Just type in *Secondhand Prose* under *Sellers*."

But he already knew that, of course.

"There's nothing like seeing books alive and close up," he purred. "And you must have some that aren't online. I'm always looking for the unusual. You know Papa Jack!"

"Aren't we all."

"I mean, I'll spend the bucks. You're located in Port Lewis?"

"Jack, I don't have a signed Rudyard Kipling if that's what you're looking for." What other fallout would there be from BookEm?

He chuckled, unconvinced. "Just furthering your education on-line, eh?"

Instead of answering, I said, "You know, I thought I saw you in Port Lewis Monday night." The proverbial shot in the dark. I should have used it with Roger, my West Indian friend.

"Port Lewis? No."

"Kind of late?"

"No. We didn't go anywhere. Stayed in with a pizza and a good flick. You can do that every night when you're retired."

"Hm. Guess it was someone who looked like you."

"How's Margaret?"

"Still unconscious. You heard about Amil?"

"Her assistant? I've been following it on Channel 12. But it still isn't clear what happened."

"I don't know either."

"What a world, huh? But listen, Delhi: If you get anything interesting, anything at all, keep me in mind!"

Just what Roger had said. Just what every bookseller on Long Island would say. Had rare books gotten that scarce? It reminded me of a short story I had read once in which the stock for sport fishing on Long Island had gotten so rare that charter captains strapped humans to the bows of their boats to attract sharks for their customers. Would that happen with books, with desirable fiction becoming so scarce that dealers had to kill each other to get it? Even the rumor that Margaret had made a find had stirred everything up.

Automatically I clicked the NEW MESSAGE button and three more came up. The first was a chatty message from my daughter, Hannah, that the brakes on her car were about to fail. The second was a BookEm question about whether taping Priority Mail envelopes was allowed. The last subject heading was blank, with an unfamiliar e-mail address of oceans9@hotmail.com. Good, a book buyer. I clicked on the icon to read the message and large green letters jarred me: *WHAT DO YOU WANT FOR IT?*

I glanced again at the subject line, as if the name of the book this rude buyer wanted would belatedly appear. But it remained blank. The oversized letters were threatening. But they couldn't be talking about Margaret's book. Lurkers on BookEm might guess I had something, but no one would know what. The e-mail address gave no clue; anyone could hide behind a Hotmail account. It was a trick question anyway. If I said it was not for sale, it sounded as if I had something. I clicked REPLY, typed in *I don't know what you're talking about.* Then I clicked SEND and waited.

Several minutes later there was a second message from oceans9@hotmail.com. A little shakily I opened it.

WHAT'S YOUR PRICE?

We pay cash.

I stared at the pulsing green letters. Someone, somewhere in the world, was sitting in front of a computer, sending aggressive messages and knowing exactly where *I* was.

Chapter Eighteen

I locked up the barn, crossed the yard, and went into the kitchen through the back door. All I wanted now was a glass of Chardonnay, my tiny frozen pizza, and an evening with Philip Roth. Throw in a cat to cuddle with and I would feel content.

Checking the answering machine, I saw that there were seven phone messages. Seven! Had Colin won an award for *Earthworks,* with newspapers calling as they had before? But the calls had all been for me. One message was the one Jack Hemingway had mentioned leaving.

The first was from my oldest friend, Gail. "Hey, Del! I'm planning my forty-fifth birthday party, one of those theme jobbies. I'm going to rent out the Egyptian Room of the Metropolitan Museum. We'll try on gold jewelry and be attended by young Nubian slaves in loincloths. Or, if that doesn't work, there's always pizza and a movie. But save the weekend of September 16th. I want you there. Bye!"

I would be there.

"Mom? It's Hannah. I e-mailed you this morning about something wrong with my car? The brakes are like making this weird noise? Can I put it on your credit card?"

You don't have a father?

"Delhi! This is Bruce Adair. I've been intrigued by something you said the other morning and I'd love to explore it over dinner. My treat, of course. You don't have to call me back; I'll try you again. This is just fair warning."

What could I have said, sitting in the Literature Department, that would have encouraged Bruce to ask me out?

"Hi there, I'm calling about a book you have listed: *Family Shoes* by Noel Streatfeild. Can you tell me if the dust jacket price is in dollars or pounds? I want the book anyway, but I'm curious."

Reaching for a corner of the newspaper, I wrote down the book's name and replayed the message to get the phone number.

Another book message, leaving me credit card information. Some people still didn't like to send their numbers over the Internet.

The last voice began softly but increased rapidly in volume. "Mrs. Laine? This is Shara Patterson. Will you please call me, please? A policeman came and took Russell away! Will you call me please?"

They had arrested Russell Patterson! I dialed her number.

The phone was answered on the second ring.

"Yes, hello?"

"Shara? This is Delhi Laine."

"Yes!"

"What happened? You said the police came?"

"Yes, they came this morning." She sounded slightly calmer than her message had. "They took Russell away."

"Do you know why?"

"It was because of the fight. Devin told them about the fight!" Her voice shook with betrayal.

"What fight?"

Silence.

"You didn't tell me about any fight," I said in my guilt-provoking voice. It had worked when my children were small.

"It was on Friday," she said reluctantly. "Russell got so angry at Amil, I thought he would hit him! But Amil ran and got into his car."

"What happened then?"

"Russell got in *his* car," she admitted.

I had an unexpected image of a chase scene into Port Lewis, of Amil taking refuge in the bookstore and Margaret attempting to intervene.

"But Russell didn't hurt him!" she insisted.

"How long was he gone?"

"He came back right away."

I didn't believe her.

Why was she defending this bully? Because she was in a foreign country with a baby and no other means of support. Yet I knew very little about her marriage, her personal life, or her relationship with Amil. Actually I didn't know her at all. I wasn't even sure why she had called me. "Is there anything I can do for you?"

"Oh. No."

"Well, call me if I can."

"Yes." She hung up.

When I went out to the barn to check the dust jacket of *Family Shoes,* I deliberately did not look at my e-mail. Instead, I called the customer back, and left a voice mail for Hannah that it would be fine to charge her car repair. What else could I do? She needed the car to get to her summer program at Cornell, and Colin *was* paying her other expenses.

I settled in with my wine and pizza, but the serenity I had imagined had gone off somewhere else.

Russell Patterson ruined my sleep. The more I thought about him, the angrier it made me. His petulant anger, his spoiled-boy temper, had ended one life and ruined the other. Even if Margaret recovered, The Old Frigate would never be the way it had been. Why had he let himself lose control and kill Amil? At least, I thought vengefully, he would be in prison forever.

Once, when I jerked awake in the darkness, I thought about how, when I told him Amil was dead, he had pretended not to believe me. But it had probably been an act. Or maybe he honestly didn't think he had hit him that hard. Yet one niggling doubt remained. How had he even known about the book closet in the basement? And why would he put him down there and leave Margaret in the store still alive?

Burrowing into the too-soft mattress of the brass bed, *le matrimoniale* as Colin called it ironically, I realized, with daylight, that it was already Friday. Some of the weekend sales were starting today and I had not even looked at *Newsday*. Summer was the time to store up books for the winter when estate sales dwindled to nothing.

Yet I couldn't even imagine leaping out of bed and making a later start. How could I pretend life was the way it had been a week ago? I closed my eyes. When I was younger and things felt all wrong, I would escape into a book as fast as I could. I would put worlds between me and whatever else was happening. Surely there was something downstairs or in the barn . . .

Like whiskey for breakfast, my father would have said. He was never dogmatic, never scolding; but when he used his favorite condemnation, "moral fiber like shredded wheat," you wanted to make sure it did not apply to you. My mother too would have tried to nudge me into doing the right thing. Although she could not knit without dropping stitches and made dinners only my father could love, she would have spent the day at Margaret's bedside, stroking her hand and offering encouragement. In the evening she would have folded Shara under her sheltering wing and given her fresh hope. Of course, if Patsy were here, she would have already solved everything: Return Margaret to consciousness—check! Set the police straight—check! Bring Amil back to life—check!

But despite the specter of my own failure, I still didn't move. There was something sinister about today, something unbearably sad, and I wasn't going to let myself think about it. The past was the past. Once the moving finger had writ, not all my wit, nor tears, could cancel out a word of it.

It was only the promise of coffee that finally roused me, though I assured myself that I could lie down on the chaise lounge by the pond to drink it and not think about anything. And by seven thirty A.M. I was lying there, watching snatches of orange fish flash in and out of chartreuse duckweed. Dressed in clean denim shorts and a SAVE THE MANATEES T-shirt, a gift from Hannah, I was listlessly staring at the *Times* crossword when I remembered Shawn. I needed to try to call him before he left for work!

Quickly I went into the barn and dialed the number Marty had given me.

"Yeah, hello?" It was the same voice! I pictured him finishing a breakfast of Pop-Tarts.

"Hi! This is Delhi Laine from Secondhand Prose? You called me last Friday about some books you were selling?"

"Yeah, right. But I'm not selling them now."

I felt a prickling along my neck. "How come?"

"I'm putting them on eBay. That's where the money is."

"But you sold some of them," I prompted.

"Nah, I just called around to see if anybody was interested."

"Are any of them children's books? The books you found?"

"Kids' books? Un-uh."

"You know. With pictures?"

"Nah. Look, I've gotta boogie."

"So you haven't sold any of those books to anyone," I persisted. "Not even to the lady in the bookstore?"

"*No—eBay.* I'm putting them on eBay. They're under my seller's name, Book Idiot."

He had *that* right. But maybe he'd said, "They're under my seller's name book, idiot!"

I said good-bye without clarifying it. Now I was thoroughly confused. I had been sure Margaret had gotten *Sambo* and other books from him. If he still had the book from the 1600s, I had been ready to make him an offer. But he sounded firm about eBay. And, to be honest, Shawn didn't sound like a person who would go to a bookstore and kill anyone.

No; that had been Russell Patterson.

What I needed to do was see Margaret at the hospital. On the way I would buy a *Newsday* and at least line up some sales for tomorrow. Should I tell her about the police arresting Russell Patterson? I wasn't sure how much she knew about Amil.

First, though, I had to check my e-mail. As I had feared, there was another message from oceans9@hotmail.com. This time the same large green letters said, *YOU KNOW YOU NEED THE MONEY.*

How? How did he know? I told myself to calm down, that everyone needed money. And if he had seen my Chevy van, he could have guessed. But Marty drove that vintage Cadillac with several dents, and The Bookie's Toyota was modest. So was the Hoovers' station wagon. More probably the writer had guessed that any used book dealer needed money.

Calming down slightly, I typed back, *Who ARE you? I need to know who I'm talking to.* I did not know how to trace the origins of messages and doubted that Hotmail would be especially cooperative. To be fair, except for the use of all caps, there was nothing threatening in the messages. I knew there were ways for people to bounce a message off an innocent third party. Unlike some people, I had no computer guru I could call on. Maybe it was time to find one.

I waited for several minutes, dawdling over my other messages, but there was no response.

I left for the hospital a few minutes before ten, stopping to buy *Newsday* and a cappuccino, and sitting in my car checking off tag sale ads. Then I drove to the hospital and parked, memorizing my van's location in the multilevel garage. Skirting the toll booth, I continued down the path to the lobby. This time I did not stop at the information desk for Margaret's room number.

When I entered room 617, Mrs. Cassidy glanced over from her television show. She was without visitors this morning. And the bed by the window had been stripped.

"Where's Margaret?" I cried.

"They moved her." Mrs. Cassidy returned her gaze to what appeared to be celebrity bowling.

"Moved her *where?* Is she okay?"

"If you call being in a coma 'okay.' I don't."

"I meant alive. Where is she?"

"You'll have to ask her nurse. Or those policemen." She sounded angry.

But why would she be so upset about Margaret? I paused at the door. "Are you okay?"

"Am I okay? No, I'm not okay! They can't get this damn disease under control so I'm going to lose a leg!"

"*God.* I'm so sorry."

"Try losing *your* leg." She began watching the television screen again.

I waited a minute longer, and then said good-bye and went to find Clarisse. The young West Indian woman was coming out of the nursing station carrying a small metal tray filled with medications.

"Clarisse?" I said.

"That's right." She studied me, her dark face bland, as if trying to remind herself who I was. Our cryptic conversation of yesterday morning might never have happened.

"You were Margaret Weller's nurse," I prompted. "She's gone?"

"Oh, right. She was moved first thing this morning."

"Moved to *where?*" I knew I sounded frantic.

"They wouldn't say. But the police want the names of anyone who comes in wanting to know where she is."

"Detective Marselli?"

"That his name?" Her expression cleared. "The one who looks like he swallowed a toad?"

I laughed.

She put a hand on my arm before I could leave. "What's this *about?*"

Didn't anyone but Jack Hemingway read the paper or watch the news? "Margaret owns a bookstore. She was attacked and her assistant was killed. I think the police are afraid someone will try and finish the job."

Clarisse nodded. "She sure was scared."

"Did she say why?"

"No, but I was watching the video screen with that police lady, and when anyone walked into the room she'd jump. She'd seem to be *looking* at them, ya know?" She made it sound creepy. "There's this man . . . he calls every day to find out how she is. He won't tell me his name though. Just said he's her friend."

That was even creepier. "Anything special about his voice?"

She thought. "No. American. I'd know it if I heard it again." She had changed her voice and demeanor to that of Bill Clinton.

I laughed.

"He's easy. So is this guy." Sounding like George W. Bush, she said "I'm good with voices."

"Wow."

"Nurses need to be entertained." She resumed her own Caribbean lilt. "It's easier for me to hear differences, because I didn't grow up in the States." Then she frowned. "Do I need to take your name?"

"It's Delhi Laine. I gave it to the policewoman yesterday. But the police know I'm trying to see Margaret whenever I can. I'm the one who found her after the attack." I didn't know why I added that, and I wished I could take it back. It sounded self-dramatizing, as if I were trying to be part of the story. "Margaret's one of my best friends," I apologized.

Clarisse tilted her head and gave me a thoughtful look. "She's one classy lady. You give her a hug from Clarisse when you see her."

"I will."

And then I had a terrible thought, one which should have occurred to me sooner.

Chapter Nineteen

What I had not thought enough about was that whoever had been sending me messages knew where I lived. My address was on the Internet, on my bookselling page. I put it there to make it easier for buyers who wanted to mail me checks and money orders. I had never considered having a post office box. It was held as common knowledge on BookEm that people had more confidence in buying from a physical address than a box number.

But that meant that if someone suspected that I had an expensive book, they would know exactly where to look for it. If they didn't find it in the barn and then went into the basement and saw a safe . . . they'd find stacks of old photographs, many copies of poetry chapbooks, and a one-hundred-year-old book. Even if they didn't know it was valuable, they'd take it because of where it was.

Now I could not move quickly enough. It took me six minutes to retrieve my car and drive home from the hospital.

When I pulled into the driveway, the front yard looked neater than I had remembered. But perhaps I was just seeing it through a thief's eyes. I gave the pots of geraniums and impatiens a glance as I ran up the porch steps, but I was focused on the dark green-painted door. It was still locked. *Good.* But had I remembered to lock the back door?

Half-tripping back down the steps, I raced along the side of the house, crunching on ivy that had grown over the path.

The backyard still lay in its morning calm, water spilling out of the gargoyle's mouth into the pond. But when I reached the glass-paned door and twisted the knob, it gave too easily. Damn! Stepping inside I expected see kitchen drawers yanked out and papers everywhere. Instead, the room appeared undisturbed. My coffee cup and newspapers were beside the avocado refrigerator, the room lit only by daylight. When I ran into the living room, it looked the same. Yet something was different. For one thing, where were the cats?

I ran upstairs to check the bedrooms. When I came back down, Miss T, my ancient tabby, emerged huffily from beneath the striped couch, a sign that something had spooked her. But she ducked away when I went to pet her and there was no sign of Raj. Hoping that he was hiding in another spot and had not escaped outside, I went over to the basement door. And then stopped. Under normal circumstances I held my breath while descending the stairs, but now I had no idea what I might find. Or not find. After all the friendship and knowledge I had gotten from Margaret, all she had asked in return was that I keep her book safe. I had not even managed to do that.

Maybe she would never regain consciousness and find out, I thought, and then pushed that idea away—a leftover from the child Delhi, trying to wriggle her way out of trouble. If the book were gone, I would feel just as bereft. Even though I had had *Sambo* only a short time, reading about its history made it very real. What if I never saw it again?

Switching on the basement light, I placed my foot slowly on the first step and called out, "Hello?" Nothing. Then a sudden squeal behind me nearly jerked me out of my skin.

Raj. Scooping him up made me feel less frightened—as if a nine-pound Siamese cat could protect me. "Come on," I said. "We might as well look."

But when I reached the bottom step, I reared back and nearly dropped him. The basement smelled not of the bookshop's after-shave from hell, but of gasoline. *Of course.* Someone had stolen the book, and then tried to burn down the house to cover the theft. I sniffed the gasoline again, and stepped onto the cement floor. At least there was not the telltale sulfur waft of matches.

The door to the safe was closed. Crossing the floor quickly, I reached for the handle, and then stopped. There might be fingerprints. Compromising, I nudged the side of the lever with my elbow and, as it gave, I pulled the door open from the top. Someone had definitely been here since this morning. The books and papers in the safe were out of kilter, different from the way I had left them.

Colin's poetry volumes were now on top instead of the old photographs. Lifting a pile of *Voices We Don't Want to Hear* and *Earthworks,* I caught my breath. *Sambo* was resting comfortably at the bottom, still wrapped in plastic.

It didn't make sense. Why hadn't whoever it was taken the book? The only reason I could think of was that when he saw *Sambo* among the old family photos, he had assumed it was a sentimental childhood treasure.

Maybe out of frustration, he had kicked the gas can, although it was now upright again near the lawnmower.

Back upstairs, with Raj and *Sambo* firmly in hand, I worried about where to put the book. As in "The Purloined Letter," I could place it in the barn on an ordinary shelf or even in the loft with the unsorted stacks. Hide a book in the midst of other books. Then I remembered how Margaret's shop basement had been ransacked. If the next searcher knew what he was looking for, he would find it quick enough. I didn't want *Sambo* that far away from me anyway. Carefully I slipped the book, still in plastic, into my bright woolen purse.

But I needed to call the police. I found Detective Marselli's card and dialed.

"Marselli," he answered, and then silence.

"Hello?" I said.

"Yes?"

"Hi, this is Delhi Laine; you came here Wednesday? I just wanted to tell you that someone searched my house."

"It wasn't the police," he said immediately.

I was taken back. That hadn't crossed my mind.

"So what's missing?"

"Nothing—that I can see. But they went through the papers in the safe."

"They break in?"

"I couldn't find any sign of that," I admitted.

A grunt. "You have an ex? Or soon-to-be ex?"

How did he know *that?* "Sort of. But—"

"Okay, then. Check for missing bank books, property deeds, see if anything's gone. But if he still owns the house it's not trespassing. He have an Order of Protection, anything like that?"

"No!" I couldn't imagine Colin guilty of domestic violence. When you knew you had Right on your side, you didn't need to get physical.

"Well, if you find any property damage, call your local precinct. But someone going through papers, that's what it always is," Marselli was saying. "Domestic incidents can get ugly. But sometimes they just take the stuff to make photocopies."

"You don't think it has to do with what happened at the bookstore?"

"With Mr. Singh?"

"Well, I knew him. And Margaret. And I have some valuable books here."

"Call your locals. And keep your doors locked." He was off the line.

I pressed the receiver to my forehead. In one short phone call I had managed to destroy not just my image as the respectable wife of a university professor, but to sound like an idiot as well.

I knew it was not Colin breaking in to look for evidence of secret bank accounts. He knew as well as I did that there weren't any.

But I called him anyway.

"Hey-lo." His normal greeting.

"Colin? It's me. Look, I was just wondering if you'd been over to the house for anything."

"You didn't notice?"

"Notice what?"

"I mowed the grass! Honestly, Delhi, the neighbors are going to lynch you if you don't take better care of the yard. That's part of the agreement."

"Okay, thanks. Did you go in the safe?"

"Did I go in the safe? I can't get things out of my own *safe?*"

"Of course you can! I just thought someone might have broken in."

"Oh. No. I needed copies of my books to apply for a grant."

"Really? Good luck."

"Thanks. Speaking of the house, we need to talk."

I winced. When a man, especially a husband, says, "We need to talk," you can bet your life savings that it's not to tell you how wonderful you are.

"Listen, you could do something for me," I said quickly.

"What's that?"

"If I mailed you a book, would you keep it really safe?"

"What is it, the Gutenberg Bible?"

I get weary of Gutenberg Bible jokes. If people actually saw one, tatty pages and uneven type, they'd probably throw it in the trash. "Not quite."

"What is it?"

"Just say yes or no. I'll send it to your post office box."

Now he was interested. "I could come pick it up."

"No! I want it out of reach for a while, in the mail. You can even leave it in your post office box if you want."

He snorted at that.

"Just keep it safe. Don't give it to anyone but me. Even if they threaten to pull out your fingernails."

"Delhi."

"Just a joke. You'll be fine."

"What *is* this book?"

"You'll see. Will you do it?"

"Oh, I'll do it." As always, he was casting himself as the long-suffering savior of mere mortals. I hated to let *Sambo* go to him or anyone else. But after those weird e-mails I was afraid to keep the book with me. What if someone came to the house tonight and threatened me personally? Started burning my books, one by one, until I gave *Sambo* up? If they actually threatened to kill me, I would hand the book right over. *You want that gift-wrapped, sir? With a nice big bow?*

It was not a position I wanted to find myself in.

Even the barn felt less safe. I bolted the door securely.

I knew I had to look through the book one more time. There was a subliminal stirring, a sense that I was overlooking something. Reaching into my bag, I retrieved it, took it out of its plastic casing, and turned the pages slowly, back to front. This time I was struck by the illustration of the tiger who had wheedled Sambo's purple shoes away from him. Wearing a pointy shoe on each ear, his front paws raised menacingly so you could see their underside, he had the look of an Oriental icon. It was a skillful rendering and brought in another cultural reference. But that was not what I was looking for.

I stopped finally at the inscription and looked, not at it, but at the illustration opposite. The picture showed Sambo bowing in the direction of the words, a quick, simple sketch with his head partially shielded by the green umbrella. Bringing it close to my face, I saw that it was not lithographed the way the other illustrations were. It was actually fainter, as if it had first been drawn in black ink, then delicately tinted with watercolors. Sliding my finger across the surface, I felt a slight texture.

I tried running my fingertips across one of the book's printed pictures, which felt completely smooth, then sat back, shaken. Had Helen Bannerman created an original painting for Kipling? If they were friends . . . But even if they weren't, he was already famous in 1899. She might have sent the little book to him in the hope of furthering its popularity, though the tone of the inscription indicated some personal familiarity.

Hoping that my e-mail channel was secure, I sent a message to a young woman I had met at a booksellers' workshop in Colorado Springs a year earlier. Katie's specialty was children's books and we had had several enthusiastic conversations. More than that, her father owned an eminent antiquarian bookstore in the Midwest. It was the kind that still produced beautiful color catalogs on glossy pages, with prices to match.

Hi Katie,

I'm not sure whether you'll remember me from the Colorado Seminar, but we talked about children's books there. In any case, I have a theoretical question for you: What do you think a first printing of THE ADVENTURES OF LITTLE BLACK SAMBO, Grant Richards, 1899, in pristine condition might be worth? And what if, say, it had an inscription from Helen Bannerman possibly to Rudyard Kipling, and a small original illustration painted by her across the page? Also what if it had "Author's Copy" stamped on the back inside cover?

Please answer off-list! Just a ballpark figure will do.
Thanks, and I hope things are going wonderfully for you.

                                    Best,
                                    Delhi

Before pressing SEND, I checked twice to make sure that I had not accidentally cc'd the message to anyone else—like the entire BookEm list—and then let it go. It would perhaps be hours before Katie turned on her computer in Chicago, but whenever she did, my question would be there.

Next I called Shara. It wasn't with the compassion my mother would have shown. I wanted to know what was happening with Russell. Although I had searched *Newsday* and checked their website, there was nothing about an arrest in the bookstore murder.

The phone was not picked up until the fourth ring. A faint "Hello?"

"Shara?"

"Yes?"

"It's Delhi Laine. Is everything okay?"

"How can everything be okay?"

"You mean the police have charged Russell?"

"Oh. No. He's back."

"You mean he's home?" I was astonished. "They let him go without charging him?"

"I don't know." She said it dully. "He won't talk to me. But—now the police want to talk to me!"

"They have to talk to everyone who knew Amil. Just tell them the truth."

"Why?"

I closed my eyes; I had no patience for temperament this morning. "Because in this country you don't get a choice. Look, I'll be in and out. Call me if anything else happens."

Then I put *Sambo* in the smallest Priority Mail box and wrapped two other books to send out.

Leaving the post office, I went up the street to the Port Lewis library. According to the card catalog online, they had the biography of Helen Bannerman, *Sambo Sahib*. Sure enough, I found the book, by Elizabeth Hay, on the shelf among the Bs.

I handled its red cover with wonder. The dust jacket illustration showed a watercolor of Sambo smiling and pointing at letters on a blackboard with his closed umbrella, teaching four small Caucasians in nursery dress. Below it and on the back were black and white caricatures of Sambo and his family portrayed, as the blurb indicated, by "later and less sympathetic illustrators."

As I expected, there were several biographies of Rudyard Kipling. I picked out three, and checked the books out.

Since it was nearly noon, I decided to have lunch near the water. Could I afford it? Of course not. But I *needed* it, and needed to be safely surrounded by other people. I settled into a white vinyl chair on the faux deck of the SS *Seascape* and ordered a lobster roll and a diet coke. By the time my sandwich came, pink and white chunks in a hot dog roll, every table was filled. Safe in the crowd, I was soon lost in Helen Bannerman's life.

Helen, a tall, rangy Scotswoman, had a good sense of humor and no aptitude for housework. Her physician husband was deeply involved in plague control around Bombay and the family was neatly divided into two older girls and two younger boys. When the girls spent the years between 1902 and 1905 in school back in Scotland, she turned her energies to her sons.

Although Helen died in 1946, before serious accusations of racism battered Sambo's reputation, the last chapter in the biography was written by Elizabeth Hay as a response to Bannerman's critics. It was a defense that transferred the blame to the coarser American illustrators. The picture of the Sambo family decorously eating their pancakes on a white tablecloth had deteriorated into Sambo alone in a bare wood shanty, scarfing down cakes like a solitary boozer. The book did not include the picture of the slender Black Mumbo in a Dorothy Lamour sari or Sambo as a freckled, redheaded American kid.

The last chapter in the biography was also the most intriguing. The initial story, that Helen Bannerman wrote *Sambo* for her daughters on the train after leaving them in Edinburgh to be educated, was not true. In 1898, she had left them temporarily at the family's second home in the hills to escape the Bombay summer when tropical ill-nesses bloomed. Yet in 1902, Janet and Day *were* left in Scotland, sep-arated from their parents for three years. It appeared that this future separation had been foreshadowed in the book by Helen, knowing it had to come.

The gifts Sambo's parents gave him helped in his temporary sepa-ration from them. More than that, they kept him from being eaten.

It wasn't until I closed the book that I realized there was no men-tion of Rudyard Kipling.

Chapter Twenty

After I paid for my lobster roll and left the restaurant, the day took another dip. Back in the barn, I called Detective Marselli and got his voice mail. I left a message saying that I wanted to see Margaret. I also wanted to know what was happening with Russell Patterson, but wasn't sure he would tell me.

Next I switched on the computer. The first e-mail told me that I had sold an expensive edition of *The Great Santini* by Pat Conroy. I should have been thrilled. The only trouble was, it was the same book I had sold in June and forgotten to remove from one of the databases. Someone who had taken the trouble to locate the book and go through the credit card process now believed he owned a Conroy first edition—and didn't. I authorized a refund and wrote an apologetic message.

As if in rebuke, there were no other book orders or inquiries.

There was, however, a response from Katie:

Dear Delhi,
So nice to hear from you!
I checked with my father who has been in the business for a thousand years. He has never had an inscribed Helen Bannerman book and thinks it is quite uncommon. With what you told me about it, including the original artwork—could you send me a scan?—he estimates its value at about $25,000. If it were a true author's copy, a unique item, the value could go up considerably, especially at auction. As you know, two collectors can drive a price into the stratosphere.

Why do you want to know? He said to tell you he would be
very interested in such a book!

Enjoy the rest of your summer,
Katie

She hadn't believed my disclaimer that it was a theoretical question; why would she? Yet it was true. The inscription was uncertain; the provenance was unknown, and it wasn't even my book. Outside of that . . . it was probably worth more than she said anyway. That was the bargaining price in case I had one to sell, the price that would give her father some margin when he resold *Sambo*. I could imagine the book highlighted on a page in one of his expensive catalogs.

When the phone rang I hoped it was Detective Marselli. "Second-hand Prose!"

It was. "You called me?" He sounded impatient.

"I wanted to know where Margaret is."

"Ms. Weller was moved to a nursing home."

"I know that. Where?"

"We're not giving out that information."

"But I want to see her!"

"It's either do it this way or post a guard. And we can't justify doing that."

"But *I'm* not a suspect."

Silence.

"Am I?"

"We don't use that terminology anymore."

"Okay. I'm not an 'alleged perp,' am I?" An unindicted co-conspirator?

An amused snort. "You don't fit the footprint."

"You have footprints?" But as soon as I said it, I realized he did not mean it literally; I would have blushed if we had been in the same room. "But what about Russell Patterson?"

There are natural pauses in a phone conversation, and there are silences so deep you can look into them, black holes rimmed with ice.

"Who told you *that?*"

"His wife. Shara?"

"Why?"

"I don't know. She didn't know anyone else to call, I guess."

"Well, she can relax. Her husband has been cleared."

"He has? But I thought—" I would have to revise what I thought. "Are you sure?"

He responded with what might have been a laugh.

"But he's a violent person. He bullies everyone!"

"Yes?" He seemed skeptical.

"He bullies her. He bullies everyone!"

"Are you afraid of him?"

"Me? No. Why would *I* be afraid of him?"

"I'll let you know about seeing Ms. Weller."

"Is she any better?"

"About the same." He hung up.

I clicked on the NEW MESSAGE icon. An order for a large Raoul Dufy art book. And another blast from oceans9:

YOU'LL BE SORRY.

That *was* a threat. But I didn't have anyone to call.

Rather than stay in the barn, I drove into Port Lewis. With two of the Kipling biographies under my arm, I walked over to the waterfront café, settling in at the same sunny table where I had sat with Roger, The Bookie. This time I ordered an icy mochaccino and watched the gargantuan white ferry, the *Moby-Dick,* arrive from Connecticut. Foot passengers streamed off first, then cars and trucks bumped gently down the gangplank and into the street. Just beyond the ferry, pleasure boats rose and fell in its wake, waiting for the weekend. Although it was mid-afternoon, a scent of fried clams came from somewhere nearby.

I missed *Sambo*. The book glowed with its own history and existence, a clear beam shining down from the past. The fact that everyone involved in writing and publishing it was long dead gave it the usual poignancy. What matters? What *really* matters? The past is sealed. The future holds annihilation. Being able to sit in the sunshine and breathe in the salty air on a summer afternoon was, in the end, all you had.

I warned myself not to go there. I did not want to go once more down the path that beckoned to me like an inexorable hand.

Instead, I escaped into the life of Rudyard Kipling, looking for the point where his world intersected with Helen Bannerman's.

Joseph Rudyard Kipling had been a sad and defiant little boy, especially after his parents left him and his younger sister, Trix, in a foster home in England. The parents dropped the children off without explaining that they would not be back for a while—six years. Their foster mother was a cold and pious woman named Mrs. Holloway who stitched a sign that said LIAR to Ruddy's jacket and forbade his reading fiction. *The tiger's pounce?* Even though Helen's daughters had been left in the loving care of family members, she would have understood that nothing can quench the yearning for the beloved parent.

I skimmed the pages to get a chronology of Kipling's life, entertaining myself with thoughts of Helen and Rudyard having tea under the hot Rangoon sun. It was hard to imagine much more. My image of Kipling was of someone stodgy and monocled, rather like Teddy Roosevelt, while Helen in her photographs was tall, pleasantly homely, and board-thin. Call me unromantic, but I could not picture anything but friendship between them.

There had not been a whisper of him in her biography. Given all the illustrated letters she sent home, if they had met she surely would have sketched Kipling—what a treasure that letter would be! Of course, she had not started writing letters to her daughters until 1902 and her book had been published in 1899.

Navigating my straw through the slushy mocha, I realized that I needed to see a map of India. Lahore, Bombay, Madras, Simla. They were familiar names—from before I could walk there had been a map of India on my father's study wall—but I could not remember very clearly where the cities were. Helen Bannerman had first arrived in India in November 1889; Rudyard Kipling, who had been working on a newspaper in Allahabad, left earlier that year for London and returned for a visit with his parents in Lahore in early 1892. I checked my notes. At that point Helen and Will Bannerman would have been in Mangalore, arriving in Madras in September 1893.

I read on. By 1892 Kipling had published *Soldiers Three, Wee Willie Winkie,* and *The Light That Failed.* The next year his parents moved from India to Wiltshire, England, though Trix married and stayed on in Simla for most of her life, suffering from emotional problems. Small wonder, given the shocks of her childhood. But though her brother worried about her, I could find no evidence that he ever went back to India again after 1893. There was no record of his ever traveling to Scotland from his London home, either. It was possible that Helen and Rudyard had met in India in 1892, but I would have to check the geography.

I pushed away my empty glass mug and wondered what Kipling would have thought of *Little Black Sambo*. He had written his *Jungle Stories* about Mowgli first. Mowgli was good with animals, but so was Sambo, in a way. It had been Sambo's good fortune that the tigers abandoned their finery and he was able to retrieve it. On the other hand, how long would a tiger be happy squeezed into a little red jacket?

Kipling's earlier success might have given Helen Bannerman more reason to send him a copy of her own effort; in a way they were double compatriots. The painting of Sambo could have been Sambo bowing to Kipling's established literary position.

Gathering up the books, I realized that I had been counting on something more conclusive. If not a documented friendship, then at least a known meeting between the two authors. Victorian writers were always being introduced to each other and going off on trips together. Indian expatriate society had been tight and chances were that they would have met if they had been at all geographically close. But India is a huge country.

Another mood dip, which meant it was time to move on. Leaving the café, I crossed the street to Cornucopia and ordered a smoked turkey wrap and a pound of mixed salad to take home. Standing in front of a deli case which had even healthier things inside, tofu lasagna and veggie burgers, I had the familiar sense that I was managing my life badly. I should have called Jane to reassure her about what had happened; I owed Jason in Santa Fe a call. At least I had told Hannah I would pay for her car repair. But this was not about my living children.

Back on the crowded sidewalk, skirting far too many tourists, I finally let myself think about what had happened on this date nineteen years ago. Picture a very young mother, five months pregnant, with three little girls in tow. A park bench in Stratford beside the calm-flowing Avon, not far from Anne Hathaway's cottage. Young men and couples row slowly by. Sitting on the bench with a two-year-old in her arms, buzzing insects and the lulling scent of honeysuckle, she is too drowsy to keep her eyes open. Her two other daughters play in the grass at her feet. Except—

"Mommy, Mommy!" Jane was tugging at my bare arm. "Caitlyn!"

"What?"

I looked around, seeing Caitlin nowhere, and then leaped up still holding Hannah, and ran to the shore. All I could see were reeds and cloudy water. The water didn't even ripple.

"Janie, did she fall in?" I scanned the grass around and behind us, trying to remember how I had dressed Hannah's twin that morning. But she was nowhere.

Jane began to cry.

"Watch Hannah!" I sat her down on the bank and waded in, then plunged abruptly deeper, thrashing my arms beneath the water and calling, calling. Other people came over right away and started searching too, and soon the police had sent divers in. But we never found her. The police suspected me briefly, I suppose, but enough people had seen us all in the park—"Such a darling tot!" one English woman told the papers—so no one thought I had done away with her somewhere else.

"So how come no one saw her fall in?" Colin agonized angrily. "How come none of these people noticed that?"

When the unthinkable happens, you still have other children to care for. Hannah didn't really know what had happened, but we couldn't get Jane, almost four, to settle down and go to sleep. I was trying to leave the girls' room when she screamed, "No! The lady will get *me*."

I stared at her. "What lady?"

"The lady who took Cate!" And she started to sob all over again.

We couldn't get any description of "the lady," though we tried. We called the police that same night; they posted her picture and reinterviewed everyone who had been in the park. No one had seen anything. A police psychologist speculated that Jane felt so guilty about letting her sister wander into the water that she had invented a "bad lady" to blame instead. My little girl's body was never found, and there were never any substantial leads to show she had been kidnapped.

Perhaps it was wrong to never talk about it again. But the alternative seemed to be getting mired in grief and recrimination forever and take the other three children there too.

Climbing into the van, I stuck the key in the ignition. But I did not go anywhere. Only four of us walked off the plane in New York that September and a month later Jason was born. Tragedy left us alone for a few years until my father died much too early, at 71, from a brain tumor. My mother was not part of the new longevity either. Even Raj, my gallant little cat, was getting on in years, his muzzle gone gray. How soon before I would be holding him on the vet's silver table, kissing him good-bye?

I crossed my arms over the steering wheel and wept. Life was a cheap trick, a fair promising penny candy to keep you from realizing what it actually was. I could not tell if my tears were for my lost little girl, my parents, for Raj, or for Amil who had died so young in a foreign country. Perhaps Margaret, whose life had been hijacked, was part of the mix. Maybe I wept too for my lost marriage, for the dreamy young mother who never thought anything so terrible could happen to her.

I took the blame for everything, letting my tears wash out every grubby corner. Finally, lifting my head, I wiped at my eyes and drove home. I wanted to call someone, but who? Not Colin, who I secretly believed had never gotten over blaming me. To my other children it was just a dream.

Only one other person had known Caitlyn.

There is a theory that if you're feeling bad anyway, you might as well get other unpleasant things out of the way. I decided it was time to talk to Patsy.

My niece, Annie Laurie, answered, and after asking, in a whisper, when I'd come out and take her to McDonald's, she put her mother on.

"Delhi?"

"Hey, Pat."

Then neither of us said anything for a moment.

"Oh, Del, I've been thinking about you all day."

"Don't make me start crying again."

"You never heard *anything?*"

"No."

More silence. Finally she sighed. "Want to tell me what's going on with Colin?"

"Sure." I told her, expecting she would have a lot of advice, tips on how she handled her own successful marriage. But all she said when I finished was, "Well, men are just dessert."

Dessert? I had a sudden memory of Ben making a fuss over me at their party, knowing how it would irritate Patsy.

"A lot of empty calories," I agreed.

When we finished the conversation I held the receiver for a moment, stunned by how much better she had made me feel. Maybe if *I* didn't come out swinging . . .

By the time I ate my turkey wrap and salad and walked out to the barn, my meltdown was fading into memory. The yard had caught pieces of sunlight, golden patches that lingered on the barn windows and the water. As I passed the pond I stopped and checked for fish, but they had retired under the blanket of bright green duckweed for the night. The evening held its breath, a Maxfield Parrish painting. I was alive inside it.

Then a blast announced the ferry's arrival, my neighbor's puppy yelped, and on the next block an ice cream truck tinkled "Turkey in the Straw."

But as soon as I went out to the barn and locked myself in, a sense of uneasiness came back.

The first thing I did was dial Jane's apartment. When her machine went on, I left another message. "Hi, it's Mom. Just wanted you to know everything's fine here. One of these days we'll catch up with each other. Love you!" After that I called Jason and was actually able to find him home. Colin was still disgusted with him for dropping out of Pratt, impatient with his struggle to find the meaning of his life. "He's not *doing* anything," Colin fumed. "He's not even painting ashtrays! Or bagging groceries. I'm giving him a year before I cut him off."

Where had I heard that before?

I worked until after ten, pricing art catalogs, and finalized my schedule for Saturday morning sales. I did not hear from oceans9 that night.

Chapter Twenty-one

Saturday began like every other Saturday in recent memory, though the ending was far different.

I was up very early and off to several estate sales in Nassau County. I don't bother with "Moving Sales" or those where a group of neighbors band together to sell off their extra stuff. But rummage sales by large organizations can be worthwhile, and the good thing about library sales is that they only have books.

During the morning I ran into Marty rushing from one house to another, cell phone plastered to his ear. Roger, the Bookie, followed him, rose-tinted glasses glinting, but he stopped long enough to order, "Meet me in Starbucks in Malverne at twelve thirty." At a house in Great Neck I had a chance to wave at the Hoovers. But I didn't see Jack Hemingway disguised as Papa, and Howard Riggs was no doubt in Port Lewis dourly tending his shop.

I was curious if Roger actually had something to tell me or if this was his idea of a date. But I waited in an overstuffed chair and, just before twelve thirty, he came in. He went to the counter for cappuccinos, then sat on the sofa on my right. "Have a good morning?"

I shrugged. "Okay. I found this copy of *The Great Gatsby* inscribed 'Dear Ernie, Stick *this* in your boxing glove, Scott.' But they wanted ten dollars, so I didn't get it."

He reared back in shock, and then saw that I was teasing him. "Yeah, shouldn't waste your money. But speaking of—it looks like Margaret's find has disappeared with her." He watched me intently.

"Don't ask me."

"No?"

"You said you thought it was black interest. But why do people want things that are caricature?"

He pounced. "Who said it was caricature?"

"A lot of those things are. And the things from well-meaning people might be even harder to take than those that were meant to be cruel."

He shrugged. "I'll take them all the way to the bank. C'mon, Delhi, I've seen it all. From Aunt Jemima, to stuff that would uncurl *your* hair. But it's all history now."

"Are most of your collectors black or white?"

"Depends. Why?"

"Just curious." But I suddenly felt as if I had *Little Black Sambo* tattooed across my forehead. Time for another subject. And then my cell phone rang. I fished around for it in my woven bag. "Hello?"

"Frank Marselli. I need to talk to you."

"Okay."

"Where are you?"

"In Nassau. I can be home in an hour."

"See you then."

What had *happened?* I took one more sip of coffee. "I have to go. That was the police about Margaret."

Frustration warred with curiosity in his face. "What's going on?"

"He didn't say."

"No, I mean—"

But I was already standing. And then I was gone.

I had hoped for time to change out of my sweaty shorts and T-shirt. But Marselli was already on my porch. Instead of his tan suit, he was wearing a white dress shirt and gray chinos.

"Hi!" I said, jumpy as a teenager meeting a blind date. "Do you want to sit out here? Or in back? We could always go inside."

He looked at me. "Here's fine. I won't keep you long."

We sat down in white wicker chairs on the front porch, a small table between us.

"How long have you known Ms. Weller?"

I thought. "I was living here when she opened the bookstore about eight years ago. Actually, it was already a bookshop, but a dive. She really fixed it up. But we didn't get to be friends until I started selling books."

"Did she ever talk about her marriage?"

"Just that it was a long time ago. She said she took back her own name."

He pursed his dark lips thoughtfully. "You knew Lily Carlyle?"

"Not well. But . . . yes."

"What kind of a relationship did she and Ms. Weller have?" The wicker creaked as he pressed back, as if he was imagining himself in a rocking chair.

"They were very close, for sisters. They did everything together. Margaret was devastated when she died."

"Sisters. They ever fight?"

"I guess."

"Ms. Weller ever tell you Lily was moving to Atlanta?"

"No!" And then I thought of the closet that had been swept bare, the glass cases with half their treasures missing.

"Ms. Weller's house was ransacked. Twice," he said, with a hard look at me.

"I didn't—" The porch, which had been in shade all day, felt chilly. I cupped my hands over my upper arms.

"Any idea what they were looking for?"

I reminded myself that I was being questioned by the police. Rubbing my hands up and down my arms to warm them, I murmured, "I think it was a book."

"What book?"

I'm sorry, Margaret. "It's *The Story of Little Black Sambo*."

"What? You mean the tigers?" He sent his hand in a circular motion. I saw that he wore a college ring with a many-faceted red stone and wondered where he had gone to school.

"The tigers," I agreed. "Margaret had a copy, a first edition. A hundred years old."

"Yeah? It's that old?"

I hesitated. "Published in 1899 and signed by the author."

"I guess she owns a lot of books."

"Sure. She has her pick of whatever comes into the shop. And books are good investments."

"Yeah?" He straightened in his chair, "But that's not what most thieves are looking for. When people find out someone's in the hospital and the house is empty, they take it as an invitation."

"Did they take a lot of things?"

"Some stuff."

"Maybe Lily sent some of it to Atlanta."

"Maybe. We'll check."

He stood up to leave.

"But when can I see Margaret?"

"Tomorrow morning. I'll call you."

"Will I need to make sure I'm not being followed?"

"No. Just go the way you usually would."

"But couldn't somebody—" Ah. If anyone followed me, the police would be there waiting. I thought of something else. "Whatever happened about the Stony Brook professor Amil had a run-in with? Ruth something?"

He shifted his eyes towards the yard as though he were going to give me his standard line about not giving out information, and then said, "She's in Dublin this summer taking a language course. People have seen her there every day."

"But you let Russell Patterson go."

He moved to the steps. "I'll call you tomorrow," he said and was gone.

I had finally done the right thing, telling him about *Little Black Sambo*. And it hadn't mattered. It probably had nothing to do with Amil anyway, and that was what Frank Marselli cared about. I suddenly remembered the threatening e-mail messages from oceans9 that I hadn't told him about. Still, they seemed to have stopped. It was almost as if the writer knew that Sambo had taken his green umbrella and left the premises.

By that evening I had carried all my Saturday purchases out to the book barn. Feeling energized—an infusion of promising books will do that to you—I settled down to work. After double-locking the door, I switched on the computer to find out if any of the books I had bought were more valuable than I thought.

I was congratulating myself for picking up an illustrated guide to mechanical banks, put out by a specialty publisher and a rarity, when I heard a noise in the yard. I stopped typing and sat very still. The noise came again. It was a different sound from the scurrying of mice and chipmunks. This sound had a human rhythm. It seemed to come from the far window, as if someone had crept into the shrubbery to watch me. Keeping my hand on the computer mouse, I strained to hear the next sound. It came as a soft rustling.

This is how it happens. There are years of predictability, everything just as expected. You assume that nothing will change. Then one day you leave your car unlocked as usual, or get on a plane, or bring coffee and a bagel to your desk on the ninety-fifth floor. You doze off on a bench in the English countryside. Or you sit isolated in an old barn with the doors locked, but the large-paned windows are flimsy enough for anyone to break one and get inside.

A jumble of thoughts. *Hide under the desk.* Call 911! As I reached toward the phone, there was the scrape of a foot on the concrete apron. Someone tried the door latch. And then they rapped politely on the door. I stopped in my half crouch. Did killers knock? It was a soft but urgent rapping, three quick taps. Perhaps it was Frank Marselli with more questions? Or some book dealer I knew? Call 911 just to be safe?

Yet remembering my terror in The Old Frigate when it had only been Roger Morris, I pushed myself up slowly. I ignored the image of someone setting fire to my books one at a time.

"Who is it?" I called out when I was close to the door.

"It's me." A woman's voice.

Leaving the chain on, I pulled back the door and almost screamed.

A tall, dim shape, and then Margaret smiling apologetically. Her unbound hair fell lankly around her face. "Delhi? I didn't mean to scare you!"

"No, no." But she had. Was she *real?* She didn't look real. Was this the visitation people talked about after someone had died? I felt thrown back into the story, "The Monkey's Paw," in which one of the old father's three wishes was that his son would come back from the dead. But when the father opened the door and saw the terrible apparition, he slammed it shut and used up another wish reinterring his child. Next I felt transported to *Salem's Lot* where the dead returned as vampires, familiar yet horribly strange. It made me think—but this was my friend!

"Wait," I cried, and then closed the door to slide off the chain and reopened it again. She stepped over the old threshold and we hugged. Not a ghost but a solid body, a body wearing an olive-checked shirt and navy linen pants, though very pale. "What are you *doing* here? How do you *feel?*"

"I'm fine. Really, I'm fine." We moved back to the desk, into the light, and she half-perched on the table, bracing herself with one slender leg.

I stood on the other side facing her, trying to put it all together. "But—I thought you were in a nursing home!"

"I was. But the whole idea was ridiculous."

"But . . . when did you come out of the coma?" And then I understood what Clarisse had been trying to tell me. Margaret had been conscious, at least toward the end. "So you know about Amil?"

She sighed. Her skin was pulled taut around her nose and mouth, giving her an almost grotesque look. Was she real? "The police were talking about it. But I can't remember anything."

"That's not unusual with a head injury," I sympathized. "But I'm so glad to see you talking! I was so afraid . . ."

"Delhi, I feel so guilty! If he hadn't come back to apologize, he wouldn't have been in the store when we were robbed."

"Is that what happened? You were robbed?"

"I—yes, but it's so confusing. I keep seeing this one guy in my mind, kind of stocky with curly red hair. But I can't remember anything else."

"You *saw* him?" It *had* been Russell! I had to let Frank Marselli know right away. "So they were after money? And not the book?"

"The book?"

"*Little Black Sambo?* And your other finds?"

She seemed to recoil. "No! They just wanted money. Why would you think they were after the book?"

Didn't she know how valuable it was?

She sighed as if reading my thoughts. "Delhi, I did something really stupid. I called Marty to see if there were specific reference works, price guides for black interest. Because of *Sambo.* And he wasn't even *curious*. He acted so patronizing, like I was this old lady bookseller who was so obviously past it, that I—" Her green-gold eyes met mine sheepishly. "I couldn't help dropping a hint or two that I had something really valuable. Then he was all over me, of course."

I laughed. "He has the same affect on me. Like I have to prove I'm good enough to swap stories with him. But where did you get it, anyway?"

"Oh, Delhi, it's complicated. And it's not as valuable as you think. But I've come to pick it up."

"Margaret, I don't have it!"

Before I could explain, she swayed with shock. I thought she would fall and I reached toward her.

"No, no, it's safe. But I was afraid someone would try to steal it from me, so I sent it somewhere to keep it safe."

"It's not here?"

She was not as well as she thought she was.

"It's somewhere very safe. I can get it for you Monday. But I was getting these weird e-mails about it and I was afraid they'd try to steal it from me."

She gave her head a quick toss, like a dog ridding itself of water after a dousing. "Doesn't matter. You can send it to me."

"I'll bring it to you."

"No, I'm going to my sister's cottage for a few days. I've got to try and sort everything out."

"Lily had a cottage?"

"No, no, Eileen. On the Jersey shore."

My Sister Eileen.

"But what about the shop?"

"What about it? It's ruined—Amil was killed there! Anyway, I can't afford it anymore. When I did the renovations, I had no idea that chains like Borders and B&N would be moving in. Or that the Internet would take so much business away."

"I know. I'm sorry." And I was. Even though I had not created the Internet, I had jumped on its shining back and galloped away. I was one of the people who had helped kill The Old Frigate.

"Silly, I don't blame *you*."

"Anyway, the store's not ruined," I argued. "You'll get past this. People count on its being there. You've got *Little Black Sambo* to help with the bills. Do you have any idea what it's worth?"

She gave me a penetrating look. "Do you?"

While I scrambled for an answer, she added, "Forget the bookstore. Tell Howard Riggs he can have the stock."

"No! Everything will work out. But you have to tell the police about the red-haired man!"

"I did."

"Good. But how are you getting to your sister's?"

She gave me a teasing smile. "Car?"

"Margaret, you can't drive. You're just getting over a head injury. You were in a coma!"

"Delhi, I'll be *fine*." She reached over and patted my arm, as if reassuring a child. My mentor again.

"Do you remember anything else? Like the ladder breaking?"

"What ladder?"

Ah. "It looked like you had been climbing up the ladder in the middle room when the rung broke and you fell backward."

"I wasn't near any ladder. I was at the counter with Amil. They made us open the cash register and took the money. Then they attacked us."

It seemed to be coming back to her more. "Maybe that's the last thing *you* remember. But the money was still there when I went in Monday, and someone had moved you into the middle room. And Amil," it was hard to say, "they put him downstairs in the basement closet."

"In the *closet?*" The overhead barn light threw a gaunt shadow across her face. I wondered if I looked grotesque to her too.

"I know it's confusing. Why don't you stay here tonight? You can't leave till tomorrow anyway."

"Thanks, but I want to be *home*. It's been almost a week!"

That made me think of something else. "Was Lily really moving to Atlanta?"

She gave me the coldest look I have ever seen, imperious and frightening. As if I were a child questioning an adult in authority. "Who said *that?*"

I didn't answer.

"Delhi? Who told you that?"

I could have lied and said it was on the news. Or risked her wrath by saying I had seen Lily's empty closets. "The police asked me about it."

She nodded grimly, as if it was just what she would expect. And then she was moving away swiftly. Before I could call her back, she was out the door.

Chapter Twenty-two

But it was all wrong. As the sound of Margaret's Volvo died away, I knew I should have never let her leave. Our usual connection had been missing, and that had thrown me off. She thought she was fine; I knew she wasn't. What if she tried to drive to New Jersey tonight?

Locking the barn, I climbed quickly into the van. At least she said she was going home first. I could drive her to her sister's cottage in the morning—if the police agreed that she could go. Would they be able to protect her as easily in another state?

When I parked at the edge of the green sloping lawn, Margaret's silver Volvo was not in the driveway. I hoped it was because she had stopped at the supermarket for food. But I was too restless to just wait and walked over to the front porch. I knocked on the carved oak door in case she was home and had garaged her car, and then peered through the lace panel covering the oval. The irony of looking through another glass door hoping to see Margaret was not lost on me.

But this time I saw nothing but the polished oak floor under beautiful woven rugs and the curving staircase to the bedrooms on the left.

Deciding to wait in the van, I retreated back down the stairs. But I had not even reached the bottom step when a voice from the darkness snapped, "Hold it!"

I know I screamed, though it was more of a startled yelp than a serious cry for help.

"Over here." Detective Marselli did not apologize for scaring me, as he stepped out from behind a tall rhododendron. "Ms. Laine."

162

I sighed. "Margaret's not back yet?"

"Back from *where?*"

"She was just at my house."

"She was at your *house?* Doing what?"

"I had a book she wanted."

He snorted at that, but his laugh was not good-humored. "Did she tell you why she left the nursing home?"

"You mean she wasn't discharged?"

At that moment, a powerfully built, gray-haired policeman approached us, a frowning man who looked ready to bend a steel bar. He glanced at Frank Marselli, excluding me. "Ms. Weller?"

"No. But she was just with her. She was at her *house.*"

"Damn! So where is she now?"

"I don't know," I answered him. "She said she was coming back here."

"She was *talking* to you?"

"Well, she was confused about some things."

They were both watching me closely. "She tell you anything about that night?"

"Yes! That a red-haired man was there. But I think she already told you that. And the last thing she remembers is being by the cash register, not the ladder."

"What else?"

"I'm not sure. But—Russell Patterson! How would she even know what he looked like if she hadn't seen him? I don't know if he was the one she was afraid of though."

"Why do you think she's afraid of someone?"

"Well, that's what Clarisse—her nurse in the hospital—told me. And I could sense it myself."

"You *interviewed* her nurse?"

"No! We were just talking when I went to see Margaret. She thought she was afraid of someone coming into her room. I guess she didn't tell you?" My voice trailed away.

"Maybe we should let you run this case." But he waved a hand to indicate he had already moved on. "Ms. Weller has been making herself very scarce where we're concerned." He turned to his partner. "Remind me never to use that nursing home again. All the trouble we went to, then they didn't even know she was gone for two hours! Didn't even notice she was wearing clothes that would have fit a midget." He shook his head, returning his gaze to me. "Tell me exactly what Ms. Weller said to you. Everything."

It was hard to remember sequences, it had been so disjointed. But I tried.

"She didn't tell you where on the Jersey shore?" Marselli asked for the third time.

"No. I didn't even know about this sister."

"Probably miles away by now," the bodybuilder muttered.

"She wouldn't go without *Sambo*. The book," I added hastily, as his eyes widened at this new traveling companion. "She said she'd let me know where to send it."

Another shared look, then Marselli turned on me. "If Ms. Weller contacts you in any way, you're to let me know immediately. Immediately! Don't mail her any books. Call the precinct, and they'll page me. Three o'clock in the morning? I want to know."

"Okay. I mean, I *will*."

"You will call me. As soon as she gets in touch with you." He looked at me as if he wished he had a tattoo to press across my forehead.

"I will." I would.

"You can go now." As if he had summoned me there!

I hesitated. I had more questions.

He turned his back on me.

I left.

It was a steamy night with no air in the bedroom. I slept horribly, jerking awake once in terror, startled by the menacing shapes of the dresser and the rocking chair. Even though the intruder outside the barn had only been Margaret, the adrenaline had not dissipated. In one dream I was at the Jersey shore, a child playing "Whack-a-Mole" at a boardwalk booth. As each brown plastic head protruded, I smashed it rapidly with the rubber mallet to earn points. Except that the moles became larger and uglier, until at last they had the faces of people. Before I could stop myself I had whacked Margaret with my mallet and screamed in horror as blood spurted out of her eyes.

When I crawled out of bed at six, my long yellow T-shirt sticking wetly to my body, I was unable to believe I had slept at all. Mechanically I fed the cats, and went out and sat on the stone bench by the pond. But awake, my thoughts were as ugly as the moles had been.

At eight I went back into the house to try and call Margaret at home. But before I could pick up the receiver, my own phone rang. It was Bruce Adair.

"Delhi! You're a hard one to get live."

My God. "I've been in and out."

"Dinner tonight?"

What was tonight? Oh. Sunday. "Uh—okay." I could not think of any reason not to go. "You wanted to talk to me about something?"

"Many things. Shoes and ships and sealing wax." His tone was flirtatious. In my fog it sounded like we were in a 1940s movie. "Mirabelle's at seven?"

I started to protest. For dinner at a restaurant that expensive, I would owe him my soul.

"It's nothing, my dear," he said smoothly. "I take visiting dignitaries there all the time. But dignitaries thin out in the summer, and I'm having withdrawal pangs."

The difference was that Bruce, not the university, would be buying my dinner. But we agreed to meet at the restaurant at seven P.M.

Before the phone could ring again, I dialed Margaret's number. The phone was picked up on the third ring. "Margaret? Thank God you're still there! I was imagining all sorts of things." As I said it, I acknowledged some of the images I had been pushing away: Margaret collapsed over the steering wheel of the Volvo, her head injury worse. Margaret attacked again—this time successfully—by Amil's killer. An exhausted Margaret crashing her car into a median on the Garden State Parkway.

"Who is this?" It was a man's voice.

"Who is *this?*" I demanded.

"Ms. Weller is not here at the moment. I'll be happy to take a message for her."

"Is this the police? Do you know where she is?"

"Give me your name, please."

"Delhi Laine. I was there last night and talked to Frank Marselli about it."

"Can you spell your name for me?"

I could. And did. I gave him my phone number when he asked. "Could you ask Detective Marselli to call me as soon as he finds her?"

"I'll give him your message."

My last call was to Howard Riggs Books. I left a message on his machine that it was important and to please call me any time after noon.

Then I stepped out onto the front porch and collected the *New York Times*. I didn't know what else to do. For the next two hours I read the paper, dozed on the chaise lounge, and filled in about half the words in the crossword puzzle. A perfect metaphor. I was still missing too much of what had happened in The Old Frigate on that Friday night.

Finally I went out to the barn and checked for book orders; there were four. The other messages were routine, comments and queries from BookEm members to each other. Why had the messages from oceans9 stopped? I tried to think what had changed. I had mailed *Sambo* to Colin and no longer physically had the book. But how would anyone know that? Unless someone were watching me with a telescope. If that were the case, then I could be putting Colin in danger.

Sitting with my elbows on the desk, propping up my weary head, I was assailed by the thoughts I had wrestled with all night. Closing my eyes, I tried to remember the names on the paintings in Margaret's house. The signature on the seascapes was easy, a literary name. Pym. Not Barbara, of course. But I thought it had started with a B, too. Becky? Something like that. The other name had been . . . Weston. W. Weston. I did not have a photographic memory, but as a book dealer I had trained myself to remember names and titles. Anyone could recognize a Hemingway; it was knowing the names connected to scarcer books, the sleepers, that kept me solvent.

I typed *Rebecca Pym* into Google and a flood of hits, pages of articles, filled the screen. It was the last thing I had been expecting. Doggedly I read for several hours—art reviews, and many other things.

In the late afternoon Colin stopped by, giving a perfunctory knock and then pulling the barn door open. In his hand was the Priority Mail box.

"How's it going, Rosie?" A reference to Secondhand Rose and one that irritated me. But we kissed anyway, two people who have known how to push each other's buttons for a long time.

"You have it already?"

"All they had to do was move it into my post office box. I figured since I was protecting it with my life I get to see what's inside."

"Sure."

He brought out his Swiss Army knife. It had accompanied him on so many digs that the red enamel was almost worn away. I had given it to him the year we got married. "You still use it," I said, distracted.

"It still works fine."

Better than our relationship.

But after he opened the flap and pulled the book out, he gave me an odd look.

"It's worth a lot of money," I said. "It's signed. But it's not mine anyway, it's Margaret's."

"So why do you have it?"

"Long story. Guess who I'm having dinner with."

"Little Black Sambo."

"No, actually, Bruce Adair."

"My old friend Bruce. How's he doing?"

"Fine, I think."

"Good. Maybe I'll come along."

I laughed then. "I don't think that's in Plan A. He's taking me to Mirabelle's."

"Really? Better be careful. People say he has his way with visiting female poets."

"I'll be okay then."

We kissed good-bye with a little more intensity, stirring feelings that I thought had departed. What were we supposed to do with so much *history?* The life we had crafted together—more like a toolshed about to collapse than an estate—was what we had. His grip on my shoulders was proprietary; Bruce had not been *that* casually dismissed.

As we moved apart, he remembered something. "You had another package, out on the front porch. I brought it in and put it on the kitchen table. They deliver on Sunday?"

"Not that I know of. Unless it's FedEx."

"Well—regards to Bruce." One of those comments that meant the opposite of what it said.

I went in through the back door, noticing that the message light was blinking. *Good.* I pressed the play button:

"Yes, this is Howard Riggs. I cannot imagine what we would have to discuss. But you may reach me at the shop in the next few minutes."

The next message was an order for a catalog of the French artist Jean Fautrier, whose abstract painting predated Jackson Pollock. Then:

"Hi, Blondie, it's Marty. This cop just interviewed me about where I was last Friday night when that guy was killed in Margaret's shop. Now they're targeting booksellers?"

The package, on the oak table, was a medium Priority Mail box but with the same red, white, and blue colors as the box I'd used for *Sambo*. Picking it up, I looked for the mailing label. There was none.

Someone had placed a book in the box and hand-delivered it to my front door. Was Margaret giving me more books to protect before she left for New Jersey? In her haste, she would not have taken the time to address it to me, knowing I was the only one who would get it.

I pulled the tape across the top, peeled back the top edge of the box and looked inside. Not a book. Maybe it wasn't meant for me.

I shook the box until the doll clattered onto the table and I yelped.

The nude Barbie with long blond hair had had her neck wrenched back; a red line was lipsticked across it, indicating a slash. On her torso was neatly printed in black marker, *Someone who kept something that wasn't hers.*

Chapter Twenty-three

Bruce was inside the pretty French restaurant when I arrived, charming the young hostess in the foyer. He was wearing a blue-striped seersucker suit and a straw bowler that managed to make him look like a little boy and Maurice Chevalier at the same time. It made me glad that I had put on my black, flower-printed dress and was wearing makeup. I had only eaten here twice, both celebrations—once for Jane's MBA and once when *Voices We Don't Want to Hear* had been on the short list for the National Book Award. Until I opened the package with the doll, I had been having pleasant fantasies about the food.

Bruce and I were escorted to a small romantic table with an embossed white cloth, and napkins the deep purple shade of eggplants. A wonderful meal of goat cheese salad and breast of duck unfolded, along with wine and Bruce's stories. As I expected, they were fascinating, many of them about people whose books I had read. I told him a few funny bookselling adventures, but my mind kept circling back to the doll.

To avoid being startled all over again, I had put the slaughtered Barbie out of sight in the dining room hutch. Somebody knew that I had *Little Black Sambo*. Somebody believed that they had a claim to the book and would slash my throat to get it.

As soon as dinner was over, I would be on the phone to Frank Marselli. This time he could not shuffle me off to my local precinct.

Over coffee and *trois-chocolat mousse* came what my friend Gail and I call "the pitch over the plate."

"You're an accomplished woman, Delhi," Bruce said, tilting his

169

head with a wistful smile. Evidently "You're a beautiful woman" had fallen into disfavor. I missed it.

"I do sell a lot of books."

"I don't mean that," he purred. "I'm talking about everything you know. And do. Your photography."

I sighed. "Bruce, I only did photography so I would have something to do on Colin's sabbaticals, besides laundry."

"I don't believe that. You're too—"

"Accomplished?"

He waved a small hand. "I've always admired women who can do many things."

"So have I."

"But you can! And look pretty besides."

Don't go there, I begged him. *You're too late.*

He did anyway. "You're quite beautiful. We're both accomplished people."

For one twinkling moment I had an image of us in Venice, Bruce a Toulouse-Lautrecian figure in the gondola, me lying back in a white lacy dress, looking appropriately pretty. Later we would tour St. Mark's and eat *fritto misto.* A scholarly, *accomplished,* nineteenth-century pair enjoying the highest communion of the mind. But then I remembered Roger's parting kiss and my response. Even Colin's good-bye embrace had stirred me more, and Colin was a leaky ship indeed. I knew I was ripe for the plucking, but the fingers had to be right.

The vision of Italy dissipated into the smoke from the plum-toned candle.

"It must be an adjustment for you, living alone," he was saying kindly, his deep blue eyes looking into mine.

"Well . . . a lot less laundry." *Bring back the cynical Bruce,* I begged.

"Less other things too."

"You know what? There's a lot of freedom living by myself, doing exactly what I want."

He considered that. "You've never lived alone before?"

"Never. I didn't even get a womb to myself."

He laughed, but added, "Will you tell me when the novelty wears off?"

"Sure."

Bruce sat back, satisfied, and I knew that at least a part of him was relieved he would not have to change his life—not tonight anyway. He would not have to give up an occasional poetic tryst or alter his dinners out.

To change the subject I said, "Do you want to see something interesting? Written by one of your countrywomen?"

"A Scotswoman? Delhi, I've had a lot of wine, but I can't think of a one."

I took the book out of my bag, removing it from its plastic protection. "Helen Bannerman?"

"Helen . . ." He twisted his head to see, recognizing the title, of course. "She was Scottish?"

"Born and raised in Edinburgh. This is a first edition."

He handled the book carefully, as I knew he would, and then handed it back. " 'The grandest tiger in the jungle,' " he mused. "I'd almost forgotten where that came from."

I took a sip of the very good dessert wine he had insisted on ordering, to be polite. "There's something else interesting." Holding the glass in my left hand, I found the painting and the inscription with my right, and then jumped my chair closer to him so he could see. "This is original art. And I think it's inscribed to Rudyard Kipling."

"Really." He was suddenly much more interested and we both looked closely at the image of Sambo bowing. We were still looking at it when the drop of condensation from my glass fell onto the side of Sambo's cheek. Brown puddled into green immediately, taking some of that color too and streaking into his red jacket. "Oh, no!" Then, "Don't!" as Bruce reached to blot it with his napkin.

"I've ruined a hundred-year-old painting," I wailed. And taken thousands off the value of the book. "How could I *do* that?" I was distraught. *Margaret would kill me! It would surely be the end of our friendship. If I hadn't been trying to show off . . .*

"Delhi." I felt Bruce's hand cover mine. "Calm down. You may have blurred this picture a little, but it's hardly a century old."

I looked at him.

"Believe me. I've examined many holographs, manuscripts that old and even older, and the color dries out completely. It might moisten up a little, but it would *never* run. You'd really have to soak something that old to get any reaction at all."

"The painting is not a hundred years old," I said numbly.

"I doubt it's a hundred days old. It hasn't cured."

"Then Helen Bannerman didn't paint it."

"Not unless she's also the world's oldest Scotswoman."

"Then who painted it?" But of course it was a question that he could not answer.

"We could test the inscription to see if it's real," he suggested.

"No!" I was terrified he would try it before I could stop him. "I mean, why smear that too?"

He brought the book close to his face, moved it away, turned it slightly. Then he looked at me. "I'd say that it is and it isn't."

"Meaning?"

" 'The tiger's pounce' and her initials look contemporaneous with the book's age. I'd put money on it that the first initials are more recent."

"You mean the JRK was added?"

"I'm afraid so."

Good-bye, Rudyard. " 'Things fall apart.' "

" 'The center will not hold.' " He completed the quotation for me with a wry smile.

Things fall apart.

What else is there to say? I left Bruce with promises to cook him a down-home dinner, fried chicken and whipped sweet potatoes, which he said were his favorite American foods, then drove back to my house. I thought about what would have happened if I hadn't blurred the painting. The book could have gotten all the way to auction or into the hands of a private collector. Would that have been so terrible? I couldn't decide. I just knew I was not ready to give up the image of Helen Bannerman creating the charming little picture for Rudyard Kipling.

But when I pulled the van into the driveway, the memory of the Barbie doll cut through the haze of exquisite food and wine like the moon knifing through clouds. What was I doing? Perhaps the sender was right now sitting at my kitchen table, patiently holding a knife, ready to threaten me into giving up the book. Going into the house could be the stupidest thing I had ever done. I would call Frank Marselli—but not from my home phone.

I backed out of the driveway and drove downtown into Port Lewis, parking illegally over some white cautionary stripes. With tourists crisscrossing the street in front of me, I felt safe enough to check my answering machine for any threats.

There was one message

"Delhi? I guess you're out, but I have to see you. I need the book as soon as possible. Can you bring it tomorrow morning or as soon as you get it back? I'm sorry to involve you, but you're the only one I trust. I'm in Montauk." She gave me the name of a motel and a room number.

I was so startled that I had to play the message again to write down the information. Then I sat staring at my cell phone.

I knew what I had to do. I had been given an order that even a five-year-old child could not misinterpret. "You *will* call me."

Reaching into my woven bag, I found the wallet which held Frank Marselli's card, and then stopped. I had promised to call him when I knew where Margaret was. And I would. But that did not mean I had to call him from Port Lewis. All I needed was a few minutes with Margaret, a chance to give her the book and see how she was. There would be chaos once the police arrived.

I couldn't go back to my house anyway, not with the mutilated doll. And I couldn't call Frank Marselli about it without telling him about Margaret. He hadn't told me I couldn't talk to her; he just told me to tell him where she was. I'd be in and out before he even arrived.

In the end, I was my parents' daughter. I could no more disobey a police order than smuggle flowers out of a botanical garden or speed away after causing an accident. Or smuggle rare books out of a library.

I stopped and bought the largest size coffee possible at Qwikjava, and then worked my way to Nicolls Road, keeping to the speed limit until I reached the road to the south fork, Sunrise Highway, and turned east. This Sunday night most of the traffic was going in the opposite direction, a slow slog of cars returning to Manhattan after the weekend. I exited at Bellport and found a convenience store. Then I extracted Frank Marselli's card and dialed.

"Homicide."

"Detective Marselli?"

"No. What's it in reference to?"

"The murder in Port Lewis? He wanted to know when I heard from Margaret Weller."

"Right, I'll patch you through."

I squeezed the little telephone in my hand. With the glow of the wine gone, I felt a jittery dread. Terrible things were being set in motion, even worse things than receiving a mutilated doll. Across the parking lot three young men in muscle shirts and head kerchiefs leaned on the hood of a Jeep, smoking and watching me. They did not look menacing, but any approach from them would have shoved me over the edge.

Several clicks on the line. "Marselli."

"Hi. It's Delhi Laine."

"You heard from Ms. Weller?"

"Yes. She left a message on my answering machine. She's still on the Island."

"Where?"

"Montauk Point. At someplace called the Captain's Comfort Motel. Room 16."

"Montauk? Sheesh! Why didn't she just swim to Block Island? Where are you?"

"In Bellport."

"Bellport?"

"I was having dinner with a friend." A non sequitur, though he did not know it.

"Go back to Port Lewis. I'll call you later."

"But—"

And then my finger slipped onto the END button, cutting us off.

To conserve the battery, I turned off the phone.

To stay alert I tuned into an oldies station and listened to Frank, Ella, and Bing. But even with the music on I obsessed about what I would say to Margaret. How could I tell her that the book she was counting on was a forgery—and that I had ruined even that? If I hadn't sent it to Colin, if it had still been in my bag when she came for it, this never would have happened. The book would be as pristine as when she had mailed it to me.

But if she's an artist, she can just repair it, my inner cynic pointed out.

That was ridiculous; there was no point in repairing a fake.

I kept to the various speed limits and braked whenever traffic lights turned yellow. In Southampton the road changed from a tree-lined parkway to one lane of restaurants, plant nurseries, and inns. The brief glitter of Bridgehampton gave way to a quieter stretch before the placid village of East Hampton with its canal. After that, the road wound through pools of darkness, broken only occasionally by house lights. Amagansett came next, and then the emptiest stretch of all before the lights of Montauk pointed the way into the Atlantic.

I was wondering if I would have to drive into the village itself when I saw the sign for Captain's Comfort—a painted board with the usual grizzled face in a yellow slicker. It was illuminated by a spotlight and the neon word NO was lit up next to VACANCY.

As it was, I almost missed the turnoff into the parking lot. Thankfully there was no one on the road behind me; I braked quickly and slipped in, bouncing over broken clam shells. The white stucco building had been built in an arc so that every room faced the ocean. But this was no resort. Beside the office door, a painted wooden Dutch boy and girl leaned together, bottoms out, engaged in the world's most boring kiss. A large plastic swordfish was mounted to the door's right and I guessed the motel had been built in the 1950s for sport fishermen.

The parking lot was full. It was after eleven P.M. and most of the cars looked snugged in for the night. Pulling into the only available space, farthest away in the shadows by the road, I climbed down from the van, shocked to find that my first steps were a cramped stagger. The ride had taken two tense hours. I was heading for the cement walk that led past the front doors of the units when I saw an East Hampton Town police car angled in front of the path. Had they already approached Margaret? Or had Frank Marselli contacted them to make sure no one left the motel room—or went in—before he got there?

Fishing in my bag as if looking for a room key, I turned and walked in the opposite direction. At the edge of the highway, the shoulder was paved with more clam shells that crunched loudly under my black sandals. Unaccustomed to high heels, I felt as if I were walking on stilts. But I kept my shoes on until I reached the property where another motel, The Montauk Light Inn, began. Then, stepping out of the sandals, I crossed the grass that divided the two buildings. I moved steadily ahead until I reached the beach and stepped onto the sand.

Instinctively, I jerked my foot back. The sand felt cold, even clammy. Although the beach was unlit, I could see from the glow of the full moon that it was deserted. An empty lifeguard's chair tilted like an abandoned toy. As if the ocean had been given a reprieve from performing, the waves barely rose and fell, making a soft plash. A wrinkled reflection of the moon bobbed near the horizon like a deflated beach ball. Only the crisp sea salt smell was strong.

As I trudged past windows with closed Venetian blinds, I could hear snatches of TV, a baby crying, a couple arguing in sharp, staccato bursts. *You're the one who had the bright idea to come.* But most of the rooms were silent, and some were already dark. Margaret's door, identified by tarnished brass numbers, was louvered with white-painted slats. A small life preserver hung to one side. It was not a place I would have imagined her staying.

Although room 16 was dark, I rapped on the louvers. "Margaret?" I called softly.

Nothing.

I knocked a little more urgently. "Margaret!"

Still nothing, and then the door was jerked back.

"*Delhi?* I didn't think you'd come tonight." Her forehead crinkled as if it wasn't the correct thing to do, as if she wasn't sure she should even let me in. She was still dressed, in white slacks and a pink striped shirt, and her rich brown hair was clasped back as usual. "Why are you here now?"

I couldn't tell her why I hadn't waited. Glancing to where the police car was still parked, I said, "Margaret, we have to talk. Now."

Looking dubious, she pulled back the door further and I stepped inside. "Lock the door," I commanded.

She picked up on my alarm. "Why—what?" But she moved very quickly.

Instead of answering, I started to cough. The air was like a storm cloud, heavy with cigarette smoke. I knew Margaret still smoked, though never around the books. But we might as well have been in a Turkish bar. Only a back bathroom light cast a glow out onto a cheap wooden wardrobe. In the remaining dimness, I could just make out two double beds and a round white plastic table near the door. Margaret must have been sitting in the dark, smoking.

I pulled out a yellow canvas director's chair and sat down, putting my purse on the table, the bag's opening facing into the room. Imagining *Sambo* leaping out, I pressed the yarn edge down. It sprang back up like a willful child.

Margaret sat down on the edge of the bed opposite me; I could barely see her face in the half-light. "Things seem so different at night." Her speckled eyes, framed by lashes that seemed darker than usual, were wide with unhappy wonder. She looked as if she had just seen something that she had thought was a myth. "In the daytime, anything's possible. But by nighttime—"

We didn't have time for a philosophical discussion. "Margaret, who are you afraid of? If you talk to the police, tell them the whole story, and they can arrest him and you can go home."

She didn't answer. In the dimness I saw that she was patting the plaid bedspread for her pack of Dorals. When her hand found the cigarettes, though, she didn't pull one out. Instead, she began to squeeze the cellophane package open and shut as if it were an exercise grip.

"Someone double-crossed you. It was supposed to look like a burglary, I guess, you and Amil on the floor and the cash drawer empty—was it for the insurance? But after he knocked you out, he switched everything around."

She put her hands to her ears to shut me out. "Don't! I can't *think.*"

I leaned toward her. "I'm telling you that someone put Amil in the basement and the money back in the register. And dragged you over to the ladder to make it look like you fell."

"Why are you saying this? I thought you were my friend!"

"I *am* your friend. I'm trying to help you sort it out."

"But you're saying I planned it!"

"Even if you did, what he did was worse."

"You have no idea what happened." This time she did shake out a cigarette, but started rolling it between her palms instead of lighting it. "You show up here in the middle of the night with all kinds of . . . accusations. Did you bring the book? Just give it to me and leave."

I blinked at the loathing in her voice. Perhaps because we were sitting in the dark, our voices were low, almost whispering. But I wasn't imagining the scorn.

"Where did you get *Sambo?*"

"I don't think that's any of your business." She looked at the white cylinder, as if thinking about what she would have to do to light it. "You think life's a treasure hunt, with everybody else supplying the clues."

This wasn't Margaret, Margaret my friend. But I already knew that.

"I know who you really are."

"What?" She imprisoned my wrist with her fingers. "What are you talking about?"

"You're Rebecca Pym. You escaped from California before you could go to jail."

Her grip was strong. Why was I telling her this, regurgitating everything I'd learned online? But I couldn't stop. "You were going to be put on trial for killing your husband and you disappeared." In the news photographs she'd looked younger, wilder, different. But if you were looking for similarities, you found them.

"You've been in my house! Who said you could go in my house? Anyway, it's all a lie!"

"Do the police know? Is *that* why they're trying to find you?"

And then, as if this were a bad play, there was a scraping on the cement stoop outside and the click of the door handle being tried. I looked quickly at Margaret to see if she had heard the sound.

She had.

Two quick knocks on the door. "Police! Open up!"

With an incredulous look at me, Margaret leaped up, jarring the mattress. Still holding my arm, she yanked me off the chair, drawing me further into the room. I was too surprised at first to resist.

The police must have had a master key. Margaret had just pulled us into the bathroom and clicked the lock when they were outside that door too, pounding on the fragile wood.

Margaret's arm was crooked around my neck, her forearm pressing hard into my throat. "You told them I was here! This was a trap, wasn't it? I was supposed to confess while they waited outside. You're probably wearing a wire."

With each accusation, she squeezed my neck harder. With my breath cut off, I couldn't even answer. Frantically I tried to wrench my head away. I started kicking backward, hitting her legs.

"Police! Open up, Ms. Weller. If you don't we'll break it down."

"Try it! I have Delhi Laine and a knife. If you try to break in, I'll slit her throat."

She was moving us backward. I tried to stay limp and resist, but black spots were swimming in front of my eyes. My body felt lighter and lighter.

"Ms. Laine, are you in there?"

In desperation I started kicking forward, my foot hitting against the door. She had lied to them. If they *didn't* break in, I would die.

In answer, something heavier banged against the wood.

Then I was free, dropping backward onto the tiles. Behind me I heard the rustle of plastic, the metal creak of a sliding door. Arching my head painfully back, I saw Margaret slip sideways through it. Not even a door, more just an opening, a place for fishermen to stash their catch.

At that moment the wooden door cracked open and pieces hit the floor. Marselli's partner, the bruiser who hated me, tripped on my legs and landed on me heavily. *Damn these motel bathrooms,* I thought. Then my eyes closed.

I felt myself being lifted, half-dragged, and then finally pushed with no gentleness onto a bed.

Chapter Twenty-four

When I opened my eyes, my throat was on fire.

Marselli and a young East Hampton officer were standing just inside the door, the younger officer's face pressed against a walkie-talkie. He must have been checking with the cop in the cruiser, because he turned to Frank to report, "Nobody's left the area."

"Silver Volvo sedan, 2005, plate 509 SID," Frank snapped at the young man. "Make sure no one leaves on foot either. We're taking care of the road."

He relayed the message, and then looked unhappy.

"What?"

"He wants to know if you're looking for a woman in white."

Marselli glared in my direction.

I nodded, unable to even whisper.

"Uh—he says someone ran into the water a few minutes ago."

Frank Marselli's face would have frightened a samurai. But he was off, racing out the door.

I pushed myself up from the bed, not sure if I had the strength to stand. My body ached in a multitude of places, but I limped to the door.

"She ran down the beach and dove right in," the young cop told me plaintively. Both being in trouble with Marselli made us allies in some odd way.

I pressed my hand against my throat to keep it from hurting when I spoke. "Did she start swimming? Or go under?"

"He didn't say. Joe? You see her after?" He listened, and turned to me. "She got out just past the breakers, and started swimming east."

180

Then, realizing what he knew, he ran down to the beach to tell Frank Marselli.

The response crew arrived in a few minutes, setting up equipment rapidly as if they did it every day. Their circle of lights in the sand glowed like a bonfire. But when the searchlights began playing over the water, porch lights snapped on too and people crept out of their rooms. I sank down on the cold sand and prayed, though I didn't know what to ask for or who to ask. Margaret would have killed me, I knew. I'd felt it in the fury of her arm crushing my throat.

She was desperate. Ironically, even if she had done nothing wrong in the bookstore, she would face charges for almost killing me. And there would be extradition back to California. If she survived.

The lower part of my flowered dress was soaked from when I had rushed into the water, just before the response crew arrived. I thought I had seen the white curve of an arm. Plunging through the foam, I reached it—a broken piece of white Styrofoam float. The feeling of groping through water looking for something human was unbearable, pulling me like a tide into the past. I dropped the white plastic at the shoreline and turned my back on the water.

At the sound of a motor, I finally turned back and saw two Coast Guard boats trawling the ocean just east of us. Probably other officers were patrolling the beaches, in case she tried to reach land and hide. But Long Island's south shore was *all* beach. It would take thousands of watchers to cover it all.

There was time then to think about all the wrong assumptions I had made about Margaret. Falling for her calm, at times prim, bookseller persona, I had endowed her with power and knowledge that she didn't really possess. If I hadn't been so intent on making her a role model, a cultured woman with a beautiful successful shop, I might have paid more attention to the clues. All those worthless books in the basement; she must have bought them in the beginning when she didn't know any better. The books in her glass cases— books with *some* value, but mostly dogs. From her constant complaints about money, even from Derek's comments, I should have guessed that the bookshop was a beautiful facade, but close to collapse.

And our friendship? But I stubbornly refused to trash that. She was the one who had first encouraged me to sell books, made me believe that I could do it.

Something damp touched my shoulder. I screamed, whirling around, and saw Frank Marselli. "You—*you* come with me."

He held my elbow as we plodded through the sand, as if I were going to break free. People stared at us from a dozen open doors.

I did not want to go back inside Margaret's room, but Frank Marselli opened the door and pushed me in. The tobacco smoke was fainter; perversely that made me sad, as if Margaret were already fading out of life.

Get over it, Delhi. She tried to kill you.

He switched on the overhead light, then gestured at me. "You have other clothes in your car?"

I looked where he was looking. My flowered black dress was crinkled and sandy, soaked and ruined. I lifted it off my legs again, and then let it fall back. "No."

He looked toward Margaret's open suitcase, but did not tell me to put on anything from there. I wouldn't have anyway.

Finally I sat down at the white plastic table again. He loomed over me, and then perched on the edge of the bed just where Margaret had sat, our knees almost touching. My stomach turned over.

We stared at each other.

"I hope you have a good attorney, Ms. Laine."

I tried to feel indignant or frightened or remorseful, the way I was trying to feel angry with Margaret. But I wasn't feeling much of anything at all. I stared at my ruined dress.

"Did I or did I not tell you not to come out here? Why would you disobey an order?"

"I didn't know it was an order." My voice was still raspy. "You just said I should go home."

He gave his hand an impatient wave. "But you didn't. Instead you put yourself in the position of being a hostage and totally screwed up what should have been a routine arrest. Now God knows where she is!"

I bowed my head. "I'm really sorry. She said she had to see me. I didn't think—"

"No, you didn't think. That's the trouble. Nobody *thinks*."

We sat silently for a moment. Then he sighed and took out his small black notebook and a pen. One of his knees started jiggling, almost bumping mine. I could smell wintergreen, but I didn't know if it was coming from him or somewhere in the room. "Did she tell you anything helpful?"

"No. She just denied everything. I mean, she admitted it was supposed to look like a robbery. But she wouldn't tell me who else was involved, the person who put her by the ladder or carried Amil into the basement."

"She did. She probably didn't mean to hit her head that hard."

"But she couldn't have hit herself. That angle, that's what the doctors said."

"I know what the doctors said. But people have ingenious ways of doing things to themselves. The *doctors*"—he lit up the word with scorn—"the doctors also thought that some deep trauma was keeping her from consciousness. Until she put on her roommate's clothes and walked right out of that nursing home. I think she was faking it all along."

I didn't argue with him. But I had seen Margaret's crumpled body and I didn't think you could fake that pallor, that kind of inertness. "But who put the shirt under her head?"

"She did. If you're lying on the floor waiting to be discovered, you want to make yourself comfortable."

It made sense. Putting my hands to my head, I pressed hard; my temples were pulsing, blurring my thoughts. "But she couldn't have carried Amil down by herself. She just wasn't that strong."

"Oh no? People do amazing things when the need arises," he said mildly. "Or, she may have dragged him."

"So why wasn't there any blood on the floor? I was there before anyone else and didn't see any." But a memory flashed across my mind: Margaret on the floor with paper towels, frantically sopping up coffee, terrified that the finish would be marred.

"Ms. Laine?"

I came back.

"I need you to tell me about Ms. Weller's relationship with Mr. Singh. And I want the *truth*."

He was going to be disappointed. "He worked for her." Yet even as I said it I remembered her flirtatious tone as she raised the latte in Amil's direction before she saw me. "She thought he was attractive—everyone did—but she wasn't interested in him that way."

"Why not?"

"For one thing, there was a huge age difference. Almost thirty years!"

He shrugged. "They spent long hours together. You never heard of young men preying on older women? Port Lewis must be a very sheltered place."

"Of course I have!" But it just did not ring true.

"You said yourself he had a way with women." He looked at the acoustical ceiling, thinking out loud. "He works for her, he charms her, they get involved. After a while he gets tired of her. Old story. But she won't leave him alone and maybe he threatens sexual harassment. It worked once. So she becomes infuriated and shoves him against the marble fireplace. If that doesn't kill him, she finishes him off with a bookend. And then she has to cover up what happened."

"A bookend? She hit him with a *bookend?*" I was veering toward hysteria.

He narrowed his eyes in disgust at me. "You use what you have. Six-pound cast iron. *The Thinker*. It had been wiped clean of prints."

I was feeling like Alice down the rabbit hole. Of course I knew which bookend he meant. It was kept on a shelf in the front room. "But why would she wipe her own prints off? You'd expect her prints to be on it."

"Maybe she panicked. She probably used it to hit her own head and wiped it so we'd think someone else had done it. Unfortunately she and Mr. Singh are both type O, so we're still doing tests."

She hit herself so hard she was unconscious, and then somehow replaced the bookend on the shelf. I knew it hadn't been in the room with the ladder when she was found. Pressing my hands against my damp skirt, I shut my eyes.

"And we have an eyewitness. If he can be believed," he added cynically, as if to himself.

I brought my hand to my face. "Someone saw her attack him?"

"Someone who puts them in the shop together Friday night. Alone."

Russell Patterson. "And you believe *him?*"

"You're really gunning for this guy, aren't you?"

"Well, Margaret and Amil weren't having an affair." As he himself would say, there was no footprint. There are a hundred ways people betray themselves: a shared reference, eyes quickly meeting, studiedly casual touches. Watching Colin in action had taught me all of them. Like a radio, even though it had been temporarily snapped off now, I would forever be tuned to that frequency. I had picked up no waves between Margaret and Amil. "You're assuming that you can't put any man and any woman together for any length of time without something happening. Why do men always think that?"

He started to answer, but I plowed on. "Because that's what men are always thinking about. You're saying that if you and I worked together, we'd end up in bed. Just because we're a man and a woman."

I had meant to point up the absurdity of his belief, but the moment I said it I felt embarrassed. My inner cynic laughed: *Why don't you just invite him home?*

He seemed close to smiling in that surreal light. "Ms. Laine, I wouldn't put myself in that position with you. I'm a cop. I value my job. And the time I get with my kids."

"Good. That's good."

"But ordinary people . . ." He flicked his hand to assert what he felt about the rest of the world.

I did not get to hear any more of his philosophy because Marselli's partner, Reilly, opened the door and pushed in. "They've covered the whole area," he said tightly.

"They didn't find her?" I asked.

He turned away, his hamlike fist balled, as if to keep himself from attacking me.

"And?" prodded Marselli.

"Nada. They did a full sweep. If she's out there, she's fish food."

"Oh, God." I huddled in on myself, cold as the deep black ocean.

"Nothing on the beaches?" Marselli asked.

"Inconclusive. They found some prints in wet sand on West Beach coming out of the water. But hell—this is summer on Long Island."

"They preserve them?"

"Yeah."

"You mean she could—" I didn't want Margaret dead, drowned. But I didn't want her vengeful and at large either. And I still had the book.

"They done on the beach?"

"Yeah. Packed up tighter than a bloody tick."

What? I pushed myself out of the plastic chair. "Can I go?"

Marselli remembered again that I was there. "Can you *go?* You mean get in your car and drive home? No, you can't go! You're in shock. You'd run that van right off the road!"

I stared at him hopelessly.

"I've already saved your life once tonight. I'll drive you. In your van. George will follow us."

George Reilly glared at me.

On the ride home from Montauk, I tried to stay awake. But the darkness was seductive, a velvet pillow urging sleep. I kept dozing off, waking to blackness. Most of the time, I didn't see any other cars. Around Shoreham, I jerked awake and told Frank Marselli, "She was really frightened of someone."

"Of the police. Getting arrested. There are things about her you don't know."

But I did. Becca Pym's husband, a top Hollywood cameraman, had been found dead in his garage from carbon monoxide poisoning eleven years earlier. She said he had been depressed and threatening to kill himself. His assistant claimed he had been about to leave her for a young actress. And he had strychnine in his system. The case had been headed for a Grand Jury with probable arrest when Becca disappeared.

But I said, "What doesn't make sense is her sawing through the ladder step. Margaret would never have ruined her own property; she was still paying for it. Did you find the saw in the trash? And if

Margaret had done it, she would have at least chosen the right step."

He kept his eyes on the road.

Finally we were passing through the quiet streets of my neighborhood. Except for a yellow bug light mounted near a garage, everything was dark. People feeling calm and safe were sleeping in these houses.

Frank Marselli pulled the van into my driveway and we both climbed out. Reilly revved the navy Ford Taurus impatiently at the curb. But I held Frank with my eyes. There was something else I had to tell him, but my mind refused to disclose what it was.

"You okay?" he asked.

"I don't know."

"You have someone to call?"

"Sure." But I knew I wouldn't. I started to yawn, interrupted myself, and asked, "What time is it?"

He checked. "Three forty-two."

The Taurus engine raced angrily.

He put his hand on my arm. "Listen to me. If your friend did survive—which I doubt—and she contacts you, let me know. Immediately." He must have seen my overwhelming agreement, because he added, "*Did* she have a knife in there?"

"No. She was strangling me. If you hadn't broken down the door . . ." I wasn't ready to go there.

"When you started kicking, it seemed like a signal."

Thank God. "Just tell me one thing: If you didn't think someone else was involved in the bookstore, why were you giving Margaret police protection?"

"Police protection?"

"You were guarding her in the hospital."

A trace of a smile that I could just see from the streetlight. "That wasn't protection; that was surveillance. We had her prints from California. We needed to question her about Lily Carlyle and Mr. Singh."

George gave a long horn honk, exactly what you didn't do in my neighborhood in the middle of the night.

Frank dropped his arm, turned, and walked down the driveway.

He climbed into the Taurus and it careened away, dislodging a sheaf of stones.

Rubbing my goose-bumped arms, I started up the gravel driveway. First I would take a hot bath. Then I would pour a glass of medicinal red wine and read something soothing—*Remembrance of Things Past* or the Bible. Then I remembered the package with the threatening doll.

Chapter Twenty-five

Somehow I made it up the porch steps and collapsed across the cushions of the wicker settee. In retrospect, that sounds crazy. I was afraid of what I would find in the house, but was lying outside any safer? Perhaps I thought nothing else could happen. But dozing on and off, my cheek against the rough cushion, I kept replaying the events of the night. If I hadn't gone out there . . . but Margaret already had her escape route planned. She knew the police might arrive any time. Except that then it wouldn't have been *my* fault.

Would she really have pressed the life out of me? She had accused me of being a spy for the police. And people under pressure did unthinkable things.

When I woke for the last time in early daylight, I was shocked by the night before all over again. But I was no longer afraid to go inside my house. Daylight shrinks fear into scraps. Now I was more worried about dog walkers and runners seeing me. They might think I had had a heart attack and rush to help. More likely they would think I had passed out in a drunken stupor. *Poor thing, she hasn't been the same since he left.*

But it actually took the voice of my next-door neighbor, Sam, talking cheerfully to their golden retriever, to make me push up dizzily from the settee and search for my keys. Locking the front door behind me, I climbed the stairs and started running a bath, and then came back down and made coffee. I poured it into the largest mug that I could find, a Laurel Burch creation of two brilliantly colored cats that Margaret had given me. *Margaret.* Then I went upstairs and submerged myself.

A kaleidoscope of images: Margaret listening sympathetically to my wails about Colin moving out, never confiding that she had faced the same thing. Margaret and her beautiful ordered life had floated slightly above other mortals. She could have admitted that she was still learning about books too instead of letting me believe she had been doing it all her life. It would have changed our friendship, made it richer and more equal. But she hadn't wanted that.

By the time the water cooled off and my coffee cup was empty, I had focused on four questions. What had happened during the time Margaret and I were having coffee to make Amil so angry? Who had attacked me in the bookshop, sent the e-mail messages, and left the mutilated doll? Who had killed Amil and stuffed him in the basement closet, and then posed Margaret under the ladder? Where had *Little Black Sambo* come from?

Big questions. All I knew for certain when I went in search of clean clothes was that Margaret and Amil had not been physically involved. Her uneasiness at seeing Amil talking to me in the bookshop had not been about jealousy. She was no pathetic spinster seduced by his charm. She had been married, for God's sake—and maybe even murdered her husband.

Dressing in striped capri pants and a plain navy T-shirt, I wove my hair into a single braid. My black flowered dress lay like a dead animal on the floor. I knew I would never wear it again.

Start with Shara Patterson, my instinct told me. But when I reached the student house and rang the bell, no one came to the door. I had a flash of fear that she had disappeared back into the vastness of India, taking some answers with her. The idea of Amil rising from the dead and spiriting her away did not seem much stranger than the staid Margaret Weller plunging into the ocean to escape from the police.

Shara *had* to be home. Finally I walked along a cement side path to the backyard and looked over the edge of a white picket fence. A flash of movement. Shara was standing at an old-fashioned rotary clothes hanger pinning up multiple pairs of men's jockey shorts. Americanized today, she had on a plain white T-shirt and navy shorts. Billy was playing with a stack of plastic blocks on the neat, uninspired cement patio. When she saw me, I couldn't tell what she was feeling. But she moved to open the gate latch.

We faced off on the benches of a redwood picnic table.

"Russell has a lot of underwear."

"Oh, that isn't Russell's only. It is Devin's too. And the others."

"You do everyone's laundry?"

She lowered her eyes primly. "They work very hard."

Give me a break.

"I guess you do all the cleaning too."

Shara nodded.

"But aren't you a graduate student too?"

"Me?" She looked incredulous.

"But how did you get here then?"

"Russell brought me."

For a dizzying moment I thought she had said Russell *bought* me.

"Oh. Did you meet in India?"

She traced her fingernail in one of the table's ridges.

I didn't have time to be tactful. "Don't tell me it was one of those Internet sites!" A colleague of Colin's, unpleasant as a scrappy little terrier, had imported a bride from Vietnam—with the understanding that she would keep house, pleasure him unceasingly, and never answer back. As far as I knew, she did.

Shara glared at me. "What do you know about it? They hate girls in Bangalore! They put girls in those houses; they sell them to farmers. Because they killed the girl babies, there are no brides for men."

"I wasn't criticizing you. But a girl as beautiful as you . . ."

She waved that away. "My family had no money! So I came here. And now I'm an American slave."

"But was Russell always such a bully? Or did it start when he found out you were going to leave him?"

She stared at me, mouth open, as if I had morphed into some kind of fortune-teller. And then tears began to run down her face and onto the table, darkening the cedar. She lowered her head on her arms and sobbed.

I let her cry.

Finally she raised her head. She brought her heavy braid around to the front, clutching it with both hands. "Why did Amil have to *die?* He was going to take me home, me and Billy."

"But—" I looked down at the beautiful little boy, now squatting and patting the grass energetically with a summer-tanned arm, stared at the reddish-gold glints in his hair. Russell would never have let him go.

"Amil had to go back; he lost his student visa when he wasn't in school. But it was okay, his family is rich. They live in Lahore."

Lahore? And then I was seeing the shape of another truth. A lesson from Colin, a memory of the early days when he still brought slides home from digs. There would be a terra-cotta glaze on the screen at first, other unidentifiable colors, blurred nonsense. Then as he turned the focus knob the picture would straighten into recognizable shapes. You knew what you were seeing and where you were.

"Little Black Sambo," I said. "It was *Amil's* book."

She reared back.

"You know about that?" I pressed.

"No! He said never to tell. A silly story, about tigers." But she put her chin in her hand, her fingers over her mouth, demonstrating that she would not say another word.

But there were things I needed to know. "You don't have to talk about it. Just shake your head yes or no, okay?"

Her eyes stared back at me, beautiful and lost.

"Did Amil give it to Margaret, the woman in the bookstore?"

She shook her head.

"But—did he sell it to her?"

Now she nodded.

So that was that.

"But he had to get it back, or he couldn't go home!" Shara blurted out. "She gave him money for it, four hundred dollars to fix his car. She said she would hold it for him. But then his father sent him money, a lot of money, and she wouldn't give it back!" The words would not stay inside. "She said she didn't have it anymore. But it was a family treasure, a, a—"

"Heirloom?"

"Yes! It was from his grandmother's mother; she knew the woman who wrote the story. Perhaps she worked for her."

No wonder Margaret had not mentioned her find to me.

I looked across the perfect square of backyard, a lawn that would have met with Colin's approval. So the book did have a provenance.

Margaret had recognized it as a first edition and of value, especially as it was signed, and stamped as a rare author's proof. But then, using her skill as an artist, she decided to gild the lily a bit, dress the book up to increase its value.

No real bookseller would ever do that.

More words tumbled out. "When the lady left the shop, Amil found the book right in her purse—all ruined! She wrote other things in it, so the book was not for his great-grandmother anymore. He was so upset, he came home and said, 'How can we go back?' And I told him he should buy the book anyway. But Russell heard. And then he *knew*. And Amil had been his best friend. They started screaming!" She put her hand to her mouth as if she could not speak about that either.

"That's when they ran out and got in their cars?"

No answer.

We sat in the early summer morning, Shara looking beyond me to the brightly colored underwear on the line, hanging as limply as the dispirited flags of many countries. Was she seeing her future?

And what was I seeing? Another young woman, also pretty, who had miscalculated too. I had been less innocent, a thousand times more privileged, when I thought it was adventure calling to me.

"Russell says he's going to take *Billy* away," she wept. "He says I'll never see him again."

Reaching across the table, I stroked her arm. "He can't. We'll think of something. I have to do something now, but we'll figure it out."

She looked at me with the hopefulness of the young.

I drove back home and went to my answering machine. Pushing the PLAY button, I listened to and deleted several old messages. Then I opened the plastic lid to remove the tape, hesitated, and then closed it. Unplugging the entire machine, I put it in a white plastic Stop & Shop bag.

At the hospital, Clarisse was reinserting an IV for a patient, so I waited by the counter at the nurses' station. Today she remembered who I was.

"How's our friend?" she asked, rubbing her hands automatically on her flowered smock.

"Not so good." I did not want to talk about Margaret.

"No?"

"Do you have a minute to listen to something?"

She shook her head. "I don't get a break for another hour."

"This is really important," I pleaded.

"Oh, okay. You know what? You look like hell."

"I know. I'll need an outlet to plug something in."

"Okay."

I followed her into what appeared to be a patients' lounge, which had a wall of windows, tan vinyl easy chairs, and two square tables with built-in seats.

Clarisse gestured at an outlet and I knelt and plugged the machine in. Looking up at her I said, "Remember how you said you'd recognize the voice of the man who was calling about Margaret?"

"Uh-huh. I said that." She hunkered down beside me.

"Just listen and tell me if any of these sound familiar." I had erased all but three messages. Pressing PLAY, I watched her face.

At the end of the final voice, she said, "Do it again."

This time she stopped me at the one she recognized.

I knew that Frank Marselli worked in Hauppauge where most of the county offices were located. But because I wasn't sure which building was his, I called first.

"Marselli." His voice was flat.

"Oh great, you're there. I have to see you!"

"I don't have time this morning."

"It's really *important.*"

As Clarisse had, he recognized something desperate in my voice. "Okay." He gave me directions to the buildings on Veterans Highway.

The police offices were located in an uninspired Suffolk County building, two-story brick, with a border of generic evergreens. Inside were pale green walls, gunmetal desks, and a complete lack of posters or decorated coffee mugs. The reception desk was a raised wooden block.

I spoke to an officer no older than Alex Kazazian.

When Frank appeared to escort me in, he was wearing the same white shirt, grimy now, the sleeves crushed halfway up his arms.

"We have to make a phone call," I said. "Can you tape it?"

He looked exhausted, his chin pinpricks of stubble. "No. I can listen."

"Haven't you been home at all?"

"We still haven't located Ms. Weller. That's not why you're here, is it?"

"No."

I followed him, not to his desk as I had expected, but into a small interview room with a scratched wooden table, several metal folding chairs, and two phones. The only thing on the pastel wall was a building evacuation diagram. We sat down facing each other. Then I reached into my pants pocket and took out the number I had copied down from the tape.

"What's this about anyway?" But he seemed at a level of fatigue where it did not matter.

I hesitated, and then started pressing in numbers. Marselli picked up his own receiver.

Be there, I prayed.

"Hello?" I recognized the rich, confident tone at once.

"Jack? It's Delhi Laine."

"Delhi! Hi. You have something for me?"

"Sort of. But I just wanted to know if you wanted your doll back."

"My *doll?*"

"Your Barbie."

"Delhi, *what* are you talking about?"

"Somebody left a package at my house yesterday with a mutilated doll. As a warning. I thought it was you."

"Is this a joke? I haven't been near your house. I don't know where your house *is.*"

Marselli gave me a weary look.

But it was an old parental trick I hadn't used for some time: First accuse a child of something he did not do—the doll was not Jack's style—and he'll confess to whatever he has done.

"But you knew I had the book. You were the only one who picked up the Kipling connection on BookEm." It wasn't only that. I re-membered how, at the Oyster Bay sale, Jack had goaded me into go-ing to the shop to look for Margaret to make her explain her "great find" to me. I had been meant to find her body instead.

"So? I've already written a piece about the book. It was an au-thor's proof with an original painting by Helen Bannerman! *And* a Kipling connection. It's one-of-a-kind. The article's been accepted. It'll introduce the book, and I'll get a small commission when it's sold. Nothing wrong with that."

"So what went wrong?"

"You tell me." His book-snatching voice.

"Okay. Amil Singh wanted his book back. And you and Margaret didn't want to give it to him."

The sound of breathing. "He sold it to her fair and square!"

"When you went to the shop Friday night, you had a fight with him about it."

"Now wait a minute, Delhi! When I got there he was already—out of it. Evidently he'd gotten violent with Margaret, and she'd knocked him against the fireplace in self-defense. At least that's what she told me. But *I* didn't do anything wrong."

Frank Marselli put his finger to his lips to warn me not to contra-dict Jack, and I nodded. "But then you knocked her out."

"That was her idea. To make it look like a robbery, both of them just lying there. I didn't hit her hard. I know, it sounds crazy." Rue-ful now. "But you'd have done the same if you'd seen her so upset. She and I were friends for ten years."

"But why did you—"

Frank was shaking his head frantically at me. I stopped.

"—change things around?" was what I was going to ask.

"Delhi? This conversation didn't happen. I'd love to have the book, but I didn't do anything wrong. I offered to pay you for it, you know. I still will."

"I know. But I don't have it anymore." The damaged book I had was not the one he wanted.

"What the hell are you talking about? Margaret *said*—"

"Sorry."

"If you're playing games—" But the phone crashed down in my ear.

Frank Marselli's olive face seemed more bewildered than anything else. "Who is this guy?"

"Jack Hemingway. He collects books and writes about them."

"But how did you know he was there?"

Instead of telling him about Clarisse and the voice identification, I said, "I think he *did* hit her hard. If she died he could just keep the book himself. Even if she didn't, he switched things around so she couldn't claim she was the victim of a robbery. And he could hold Amil's death over her head." *Little Black Sambo* would probably have been his price. I remembered how implacable he had been when he wrested the Chan book from me.

Frank squinted at me. "Maybe *he* killed Amil and wanted her to take the fall."

I shivered at the specter of Margaret's innocence. But she needed Amil dead more than Jack knew. She could not have risked his telling anyone that the inscription and the painting were forgeries. It would devalue the book; Margaret's reputation for integrity would be ruined. There would be scandal and disgrace. She could especially not let Amil tell Jack, who believed the book was genuine. Maybe she had lured Amil to the shop Friday night by promising he could have the book back, even altered.

I sighed. "No, I think she killed him, and then panicked and called Jack. Maybe Russell did follow him to the shop and try to get in—how else would Margaret know what he looked like? Maybe seeing him trying to get in even gave her the idea for the robbery. She just didn't know that Jack would have a plan of his own." It must have driven Jack crazy searching the shop and her house and not finding the book. Those e-mails meant to frighten me had started after my post to BookEm about Kipling.

"Sounds like Mr. Hemingway and I should have a conversation. Maybe I should pick up a search warrant first."

"Maybe you should shave first."

He almost smiled.

"But how about Lily Carlyle? How does she fit in?" I said as he started to stand up.

He sat back down. "She doesn't. Not to this anyway. When we interviewed her coworkers at the Metropolitan about her being depressed, they were shocked. She'd already resigned from the museum and taken a curator's job in Atlanta that she was excited about. She was supposed to start the following Monday."

"But I thought she left a note." That Margaret had not been allowed to see. "Was that a forgery?"

"Oh, no. It was in her handwriting."

"But . . ."

He relented. "It's in the evidence room. It said something like, 'Margaret, I'm sorry to disappoint you. But I *have* to go. Love, Lily.' We just misinterpreted where she was going. When we checked their finances, though, we saw it would bankrupt Ms. Weller if Lily stopped paying the mortgage. But the will left her everything. Generous, considering they weren't related."

Had everything been a lie? "They weren't sisters?"

"Just old friends. But it was a good cover story for Becca Pym. You don't think of someone living a respectable life with her sister as being a fugitive." This time he did stand up.

At the double front doors, he opened one and stopped to let me pass, but I didn't.

"Jack said something odd. When he talked about being friends with Margaret, he used the past tense. He said they *were* friends for nearly ten years."

"People use bad grammar sometimes." But he was listening.

"Not Jack. He taught college literature."

"I'll see what calls there were to his line last night. Or if he's made any trips to Montauk lately."

Margaret's body was found the next morning when a garbage truck was emptying a dumpster behind the Amagansett shopping center and a worker saw a flash of skin. The side of her head had been smashed in. The tiger's pounce had turned fatal.

There was no funeral for either Lily or Margaret. But in the way of the twenty-first century, candles, notes, and literary stuffed animals—Paddington Bear, The Cat in the Hat, Winnie the Pooh— began to crowd the doorway of The Old Frigate. A real village idol. I still mourned our friendship, the times we had laughed together in understanding. But whenever I approached the bookstore, my stomach would turn over and my throat start to feel sore.

I had no sympathy for Jack. When Frank Marselli called to say they had found a saw in his garage with bits of fresh sawdust that matched the wood and tooth marks from the library ladder, and they arrested him for her murder in Montauk, I savored the taste of vindication. Evidently she had survived the Atlantic, reversing her direction and swimming slightly west, and then called on Jack once again for help. But saving Margaret was not in his best interest. He claimed he had hit her in self-defense. After all, she was the killer, wasn't she?

I worked hard to rekindle my passion for selling books. But there was no joy. When the phone rang Thursday morning of that week, I answered on the fifth ring, "Secondhand Prose."

"Good morning. This is Howard Riggs." Something in his tone indicated that he did not want to recognize me as a person by using my name, that he would not even be calling if there had been any alternative.

But I was tired of that. "Hello, Howard." *You Howard, me Jane.*

"Yes, well, I've had a letter from Margaret Weller. She said to open it. If she passed."

A letter? When had she had time to write a letter? I didn't believe him.

"It seems she's left me her books."

Right. "Congratulations."

"But you still have one?"

No! My eyes stung unexpectedly with tears. Hadn't she liked me at all? "What did she say?"

"What is it?"

"It's . . . nothing."

"I mean, what is the *book?*"

"She didn't tell you?" That was odd. "What did she say about it?"

"Are you going to tell me what the book is, or not?"

But the time for being intimidated by a "real bookseller" was over. "Not until you read me what she wrote."

"It's a letter to *me*."

"Fine. I have to go now."

"Wait. Just wait, will you? She mentions you having this book. That's all."

"Read me what she says." I was not turning over *Sambo* until I heard Margaret's own words ordering me to do it.

He sighed and took his time, rustling papers. " 'Please tell Delhi Laine that she should keep the book of mine she has. I hope it's the find she's always wanted. Maybe it will make up for that stupid doll. I just started feeling paranoid about getting the book back.' That's it."

I had been so primed to hear him read, "Please tell Delhi Laine to give you the book she's holding," that I couldn't say anything for a moment. "She's giving it to me."

"So she says. But I have to make sure that it's not part of the store stock that's mine."

I felt a familiar red heat creeping up the back of my neck. "Wait a minute, Howard. If you're going to accept the part of her letter giving her books to you, you have to accept the part giving that book to me."

"Not if it's part of the store stock she's given me!"

The red tide exploded. "Well, I can set your mind at rest. It was never in the store."

"Was it her so-called find?" Out in the open now.

"Not that valuable." I paused. "What if I said it was a first printing of *Ulysses,* but only the paperback—in white paper covers, by Shakespeare & Co." I expected him to know that there had not been a hardcover printing, that this was the true first of 750 copies. "What makes it so interesting, though, is that Picasso made a little sketch of Gertrude Stein on the inside back cover, probably when he was getting ready to paint her portrait. Maybe he thought that signing *his* name would give the book some value." I gave a laugh. "Little did he know." As I heard Howard's gasp, I added, "Sorry, someone's here," and hung up.

Well, I hadn't said I *had* such a book. But of course Howard would think that the book had to be real, since I would be too dumb to know those details myself.

The phone rang again immediately, and then a few more times. I let the machine in the house pick up the calls.

Then I gave myself time to think about what Margaret had done. *Sambo* was really mine.

So why wasn't I dancing around the barn? Selling the book would finally give me some financial security. Katie's father might or might not be interested, but Roger Morris, The Bookie, certainly would. So would any of the others, for that matter; Marty, the Hoovers, though they couldn't afford it, dealers I didn't even know. Jack, of course, would be spending his disposable income on a lawyer.

But I didn't move. The book had caused the deaths of two people. The larger truth was that it could never be mine. The only time it had belonged to me was when I was five years old and imagined vanquishing tigers too.

I reached into my woven bag and pulled out the small, white-jacketed book. Holding it gently in my palm, it weighed no more than a soul.

Then, pushing up from the chair, I went into the kitchenette for a glass of water, a child's small paintbrush, and a handful of paper towels. Back at my library table I opened the book to the front and began to work carefully. First I removed the *To JRK* inscription using tiny drops of water and an absorbent towel. It came up better than I would have expected. Once, when a droplet rolled across the word *pounce,* nothing happened. Bruce Adair knew his time frames.

The painting itself was more difficult. Even though the paper was glazed, bits of color seemed to have gotten inside and refused to come out. I knew that I could not get the paper too wet or it would swell and buckle, so it took nearly an hour of patient work. Finally I sat back in my chair to let it dry.

My parents had never gotten to India. When I was small they believed it was only a matter of time before God sent them there as missionaries. To practice, we ate a lot of curries, made scrapbooks from *National Geographic,* and remembered Asian souls in our prayers. Then Partitioning hardened and proselytizing foreigners were not welcome. My parents scissored India out of their dreams and sent their savings to an orphanage in Calcutta.

And finally it was too late. At the end, when they had enough money to visit India and no more church responsibilities, they were cheated out of India one more time. My father developed the brain tumor that quickly stole his life. My mother made no more travel plans.

Despite my name, I had never been to India either. I had talked about it, been anxious to go, but Colin was not interested. He insisted there were archaeological places *he* needed to go first; I had not stood up for what I wanted. But that was then. I had a few thousand dollars that my parents had left me, money I had held on to in case I failed completely at bookselling. What better way to use it than to travel to the country they had only dreamed about?

As Colin had pointed out, I had no safety net. But somehow I would survive.

I had a better reason to go to India. Although I could not return Amil to his family, I could bring them their beloved book and try and help them make sense of his death. And I would bring them something else, a young woman who had loved their son and had created a child who Amil had assured them was their grandson. I knew better, of course. But Shara could tell them what she liked.

Looking down at the book, I saw that the page had dried. The JRK had vanished. There was slight wrinkling to the other page, and just the faintest shadow of a golden-skinned boy bowing out of the world.